G000057132

Masked Do

Shortly after the dawn of the new millennium, Judy and Jiaying are thrown together in a youth hostel in Seoul, both having escaped long-term relationships. Their arrival in Seoul in the first year of the 21st century coincides with passionate anti-American demonstrations on the streets of the city, as South Koreans protest against US troops being stationed in their country, western hegemony and the manipulations of arms dealers. Anti-American sentiment spreads like wildfire.

Judy's parents hail from Britain and France, meet in Paris during a volatile period in French history—the student movement of 1968—and later migrate to Australia to begin a new life. After her parents part, Judy abandons racial and cultural prejudice and, while studying in Tokyo, falls in love with Zhou, a Chinese student from Beijing. But this stormy relationship eventually culminates in violence and Judy, fleeing its demise, escapes to Seoul.

Jiaying's family are from war-torn China, which, in the 19th century had suffered invasion and colonisation by the British and French; in the 20th century had been occupied by the Japanese, under the pretext of liberating Asia from Western imperialists; and was then convulsed by a Communist revolution propped up by the Russians. Having both fought in and sought to escape the wars, Jiaying's grandparents and parents eventually settle in Taiwan, carrying with them the scars of a century of conflict. Attempting to begin a new life on this island of exiles, they struggle to come to terms with the humiliation that generations of Chinese people had suffered.

Jiaying, twelve years older than Judy, becomes her only confidante, as the younger woman pours out her frustrations. Judy still loves her Chinese boyfriend, but could never really understand him. In Judy's painful struggle to come to terms with the past, Jiaying is reminded of her own history, from which she still seeks an escape. Nationalism that has wounded and distorted history time and again over the last hundred years; violence as a consequence of sexuality repressed by Confucianism … as Jiaying began her relationship with a European man, these things had begun to seep into her life. Judy's story gives Jiaying a channel to sort out her own thoughts and gradually begin the healing process.

And yet, even as the women forge new paths through the emotional jungle of their lives, violence once again shatters the potential for peace of mind.

Shih Chiung-Yu was born in Taiwan in 1968. She grew up in Taitung, a village of aboriginal Taiwan. She has been a writer, essayist, news reporter and documentary filmmaker for many years. Her writing has garnered numerous accolades, including *China Times Literature Award* and *United Daily News Literature Award*.

Masked Dolls is her first book to be translated into English.

SHIH CHIUNG-YU

Masked Dolls

Translated from the Chinese
by Wang Xinlin and Poppy Toland

balestierpress

Balestier Press
238 Balestier Road #02-02, Singapore 329701
71-75 Shelton Street, London WC2H 9JQ
www.balestier.com

Masked Dolls
Original title: 假面娃娃
Copyright © Shih Chiung-Yu, 2002
English translation copyright © Wang Xinlin and Poppy Toland, 2016

This edition first published by Balestier Press in 2016

ISBN 978 0 9932154 6 9

All rights reserved. No part of this publication may be
reproduced, stored in a retrieval system or transmitted in
any form or by any means, electronic, mechanical, without
the prior written permission of the publisher of this book.

This book is a work of fiction. The literary perceptions and
insights are based on experience, all names, characters, places,
and incidents either are products of the author's imagination
or are used fictitiously.

Masked Dolls

Conflict One

Perhaps I'll call her Judy, because that's the name of the girl my ex-boyfriend got together with after we broke up.

I'd just moved into a six-bed female dormitory in a youth hostel located up a hidden alley in Seoul's Daehak Road, and she was my only roommate. Deciding to leave my boyfriend felt like moving out of a house full of ghosts. Every time I had this thought, I felt seized by the need escape from Taiwan and travel, and I had chosen to come here to South Korea. I'd got off at Hyehwa metro station and spent the next two hours trying to track down the place I'd read about in my travel guide. I got completely lost within the alleyways, and with my rucksack on my back in the scorching sun, I was soon drenched in sweat. Had an old man not taken pity and kindly led me to the hostel's front steps, I might still be floundering about there out on that uneven pavement.

The hostel turned out to be only ten minutes walk from the

station. "Why didn't you call me to pick you up?" asked the owner, Mr Kim, once I had arrived. "Guests are always getting themselves really lost trying to find this place."

I opened the door to the dormitory, rousing Judy, who turned in her bed and looked at me through bleary eyes. "I hope I didn't wake you," I said. Judy mumbled something, turned back round and fell asleep again.

The room was a complete mess. Judy's oblong sports bag was unzipped on the floor next to her single bed, half of her possessions were still in the bag, the other half scattered untidily across the floor. Her towel, face cloth, and dirty clothes dangled from the unoccupied top and bottom bunks across from her. What a sloppy Western girl, I grumbled to myself. It was 5.15pm, but South Korea was much further north than Taiwan and the sun was still aflame in the sky, with warm rays of sunlight darting in through the curtain slits. I decided to take advantage of the remaining daylight and make my way to the old site of Seoul National University, now a lively area full of cafés, and from there on to Daehak Road, a spot popular with idle teenagers. There I could while away the time before dinner.

At dusk Daehak Road became awash with another wave of people—the white-collar workers leaving their offices and converging in search of restaurants, bars and cafes. Night descended on midsummer Seoul, and the temperature dropped. I entered a restaurant with a shop front image of a Rose of Sharon, Korea's national flower, and ordered a bowl of cold noodle soup—a traditional North Korean dish that was propelled into international focus after a historical meeting between Kim Dae-jung and Kim Jong-Il who ingested it together in Pyongyang in a lofty show of camaraderie. After dinner I stopped off at the 7-Eleven store on the corner to buy a bottle of Soju, as well as tomorrow's breakfast, and then made my way back to the hostel. By night the youth hostel didn't look as if it belonged to an emerging Asian modern metropolis, with a rapidly growing population obsessed by style and change. It just looked frozen in time, unaffected by the currents of history, part of an old European town. There was ivy clambering unhindered over the red brick walls of the two-storey building, a secluded little courtyard, and a lawn of lush, unspoiled grass, with several deckchairs arranged around an oval table beneath a tree. Inside the house the wooden floorboards, spiral staircase, and high ceilings offered a strange contrast to the collection of abstract paintings hanging on the wall with their strong impression of modernism, painted with assertive brushstrokes in bold colours. Perhaps the oddest part was the smell of weed pervading the kitchen, bathroom and living room, and often drifting from the door crack of the loft room.

"My sweet, your smile is sweet, like flowers blossoming in the spring breeze ..."

Teresa Teng's dulcet voice floated through the air. As I stepped into the hostel's ground floor lobby, a young man with dirty blond peroxide hair, wearing a tight white T-shirt gestured for me to sit down.

"Are you from Taiwan?" he asked.

"Yes, Taipei," I answered.

"This is my favourite Chinese singer. She's got such a beautiful voice." He crooned to the tune of the song, his lyrics muffled and indistinct.

"She's called Teresa Teng." I pushed out my lips, and repeated the name in an exaggerated way, to teach him the correct Chinese pronunciation. "How did you get to know about her?" I asked, intrigued.

"From films. *Comrades: Almost a Love Story* with Leon Lai and

Maggie Cheung." That film was about two lovers who went from China to Hong Kong to find work, and were, by a stroke of luck, later reunited in America.

"Teresa Teng has been dead for a long time," I said.

"Dead?" he exclaimed. This was old news—I'd assumed he'd have known. "Dead?" he repeated, bewildered, his features twisted in anguish and his eyes glazed over, as if he'd just learned of the death of a parent or lover.

"Yeah, she died. She was on holiday in Chiang Mai in Thailand a few years back when she had a sudden asthma attack." And then in the style of a movie gossip, I told him about how after her death, Teresa's French toy-boy travelled to Taipei for her funeral, and went back to her Hong Kong mansion, a broken man, until the Teng family, who wished to convert the mansion into a memorial for their daughter, asked him to leave. During my lengthy spiel, I became aware that my revelations about his dream woman were not exactly welcome.

"She was with a Western man?"

I didn't understand why he was focusing on this aspect of the story. "Everyone loved her so much! Her funeral procession was several hundred metres long. They covered her coffin with an enormous Taiwan flag, blue of the sky, white of the sun, red of the earth. I've only witnessed such magnificence once before, at General Chiang Kai-shek's funeral when I was a child. Teresa Teng is very intriguing," I continued. "She was so delicate and feminine-looking—you'd never have guessed she rode a Harley."

He got up and quietly walked from the lobby, leaving me there on my own, staring up at the ceiling with vacant eyes. I turned my gaze once more to the wall, to one of the modernist paintings, thin scrawls. I reached into my daypack and pulled out my cigarette packet, containing my last two Virginia Slims. I lit one and took a long drag.

I didn't know what I'd said to offend him, but I felt the stifling atmosphere around me.

* * *

You ask how deeply I love you?
How fiercely and how true?
My heart is pure
My love is deep
The moon reflects my heart

The light touch of your lips against mine
Has roused my heart so true
How would I ever forget This
deep love between us?

You ask how deeply I love you?
How fiercely and how true …

Teresa Teng's voice continued to reverberate through to the lobby. *The moon reflects my heart.* A golden oldie my parents used to sing together. Some time later I gave my then boyfriend the Chyi Chin cover of this song. Why that particular cover? Because it was rumoured that Chyi Chin sang the song for Joey Wong, whom my ex-boyfriend was crazy about.

Like Teresa, I'd also been in a long-term interracial relationship once too—with a Western guy. This sort of relationship, like internet cafes, started to proliferate in every major city at the turn of the century. Just like the concepts of globalisation and the global village, these relationships started to appear among my group of friends of different cultures, nationalities and skin colours.

It was to escape the memory of this relationship that I'd gathered up my belongings yet again, taken to the road and embarked upon that journey. It was why I had found myself in that unfamiliar place.

Conflict Two

Conflicts. I guess I'm the kind who attracts conflicts but has no idea how to resolve them. I clash frequently in big ways and small ways with loved ones such as my boyfriend and my mother. Lots of my relationships have ended this way. My mother is the only one I've stayed close to, despite endless conflict. If we weren't blood relations, we'd probably have gone our separate ways in the end, too. That's partly why I was in Seoul, walking the streets of a foreign country on my own.

I'll never forget the scene: the cane in my mother's hand as she whipped it across my skinny legs in a fit of hysterical fury. Had I been eight, nine or eleven? I don't remember what led to the beating. Perhaps I'd stolen her high heels or taken her lipstick without asking and snapped it by mistake—it was Shiseido or Max Factor, considered a classy brand back then. As a child I used to devour fairy tales, traditional myths about courageous and righteous heroes. Being so young, I misinterpreted and misapplied the hero's mantra: *A warrior chooses death over humiliation.* Each time mother lashed her cane down upon my legs in a frenzy, screeching at me in fury as she did so, I would stand rooted to the ground like a statue, until I had crimson lines like shallow rivers cut across my legs and stomach. My mother must have been praying that I would be like my siblings, scrambling to take cover under beds and tables to escape their thrashings, allowing her electrifyingly hysterical performance reach an immaculate, furious finale. But not me. I was like an actor who'd veered off-script, with no regard for my lines.

I was always served a simmering bowl of pig liver and kidney after these thrashings. It nourished the blood, my mother said. I'd take the bowl of pig offal stir-fried in ginger, and lumber wordlessly into the living room to watch *Gatchaman*, my favourite Japanese cartoon. As Gatchaman spun his magic cloak and launched himself into the sky to battle Galactor, his nemesis, I'd hear my mother sigh to my father, "Jiaying is such a strange child, she never runs away from a beating."

The morning after a beating, I'd wear stockings that were usually reserved for choir competitions or extra-curricular performances. This was to save me the embarrassment of having my red and purple leg laceration from becoming a subject of scrutiny and gossip at school. During a drawn-out assembly one morning, the elastic around the knee of one of my stockings became loose. I scrambled to yank it back up without being noticed, but I was spotted by a teacher, who was new to our school and pregnant.

Let's call her Miss A. It's been a long time and I've forgotten her actual name, although I still remember her gentle voice and the way her eyes crinkled when she smiled. After assembly she tapped me on the shoulder and asked me to go with her to the sickbay. I was made to lie on a black plastic reclining seat, feeling like an indulged child as Miss A squatted in front of me and rolled down my stockings to inspect my legs. I was resistant at first.

"Did you hurt yourself? Be good and let me take a look."

"I fell off my bike yesterday and hurt myself," I mumbled stiffly, and twisted my head away, not wanting to look directly at my injuries.

Naturally Miss A didn't believe me. She lowered her head to dab purple ointment onto my wounds, blowing gently onto the raw area of split skin to stop the ointment from burning so much.

If there was such a thing as happiness, I was convinced I'd just been filled to the brim with it. Miss A finally set me down from the seat, stroked my head and told me to go back to my classroom. When she smiled she looked like one of those winged angels from stories. I bounded back to my classroom and found a long strand of Miss A's hair on my blue dress. I carefully picked it off and slid it into my copy of *Alice in Wonderland*, keeping it safe between the pages. From then on, whenever I was unhappy, I'd take the strand of hair from my book and play with it.

* * *

The year I broke up with my English boyfriend Lawrence, we'd already stopped having sex or sharing a bed. We no longer even ate together. On the rare occasion that we did, we'd sit opposite each other in silence, gazing stonily into the distance and mechanically shovelled food into our mouths with movements like cogs in a machine. We'd been having endless arguments, some serious, some trivial. After we'd finished all our finger pointing during these terrible shouting matches, I'd feel exhausted, trapped and suffocated. The gloom would be cast over every nook and cranny of our hundred square metre apartment. I had such a strong sense of suffocation. It was unrelenting. It felt like when I almost drowned in the river as a child, when the water kept crashing down onto me, crashing down, crashing down. I lashed my limbs about in a furious attempt to break for the surface, but just sunk deeper and deeper instead, until I found myself exhausted, spent ...

After one particularly fierce argument with Lawrence, I buried my head in the bedroom wardrobe and began to howl. I hadn't thought there was anything particularly odd about my behaviour. But when Lawrence's American friend Sam came over for dinner one evening, I was spying on them through a gap in the door, and overheard Lawrence telling him about my episode in the bedroom as if it were something incomprehensible:

"She was just lying there, half her body in the wardrobe, the other half on the floor. I was in the living room and I heard this terrible cry. I ran into the bedroom to see what was going on. She'd buried her head in the wardrobe like an ostrich, and was crying loud enough to wake the dead.

" 'Are you okay?' I asked her. 'Why are you crying like this?'

She stopped crying as soon as she heard me walk into the bedroom, pulled her head from the wardrobe and began to babble. At first she told me nothing was wrong and then later, she said, 'Oh, it's because my aunt passed away'.

" 'Didn't your aunt die from cancer two months ago?' I asked her. 'I don't remember you crying hysterically like this then!' She didn't say anything, just buried her head under the duvet, flopped onto the bed and refused to speak any more to me."

Lawrence chewed the end of his cigar, smoked half of it and handed the rest to Sam.

From some distance away, through the red wine glasses and scented candles, Sam's blue eyes locked with mine. He blew out a series of smoke rings, and then explained in an earnest way how many of his friends in long-term relationships had broken up with their partners, because they had dragged their heels for too long about marriage.

Was he heralding the breakup of our relationship? Or had he just then realised we were doomed?

When I think back on what happened, it's this scene in particular that fills me with rage. Most of the time I didn't understand why I was so angry. Maybe I'm just a man hater, who knows. That, too, was partly why I was in Seoul, walking the streets of that foreign country, all on my own. Perhaps I was thinking that only through self-exile, far from home, would I have the chance to figure it all out. I hope that will prove to be true.

Conflict Three

J udy wasn't one of those really beautiful Western girls. She had small brown freckles scattered across her snow white face, particularly around the bridge of her nose. Her curly brown hair, which grew a couple of centimetres past her ears, was tinged a blondish-brown at the ends. She had a very small oval face, with a light spread of fluffy blonde down her temples. Despite all these little oddities, Judy was strangely charismatic. Perhaps it was her bewildered gaze and innocent smile.

I'd been sharing a room with her at that Seoul youth hostel for two days already, but we hadn't exchanged one word yet. I only saw her when she was in bed—either tossing fretfully unable to fall asleep, or snoring softly from underneath her bed covers when she finally drifted off. One evening, after I'd emerged from the steaming shower room, we eventually spoke. "Hey, how are you doing? I've heard you're Chinese," Judy greeted me. She was in the living room watching TV, sitting among a heap of clothes laid out over the sofa to dry.

"Yes, I'm from Taiwan." It was hard to see Judy's head poking out from among the messy array of dank clothing. "So you speak Mandarin!"

It was strange to have a blond Western woman speaking Mandarin to me in a foreign country, and my remark came out sounding mistrustful.

"Only a little. I studied in Beijing a couple of months ago," she replied.

Judy's Mandarin was tinged with a strong Beijing accent, and the way she intonated words sounded jarring and ridiculous to my Taiwanese ears.

Later that night I had already fallen asleep when I was woken by Judy's footsteps as she entered the dormitory.

She opened the
door. Closed the
door. Quiet as a
cat.
Gulped down water.
Changed her clothes.
And slipped under the covers.

It must have been four in the morning. I could make out a faint whiff of alcohol within the darkness of the dormitory. Had Judy been drinking? I pondered this question drowsily and drifted straight back to sleep.

It was around midday when I finally emerged from my deep slumber. Most people had left the building and the dormitory floor was empty apart from Judy. I found her sitting at the kitchen table eating lunch. We started to chat.

Judy had been beaten up by a Chinese man. He had been her classmate while studying in Tokyo. Later they'd become lovers and moved in together.

Do you miss him? I sat down at the table opposite her and started slurping down the cup noodles and *kimchi* I'd bought from 7-Eleven.

The atmosphere within the youth hostel was calm, compared to the endless stream of traffic outside. Seoul was a city being overwhelmed by time and speed, while we felt like survivors on a deserted island, forgotten by the rest of the city. And in this space where time seemed to have stopped, I heard my question reverberate...

* * *

After he hit me, we always had this intense, long drawn-out sex. He sucked my breasts, rubbed them with his fingers, took them in his mouth. He bit my earlobes, neck, back and stomach with his warm lips, teeth and tongue.

He spread my thighs and sunk his head deep down between them, just like a devout pilgrim. Gently and meticulously, he would stroke the dense clusters of fine hair between my legs, stroke it, fondle it. With the tip of his tongue he would tease the pea-sized protrusion of my swelling clit. I'd be so wet. It would flow out in a continuous stream. Like ocean waves, he told me, salty and wet. It mixed with his saliva, soaking the bed sheets.

Do you want me to fuck you from behind? he'd always ask in an authoritative tone. This was after I'd ridden him like a wild horsewoman or a reckless racing car driver.

Tell me you want me to fuck you.

Yes. I want you to fuck me. From behind. Please. From behind.

Fuck me.

He didn't wear condoms. Ever.

He explained it in terms of traditional Chinese philosophy, which he said were different from Western philosophies about love. If he wore a condom, we wouldn't blend into one another, we wouldn't be unified.

Our fluids had to mingle. My clay would contain some of his; and his clay would contain some of me. Isn't there a Chinese song about that? He taught me to sing it. It's called *Clay Figures*, I think.

The first time he slapped me was because I had been out until late drinking in bars with friends. It was around the time we'd decided to move in together to save on rent—you must know how expensive rent is in Tokyo.

Do you know I've been out of my mind worrying about you? he said.

But I told you I was going to a bar with some of my Western friends and that I'd be home late.

Do you have any idea how dangerous it is for a woman to take a taxi home by herself in the middle of the night? So many girls get raped that way. How do you expect me not to worry? I was too scared to go to the toilet or take a shower in case I missed your call.

You're way too paranoid. What's the big deal? If you were that worried, you could have just called me on my mobile.

You think I didn't try that? But you had your phone switched off, didn't you? Greenish veins bulged from his neck and his eyes blazed with fury.

My phone had been on the whole time, but perhaps because I'd been in a basement room there had been no signal.

You clearly don't give a damn about how I feel.

I'm very touched you're so concerned about my well-being, but there was no need for you to get so worried. Of course you could have showered or used the toilet. You shouldn't have wasted your energy worrying—I'm old enough to look after myself. Please don't act like a dad.

Can you stop being so selfish and see that I'm doing this for your own good! You have no idea what men think when they see a tipsy woman. Women who drink are the ones that get raped. Isn't it better to be safe than sorry? And anyway, I hate it when you reek of booze.

But going out with friends for a drink or two is completely normal. You do it with your friends.

It's different for men.

What do you mean 'different'? What you're saying sounds a lot like male chauvinism.

Don't try and bring that old gender conflict stuff into our relationship—it's nothing like that.

I don't want to argue with you, I'm tired and I want to go to bed. If you're so worried about me, you're welcome to come along next time.

I told you so many times—those places blast their music so loudly you feel as if your eardrums are about to burst—I hate it!

It feels as if you're just trying to avoid meeting my Western friends.

Why should I meet them? Do I have to? Do I have to make small talk with these people when I don't even speak English properly? They're a strange bunch of people, aren't they, coming to Asia and carrying on speaking their own little language. They should get it into their thick skulls that they're in Japan, in Asia, not a colony of theirs! They've got some nerve to grumble about the fact that people don't speak good English here. Do you really think they talk to me because they're interested in what I have to say? All they want to ask is if I eat dog meat or monkey brain in China. Does my grandmother still bind her feet? Do I know what happened at Tiananmen Square? How can I afford the high living costs in Tokyo? Whether I'm filthy rich, with parents who are high-ranking officials. When will China start a World War against the Western powers? Does the fact that I have a Western girlfriend get me a lot of attention in China and give me kudos?

Bunch of imbeciles, he spat. White bastards. I can't be bothered to waste my time with any of them.

Do you really need to talk so aggressively? You're the crazy one.

He swung his hand hard down on my face. The sound of the slap echoed in the air. Searing heat. That was all I felt. I thought I'd lost the feeling in one half of my face. That was the first time he hit me.

Conflict Four

"Dump your Western boyfriend," I was told in a dark bar once many years ago. We had played a few games of darts, had several rounds of drinks and were all completedly wasted. I ordered a Singapore Sling, and distinctly remember feeling as if the pink cocktail was twirling me around and around. I was on tiptoes, light-footed as a ballerina. Spinning, spinning ... How I wished I could just carry on spinning, until every last trace of sorrow had been wiped from my memory.

I had a crimson cherry and a paper umbrella clipped to the rim of my Singapore Sling glass.

I gulped down a few more mouthfuls of the cocktail and the paper umbrella started to expand before my eyes. I saw it growing larger and larger...

The wooden stick of the enlarged umbrella slid into my hand.

I looked like a girl from the early Republican-era wearing a Mandarin gown, but curiously enough found myself on tiptoes, dancing the classical ballet steps I'd learnt as a child.

I danced and danced, occasionally bumping into one of the high wooden bar stools, or getting so dizzy I bashed my thigh against a bench in the gangway. I spun round and round, eventually spinning my way out of The Cave, the bar I'd been in, and onto Shuangcheng Street ... This bar district seemed to still be haunted by the American military ... Barmaids and soldiers strolled along the alleyways flirting, illuminated by the neon lights ... An elderly prostitute, her mouth smeared with cheap shiny lipstick, hooted at well-attired business travellers carrying briefcases, soliciting them as they came over to the bar for a drink.

I made my way past the sizzling smoke from the grilled sausage stand on the street corner and to the bar across the street which advertised live rock 'n' roll. I pressed my face up against its cool, dark window.

There was a heavy metal band playing on stage. The singer, guitarist, bassist and drummer all had the same shoulder-length hair and wore black leather jackets and skinny jeans. The audience moved their heads to the beat of the music, as if high on ecstasy. Their heads bobbed from side to side like clockwork dolls. I suddenly noticed that Fat Luo was there too. He was standing in front of the grabber machine, completely engrossed in the task of capturing a flannel doll. The mechanical claw descended upon its prey, with Fat Luo deftly pressing its buttons. All of a sudden he started hitting the machine out of sheer frustration. From where I was standing on the other side of the window, I saw that he'd failed to snare the doll.

Light glinted off the mechanic claw. Fat Luo seemed to have been lucky this time. His mouth curled up at the corners and I read his lips. "Heh, heh, Jiaying, I've got you this time." Jiaying? Was he talking about me? He was—the doll had a Hello Kitty-ish body, but my face. The mechanical claw gripped it around the neck, dragging it upwards, contorting its features, but there was no doubt about it—it was me.

Why was Fat Luo so intent on picking me up with the cold claws of the grabber machine? Why did he want a Hello-Kitty-ish doll version of me? I could hear him laughing nastily from inside the dark bar.

A chill ran down my spine. I turned and ran, back to the others in *The Cave*. I shoved open the door and collided with our young professor, who was on his way to the bar to get a drink. "What's wrong? Did you go outside to throw up?" he asked.

"Come and play a game of darts with me," he ordered, without waiting for me to reply.

"Didn't you see those American soldiers walking down the street, or Fat Luo in that bar playing with the grabber machine?" Strange laughter echoed around me. "Fat Luo's here, isn't he?" Someone pointed to the toilets across from the pool-table, out of which Fat Luo was emerging.

Fat Luo shrugged off the accusing finger pointing at him, and looked innocent. He dried his hands against the sides of his trousers. If Fat Luo was over here... what had I seen in that dim lighting across the road?

"Bull's Eye!" The young professor's haughty remark was accompanied by a swoosh. Like a powerful magnet, the dart appeared to be sucked towards the dartboard with incredible speed and force.

"Wow! Amazing, Professor, you're amazing." The crowd went wild. Some people bashed beer bottles against the table top, while others applauded with hands that were already red from too much clapping. The young professor was like a king surrounded by this entourage of students.

"Come over here and let me kiss you," the young professor called out to a female student, tipsy and euphoric. She had bright bronze eyes and wavy Barbie-doll hair.

"Aren't I something?" The young professor asked smugly, glancing at the fresh faced female student making her way over.

The girl began to giggle. "Amazing," she said, deliberately drawing out the word. The young professor lifted her petite face of the girl, lowered his own head and pecked her on the cheek like a little bird. Someone frowned at the shady alcohol-infused atmosphere. The young professor, dressed like a student in his white T-shirt, jeans and Nike trainers, raised his right hand once again—the same hand he'd just shot the bull's eye with—and pointed towards the bar.

"You. Come here."

Everyone looked over at me. The professor wasn't calling me, was he? Under the searing gaze of the crowd I glanced around reluctantly, trying to pretend he didn't mean me. I hesitated before dragging my feet towards the professor's dark shadow. I hung my head, feeling bashful, like a little girl who'd misbehaved. I thought that perhaps I was going to be on the receiving end of some punishment ritual, that I too might be about to receive the professor's bird-like peck on the cheek.

But I didn't. The professor noticed my mistrustful expression, and in a commandeering tone, said, "You must break up with your Western boyfriend."

I felt as if I had a fish bone lodged in my throat. I struggled to formulate a reply. I whipped my head round in silence and in that dingy lighting instinctively managed to locate Fat Luo's gaze. It must have been a murderous look I gave that big-mouthed tell-tale. Idiot! Going on and on about how he was my blood brother, but then stabbing me in the back as soon as an opportunity arose and dragging me through the mud. Asshole! Bastard! Coward! Yes. My face must have been full of this contempt and disdain as I glared up at him. Fat Luo feigned innocence, shrugging as if it were nothing to do with him. But I could see his ears had pricked up like a radio antenna as he listened, straining to hear whether I would succumb to the pressure and announce before the crowd that I would leave my boyfriend, my British boyfriend, my "Western boyfriend". Traitor!

I pursed my lips, stiffened my spine, and said nothing. Punish me then. Rosy in the film *Ryan's Daughter* endured a similar fate: they had picked up stones from the ground and pelted her with them. They had converged on her, spitting at her, calling her a slut. They had stripped her naked before a crowd to humiliate her, used scissors to savagely snip off her once beautiful and lustrous hair. All because she'd fallen in love with a man of a different race who spoke a different language. For fuck's sake!

Between the earth and sky, there is justice to abide by. Did I really just mutter that to myself, the way I used to recite lines of poetry I'd memorised from the calligraphy scrolls hanging at home. I was back to being a child, standing motionless before my mother as she caned me, challenging her to beat me to death. This unrelenting obstinacy of mine stemmed from my own unwavering and damning logic?

I won't give in. I have told you a hundred times: I will never, ever be in love with you. I will never see you as anything more than a dear friend. Give up on the thought—you've got to just give it up. Within my stubborn, unbending heart, I am carrying all the pain and the burden you have imposed upon me, but it's too much. Don't love me, I thought. Don't, don't, just don't love me. You'll stifle me to death.

I said nothing, just took the dart from the professor's hands, my head lowered to escape the scene. I made my way over to the dartboard, and with a swish I threw my dart. It missed. It struck the wall like a deflated rubber ball, and plummeted lifelessly to the floor. I had nothing of the skill of an old master. And actually came away looking like a traitor.

I'd thought that I'd been clever in throwing this dart. I thought it might help to extricate me from this embarrassing situation. But it didn't work.

It was late at night and I heard the manic barking of dogs from behind the iron gates of Shuangcheng Street apartment blocks. Alongside the barking came the howling and raving of a drunken bar patron:

I want to die! I want to jump in the Tamsui River! What are you going to do about it? Are you going to help me to die? Leave me alone! Just let me die! Just kill me and be done with it!

The man collapsed onto the road in his drunken state. As night drew deeper, Shuangcheng Street seemed possessed by more and more demons. We all seemed to be falling into the strange iridescent glass of a crystal ball. Each person sealed within the crystal fell into a narcotic trance-like state. Instincts took over as consciousness was peeled away.

The faces of the people in the bar were starting to look different. Drunken brawls broke up as demons descended. The dark night was aquiver with black shadowy souls. Wild flames of desire from their bodies. Night provided a protective cover for this unsettling, murky chaos. It allowed people to choose advantageous positions.

Fat Luo had thrown off his usual slow and blundering mannerisms and was starting to imitate the moves of a computer game boxer. He was attacking from all sides and angles, his fat plimsoll-clad feet moving nimbly back and forth. The target of his attack was the young professor, the king surrounded by his cohorts. Everyone broke into raucous laughter when they saw Fat Luo. "Go for it, Fat Luo! Go for it!" Someone slammed the bottom half of a broken beer bottle against the table. "Go for it Fat Luo! Go for it!" Fat Luo was spurred into action, like a dormant beast suddenly come back to life,. A strange gurgling sound rose from his throat.

"Wa! Hoo!" He gave long and sudden shriek and released a flying roundhouse kick. "Wahoo!" Another strange cry, his leg going for the young professor's chin. The young professor ducked out of the way, and pushed out at Fat Luo, who tumbled like a snowman and landed beneath the wooden table. The crowd gave a howl. In front of all their stunned faces, he smashed a leg off the wooden stool.

"Hah! You bastard. You want to fight with me, do you?" the young professor said. "Go home and practice for another ten years! Trying to usurp the throne, are you? Think it's that easy? Useless piece of shit!" He made as if about to spit down onto Fat Luo.

"Long live the professor! Long live the professor!" The crowd of students began to clap and cheer.

"Oh that isn't necessary!" The young professor raised his arms in a show of victory. Once again he went to stroke the cheek of the pretty fresh-faced female student, her gaze filled with admiration and longing.

"What do you think? I'm good, aren't I?"

"Amazing, you're really cool, Professor!" The female student's voice was filled with wonder, with eyes like those of the Red Guards standing at Tiananmen Square during the Cultural Revolution, looking up at Chairman Mao with adoration fit only for an emperor. The young professor chuckled at the ribbing he was receiving, and swiftly planted another bird-like kiss on her tender cheek.

The place's female owner had been standing at the bar chatting to customers, dressed in an off-the-shoulder top and a tight silk miniskirt that showed off her long slender legs. In her high heels, she clipped her way over to the source of the commotion, oozing lazy sensuality. She pressed a delicate finger, decorated with a diamond ring, into the young professor's shoulder blade.

"Oh, Gary!" she drawled in a deep, husky voice. "Who's going to pay for the chair your student just smashed up?" She pointed to where Fat Luo lay collapsed on the floor, the diamond on her finger casting a glittering light onto his face.

"You know you can put it on my bill," the young professor said gallantly. His hand slid from her waist down to her shapely behind, and began to knead at the flesh. He released a slow breath next to her ear. "Miss me, did you?" he murmured in a deep voice. Sprawled out beneath the table like a dying cockerel, Fat Luo stared back in amazement, with the expression of a foolish child. "Arsehole!" the word burst out of his mouth, but it wasn't clear whether it came from a place of admiration or envy.

The bar owner turned around just in time to see her husband, a Westerner, coming in through the revolving door, carrying a bottle of Isle of Skye Scotch whisky. She leapt up from the young professor's lap, and stroking his head she cooed, "Be a good boy. There's no hurry, I'll attend to you later."

She gave the young professor's ear a light pinch and shuffled nimbly in her high-heels, back to the bar where her husband now stood.

Conflict Five

Taomei. Her face radiated seductive energy. It was a face that ignited male desire.

Behind Taomei's clear and curious gaze was hidden the unspeakable secret we had shared since girlhood. We could look at each other, but never talk about it. It made me angry and Taomei crazy.

I liked Taomei's poetry. Quirky and evocative. Sometimes angelic, other times devilish. How she managed to flit so effortlessly between these two modes I do not know. I'd sometimes find her sitting in a corner of the Liberal Arts Department corridor at university. As the bitter mountain wind raged outside, she would read her latest poems and we would eat fast-food sandwiches and drink milk tea.

If Taomei ever decided to give up on her poetry, I always thought she should be a model, so as not to waste her God-given talent. Yet it was Taomei's beauty that inevitably led to her demise.

Taomei never thought I'd be awarded a national literary prize one day, have my debut novel published and become the envy of all my peers. I just felt that life was a huge joke. I wished none of it had happened, because it made everything look like a pile of shit.

My photo rested ghost-like on the front covers of my novel stacked up in bookshops. A picture of my face looking incredibly childish and guileless had been printed on the publicity posters on display in countless bookshops. I rushed around tirelessly speaking at writing forums on an array of different topics. So as to avoid disappointing my devoted readership, I stayed up all night writing pieces on topics chosen by my editor and of no interest to me.

Much of my time was spent receiving phone calls and learning how to say no to people. I refused five invitations from television stations to appear on their programmes. I rejected an advertising company's invitation—and a six-sum figure—to endorse their shampoo by flicking my hair in front of the camera. Overnight I found myself surrounded by literary old-timers wanting to act as my agents, and literary elders putting me down for being too young, frivolous, brash and reckless, and calling my work unintelligible. I was offered publishing contract after publishing contract, and had to really plead to make sure these publishers understood that I absolutely didn't want my photograph on the cover. My love life became a topic of discussion for gossip columns. I became the target of attack from people, many of whom I hadn't even met, alleging that I was a diva, a pain in the arse to work with, and so on.

Most of these matters were completely unrelated to writing, but took up eighty percent of my energy. My literary predecessor Eileen Chang once said that it was better to be famous as early in life as possible, as later in life fame lost its buzz. I completely disagree with her. I suppose she might have changed her mind when she was older—why else would she have hidden herself away in the United States, moving house each time she was discovered? In her later years she no longer wrote, perhaps smug in the knowledge that she had finally found an ordinary old woman's freedom.

Freedom. How precious freedom was. Even when it meant losing the will to live, when nothing made you feel happy or worth hanging on for, when even your desire to eat was gone, that freedom to just naturally slip away, not forced to live on for the sake of the public. Eileen Chang stopped eating and died a natural death; San Mao used stockings to hang herself in the hospital; Virginia Woolf ended her life by jumping into a river; Hemingway put a gun to his head; Yukio Mishima disembowelled himself like a samurai; Yasunari Kawabata died quietly with gas; Lao She drowned himself in the river; and my friend Xiaojin killed herself in Paris, at the age of twenty-six, by plunging a knife through her heart …

It was far too late to discuss any of these examples with Taomei. We had once been university roommates sharing a tiny flat lined with electric heaters and exchanging girly secrets. But there would be no more secrets to exchange with her. How I wanted to gently explain how everything we'd believed so important back then was all just a crock of shit. But Taomei would never listen to such a show of sincerity from me again, nor would she be willing to go back over everything that had happened, dredging up all those past thoughts and feelings. I wanted to tell her how each time as I saw my self-important face staring ghost-like back at me like a commodity in the bookshop, I was seized by the impulse to take a knife and slash my own face or shave all the long thick black hair from my head. I didn't want people discussing my beauty in the same way they discussed the lithe figure of some *Playboy* magazine model without giving a crap about what she thought. I blamed my mother for giving me my beautiful face, making my load heavier and giving me the potential to sin.

I lost Taomei's friendship, though I'm not sure exactly when.

* * *

Seeing Judy reminded me of my long-lost friend. A Taiwanese girl and a Westerner—how did they manage to look alike?

Sitting at the kitchen table of the youth hostel in Seoul and examining Judy's face, I felt myself starting to zone out. Taomei was more beautiful than Judy, with features that were delicate and refined. Those big bright eyes of hers shone with purity and a sparkle of childlike bewilderment. Taomei was spontaneous and scatter-brained. Her animated gaze could not conceal her simple desires. Her hair was soft and voluminous and blondish, like the curls on a Barbie doll.

I saw the two of them, young and alluring, shrouded in a soft white see-through veil. Lured by witchcraft through the dark and tempestuous night, under the searing gaze of the crowd, being led step by step towards the altar.

No! I cried out loudly, reaching out to grasp their arms.

"It's nothing to do with you, bitch," the young professor turned around and said nastily.

"You shameless little whores," spat my old classmate Fat Luo, who used to inundate Taomei and me with love letters.

I had no way to stop the girls. They just continued walking step by step towards the fiery altar.

Ah. I must be dreaming.

Oh, if only it were all just a dream.

One afternoon, a few years after this unspeakable event between

Taomei and me, on an urge I grabbed my college address book, and headed to Taipei Bus Station. I boarded the southbound Zhongxing bus, changed to a local bus, and then caught a cab, finally arriving at the address in the book.

It was a traditional courtyard house, the sort you no longer see in Taipei. Her parents were crop growers, and had the simple way of farmers.

"Our Taomei has been infected by bad ways in Taipei," they muttered in low voices in the presence of their daughter's close friend.

Taomei didn't recognise me at all.

"Taomei, it's me, Jiaying."

"Taomei, it's Jiaying, you remember, we used to read magazines together in 7–Eleven on the sly." I moved my hand up and down in front of her eyes, trying to get her to acknowledge my presence. "Oh. Jiaying." Her reply was so brief that it didn't seem like an answer at all. She turned her head and looked towards the window, completely ignoring that I was there.

I followed her gaze out the window. Snow-white plum blossoms flowered along the bumpy slopes, a dreamscape dotting the hills and valleys.

That strange and mischievous girl who used to play incessant practical jokes, who'd smack the arses of the most straight-laced boys in our class, causing us both to explode into fits of laughter as we fled away—my friend Taomei. She was gone.

Conflict Six

Taomei's face intermingled with Judy's. Fading in and out. Like two film shots being spliced together, the image of one face being overlaid on another. The merged face slowly moved away from the camera, or perhaps more accurately the camera gradually pulled away from the face. Their bodies started to recede, as if they were performing some secret ritual, walking step by step towards that mysterious altar stained dark red with the blood of virgins …

Judy sat opposite me moaning on about her Chinese boyfriend in Tokyo, the love of her life. As she descended into this vague, relatively fresh grief, I saw ther face morphing into that of my girlhood friend, Taomei. Judy was oblivious as she continued to regale me with the details of her life in the Tokyo—a life separated by the sea now, and a Chinese lover who used to beat her.

* * *

We lived in Ikebukuro, northwest Tokyo. Our place was on the ninth floor of an apartment block. It was small, with a tiny kitchen and bathroom, and the rent was extortionate. I come from Australia, which is massive, and we're used to large living spaces. Squeezed into an apartment where the bedroom was also the living room made me feel cramped and stifled. Coming back to the apartment after class each night, we'd turn right out of the subway station and glimpse hoards of youngsters loitering on the pavement. Even on cold winter nights you'd see teenage girls in ultra-short miniskirts wandering the streets.

Do you know what they were doing? Judy's eyes blazed with excitement, as she tried to reel me in with her story.

"What were they up to?" I already knew the answer, but tried not to show it in my voice so as not to disappoint her.

Business. The primitive business of flesh. You know how crazy Japanese people are about Western luxury goods? To get their hands on these exorbitantly priced designer bags, these girls would trade their flesh to rich men, without even batting an eyelid.

I responded with another polite "Ah," to show that I was listening.

It's insane how much they worship the west! Judy said in an incredulous tone, giggling.

I had a degree in East Asian Languages from Sydney University, she continued, but everyone in Tokyo was way more interested in learning English from me and going to live in the west. I was a bit bummed out about that at first. Judy's face broke into another childish grin.

"That's pretty common. People idealise what it might be like to live in a faraway place." I heard myself sounding like a wise old woman as I comforted her.

Sometimes I miss life in Australia, especially the wide-open spaces and being close to nature. But I don't want to go back.

Australia is way too boring. Judy paused. As she said the word 'boring', she sounded as if her mind was drifting off somewhere.

"I've no idea if Australia is boring," I said. "I've only ever been to Sydney, but one interesting thing I found there was that the place names were derived from where the early settlers came from. Oxford Street, for example, King's Cross, Liverpool Street and Hyde Park. In some way it reflects the deep nostalgia the early settlers felt towards Britain. You see a similar sense of nostalgia towards China in my home town, Taipei."

I thought my comment would garner some response from Judy, but she didn't say a word. Perhaps never having been to Taipei, she found it hard to understand what I was saying. Perhaps she was just missing her ex-boyfriend in Tokyo, and had unwittingly sunk deep into sorrow. Or perhaps all Judy wanted in this foreign country was to talk to somebody in her mother tongue, and my role was simply to listen, not respond.

Ah. Yes, Judy said, before beginning a monologue which led her back to that Chinese lover who had beaten her so badly. In Tokyo.

But. I couldn't completely fall in love with Tokyo's way of life.

I've told you about my apartment in Ikebukuro. I really didn't like it at all. It was too small and cramped. I wanted to move to the suburbs where you could rent bigger apartments in a better environment for the same price. But my Chinese boyfriend didn't want that. He had two jobs, one at a Japanese bar near Ikebukuro bus station, as well as occasional translation work.

I knew he was exhausted, so I suggested paying a bigger portion of the rent. He said he may be poor but he still had backbone.

This was the tradition of Chinese intellectuals, he explained. I never anticipated it might become a cause of conflict between us. After every argument he would go out to the balcony to smoke, without saying a word. I didn't like the atmosphere. I preferred to talk things through and clear the air, to take action if needed. Perhaps he found me too forthright.

Money wasn't the problem. If I'd been living on my own in Tokyo I would have rented a similar-sized apartment and paid roughly the same amount. Tokyo's rent might be exorbitant, but that didn't mean we had to lower our quality of life, did it? I told him I wouldn't mind paying a bit more if it meant we could live more comfortably.

I don't think we have a poor quality of life, he replied. And this apartment is so close to my work, which saves me a long commute. Plus it's not far from the university, he said.

Don't you think the bar job takes up too much of your time? And it's not going to help your career, is it?

Listen here, missy, do you think I can teach English like you, make easy money by the hour? You're like the emperor in the Chinese proverb who hears that the people didn't have enough rice to eat and asks, "Well, why don't they eat meat then?"

I'm only thinking of you. You could definitely find another job, one with better working conditions. You don't have to work like a dog in that cramped place filled with barbecue smoke, do you?

You obviously look down on my work, don't you? Can't you be happy that I'm making money? And you eat those barbecues, how can you say you hate the place?

I'm not saying your job's bad. I just think you could work in a better environment. It's like the place we're living in right now: cramped. It's not a big problem, but we can still strive for somewhere better.

You look down on me. I don't. Subconsciously you do. I don't. Don't denigrate me. Your lack of respect is obvious from the way you look and talk. I do respect you—how many times do I have to tell you? Don't you understand what I'm saying? You really don't understand the way I feel.

Do I have to be responsible for the way you feel each time you kick up a fuss for no reason? Can't you see you're making a mountain out of a molehill? And yet for some reason you want me to be responsible for it? Does that sound fair to you?

Go back to Australia if you want to live in a first world country. Don't measure your first world standards against the lives of third world people.

"And then?" I asked.

And then he hit me.

"Ah," I said. "And then?"

I left our apartment and ran out into the street. I spent the whole night in a bar drinking. But it was freezing outside and so I had no choice but to go back to our apartment.

He told me he was sorry. He held me and promised not to hurt me again. We both cried.

"Ah. And then?" I pursued the outcome of the story like a robot, devoid of warmth or emotion.

Then we curled up on the floor and had mind-blowing sex. We were in this uncontrollably euphoric state where we had to make passionate love at least three times a night. It was as if we were unable to prove our love for each other without it.

"Oh," I said.

Conflict Seven

Do all conflicts lead to violence? Are people with higher testosterone levels really more aggressive?

Years ago I asked my father the same question. My father had followed the army from mainland China to the dank and humid southern island of Taiwan. Why did you kill people with your gun and bayonet when you were younger? My question must have seemed absurd to him, alien. My whole family had been sitting at the marble table eating dinner when I asked. My father enjoyed cooking and craved certain dishes. A reflection of the deep nostalgic longing of one who had wandered far from a home he could not return to. He craved pea tofu. Papaya chicken. Light crispy pancakes. He wanted to eat brown garlic chicken and fried pork.

He asked a friend from the mainland to bring over ingredients from the Yunnan-Guizhou Plateau when he visited. My father handled these items as if they were precious herbs, like ginseng. He holed himself up in the kitchen and spent ages cooking up his regional dishes. Sometimes walking past the kitchen, I'd hear him mutter to himself as he used his spatula to scoop a little food from the wok. He lifted it to the corner of his mouth to taste, and then shook his head saying, Why doesn't it taste like grandma's cooking?

My father began to get lost in a maze of memories.

He told me that my grandfather used to do business on the Burmese border. He did business with English colonial businessmen in Burma and sometimes crossed into Vietnam to do business with French colonists.

When my grandfather went away it was often for months on end. During this time, our family land, our shop, and all the household affairs—including dealings with our dozen or so workers, was tended to by my tough-as-nails grandmother. Whenever he reminisced about his childhood, sneaking out into the fields to steal food with friends and being pursued by my grandmother with her cane in her hand, my father would start to chuckle, and exclaim what an energetic lady she'd been. He recounted how his father's return was always marked by suitcases full of rare and expensive trinkets that couldn't be found at home. Once his father brought him a pair of shoes, English black leather Oxfords, which my young father proudly wore to school. When no one took any notice or even mentioned them, my father gave one classmate such a hard kick with the shoe that they finally became a talking point. My father even wore his Oxfords into the playing fields after class for a game of football with friends. I wore leather Oxfords to play football, he said, laughing so hard tears welled up in the corners of his eyes.

Lots of calligraphy scrolls adorned the hall of our home in

Yunnan, he told me. They were paintings my grandfather had collected with the money from his business deals. No matter how hard he tried, my father couldn't remember the verses painted onto these huge wall scrolls, despite having seen them in the hall every day for years. My father racked his brains in pure frustration as he tried to remember, but in vain. When our family was gathered in the living room, our attention focused on the TV, my father suddenly seemed to have inhabited another place entirely. He told me how after dinner his schoolmates used to bring their musical instruments and they would go up to the balcony of his old home and play together under the stars.

"What?"

My gaze flickered from the TV screen up to my father who was talking. I had no idea what he was talking about. What balcony and which instruments? I asked.

"We had a small band! We would get together every couple of days to play our local folk music."

Sometimes my father would ramble on, telling me how, not long after coming to Taiwan, he had acquired a German Leica camera. Then unmarried, he would round up a group of his military friends, and travel round the humid new island with his camera in hand, looking for things to photograph.

"We should develop these photos to show the people back home. The camera can be their eyes!" My uncle was working as a spy in North Korea at that time. He was my father's little brother, his only brother, and had been a guerrilla fighter with him in northern Thailand before they'd both made their way to Taiwan. My uncle earned a big salary as a spy—paid in American dollars. He was the one who provided the money for my father to buy the Leica, a very sought-after brand in those days. My uncle would write letters to my father from the frontlines of the Korean War, reminding him to take lots of photos, particularly of Taiwan's local scenery and culture, to show the people back home.

My father squandered all the money my uncle made as a spy, though he never told me that part. 38 degrees parallel north, with little chance of survival, my uncle trekked through wind and snow, stepping over the ruins of burnt-out tanks filled with human bones, and made his escape from North Korea into South Korea, through the deathly ruins of Panmunjom, and finally back to Taiwan. One sticky and sweltering Taiwan summer afternoon many years later, my uncle no longer able to contain what he was feeling, had told me all about it.

"Father, why did you kill when you were young? Isn't murder horrible and violent?" I asked.

What I'd actually wanted to say was, no one on this island really thanked you for it, did they? My father was still heartbroken over the words of the then-president, Lee Teng-hui.

"So Lee Teng-hui thinks he's more Japanese than Chinese, does he?" My father was driven to distraction. It was as if he had suddenly been awakened to all those years of deceit. He'd often implore me to take him to the National Palace Museum in Taipei. He'd stand rooted in the dark, maze-like building for ages, facing all those thousand-year old cultural relics and treasures, perhaps letting out a sigh. Muggy afternoon after muggy afternoon was spent with him in that dark maze. I was sometimes scared that setting eyes on the *Jadeite Cabbage, Travellers Among Mountains and Streams,* or Song Huizong's calligraphy scrolls would inadvertently move him to tears.

"If you don't kill them, they kill you!" My father told me in a fit of righteous indignation, as if to a child who knew nothing of how the world worked. "Should you stand around and do nothing when they pillage the place you call home?" he asked furiously, as if I had riled him up and flustered him with all my ridiculous questions.

A historian friend of mine once told me that the impacts of war weren't necessarily negative. There were examples of splendid civilisations that had sprung up as the result of clashes and battles.

"Did your father beat you when you were little?" I asked. "Of course. He beat the crap out of me," he said.

"How did it make you feel?" I asked.

"I was cursing him in my head. Then one day, when I'd grown taller and stronger than him, I lifted him up by the collar and give him a good thrashing."

"Did you beat him again after that?"

"No."

"Why not?"

"Because he was old. He couldn't have taken a single blow," he said.

"So you don't hate him anymore?" I asked.

"No, but I don't love him either. I can just ignore him now. He has no more power over me."

White clouds drifted overhead in the sunny skies of Seoul, changing shape as the earth turned. I'd often gaze foolishly at these graceful, unfettered, ever-changing clouds, believing that someday I might sit astride one and sail off into the distance, and that all those unspeakable things would finally dissipate like dark clouds into the air. I would be like Monkey King in the cartoon, riding off on the clouds and mist, and vanishing without a trace. I lived with my uncle for a whole year. He had suffered a devastating double loss—first his son died then his wife left him. On the outside I was no different from any other fresh-faced, wide-eyed girl. I started wearing bras, exchanging secret love letters with boys. I would spend half an hour in the shower, just so I could inspect my body in the mirror. Following each fierce quarrel with my mother I would slam the bedroom door with all my might and lock myself in. If you were to flick through photos of me in my adolescent years, you would find that my pleasant, agreeable face had been fitted with a gaze that belied my age, thoughtful but rebellious, defying and challenging everything. That was me. Me back then. Defying everything, challenging everything. Where did all that energy come from? I really can't say. Just rampaging hormones I suppose.

By the time I moved in with my uncle, my rebellious streak had run its course. In that dingy hall stuck in time, we'd sit opposite each other, eating our meals without a word. His eyes were always brimming with sorrow, an indescribable sadness that was transmitted to me. Sometimes I worried I'd grown old before my time.

Like my mother, I was a child who had been abandoned, banished from the house. Instead I calmly took on the burden of this lonely middle-aged man's silent grief. I often came across my uncle alone, a spatula in his hand, as he stood in his dingy kitchen, making dinner. I witnessed him aging prematurely, his back hunched as he strolled through the dim-lit alleys on his own after the meal. He never mentioned my cousin, who had drowned in a nearby river, or where my aunt, who had left him, had disappeared to.

And I didn't ask. Perhaps being in a new environment had taught me to just observe and say nothing.

All good things came from elsewhere. It was hard to imagine that my uncle, with his primitive way of life, had once lived like a prince in some far off land. It was hard to imagine him having been a member of the secret service in South Korea, and living an extravagant life.

"Life is ephemeral!" On one occasion my usually silent uncle became animated and began to recount his life as an intelligence agent during the outbreak of the Korean War.

"They had to pick one person from a group of ten thousand and that one person was me. They sent us all to Okinawa to undergo US military training, after which we were dispatched to the Korean peninsula."

"I was the only person from my unit who came back alive." My uncle sighed. "Most were killed in the Korea," he continued, "while one or two were captured by the Communists and sent to the mainland after surrendering."

"They paid us a very good salary—in American dollars. It was the price for our lives." My uncle gazed into the middle distance, his narrow eyes squeezed into arches.

"We were living in the fast lane, leading completely debauched lives. Because at the back of our minds we always knew that today might be our last," my uncle said.

"What was your mission there?" I asked. "To take photographs," my uncle replied. "To photograph North Korea's military bases—airports, bridges, roads, ports, ammunition depots. Some of our cameras were the size of watches. We'd lift our wrists, pretending to check the time, when in actual fact the camera was snapping away. Some people wore caps fitted with micro-cameras. We'd parachute from helicopters and fighter jets to carry out our espionage. Each mission was like a rendezvous with death.

"Someone with your father's personality wouldn't have made it as an intelligence agent. You had be careful, cautious, serious and tight-lipped," my uncle said.

But, my uncle said, it had been my father's letters, delivered one after another to the frontline of the Korean War, that had made him determined, against all odds, to return to Taiwan.

"You must—the least you can do for me—is to return to Taiwan alive. I want to see you with my own eyes, alive and kicking, the way you were as a mischievous teenager. Together we'll make our way back to the mainland, to Yunnan, our home. As brothers we've stuck together through thick and thin, leaving the mainland for the Burmese borders as guerrilla fighters, before retreating to Taiwan. Countless people have perished in the fires of war, but you must remain strong—come back to Taiwan. There is a lot of work to be done—we need to defeat the Communists and save China."

And so my father's succession of letters, instructing my uncle to hold on, keep strong and make it back to Taiwan alive, arrived at the smoke-filled battlefields of the Korean peninsula where the war was still raging.

Could letters really have magical powers? Could they endow a person on the borderline between life and death with an intense will to live, so as to escape death by a whisker, defying all perils and returning home? Miraculously, against all the odds, my uncle made it back to Taiwan. My uncle told my father how grateful he was for being rescued from the gates of hell. Even though his older brother often infuriated him so much he'd gnash his teeth —for squandering his hard-earned American dollars, lending them out to a group of fellow guerrilla fighters who'd come to Taiwan, and who never returned a cent. My uncle felt suspicion and resentment towards his brother, a good-for-nothing rich boy who was always getting into fights. It was my father, he said, who had talked him into joining the military to save the country, an act which had later embroiled him in the retreat from Yunnan down to northern Burma where several years of guerrilla warfare nearly cost them their lives.

In that leech-infested wilderness, that foreign mountainous

terrain full of prowling tigers, with no food and supplies, my uncle had become addicted to opium.

He experienced severe mental anguish. He found himself on the disputed China-Burma border, in an area three times the size of Taiwan. His home was just beyond the lofty peaks of the high mountains, but he could not return.

With his gun, he fought and killed people who spoke his language, and at night he had nightmares, often waking with a face wet with tears. He was only twenty, a mere boy, with no understanding of the world. Why was he crying? He could never explain what he was crying about. Missing his family? Mourning his dead friends? Being separated and displaced by the flames of war? Or was it that he had already experienced so much despite his young age? It was all of these things and none of them.

The first time he used opium it had been to alleviate the pain of his battle wounds. Naturally he became hooked.

My father had been the one who had led him to leave their home. He'd called up large numbers of young people to join the army and save the country, and had later served as deputy commander of the guerrilla army. The same man, on discovering that his little brother was addicted to opium, had bound him up like a pig and locked him in a tiny room used to confine prisoners. No matter how my uncle screamed and howled, or how much his guerrilla buddies pleaded for him, my father's heart was like steel, and he refused point blank to release him.

"Sadist."

"You have no conscience."

"Heartless fiend."

"When we go home I'll tell mother how you've treated me!"

"Bastard!"

"Son of a bitch."

While going cold turkey, my uncle called my father every name in the book. But he remained locked in that bamboo cell, howling, shrieking, tearing and clawing … Days dragged on like years, and my uncle didn't know how long had elapsed before he finally overcame his addiction.

"Your father saved my life," my uncle said.

That was the way it was in wartime.

Conflict Eight

The Seoul my uncle saw was one occupied by the North Korean army, its skies filled with flames and shrill cries—a city shrouded in gloom. The Seoul I saw was a modern metropolis with a population of over ten million, living at a fast and furious pace, people rushing through the streets talking on their mobile phones, without even a minute to waste—a stylish emerging Asian city.

After breakfast and a cup of coffee at the youth hostel, I set out with my navy rucksack and headed to Everland.

Everland was about 40 minutes drive from central Seoul, on the outskirts of the city, a place called Yongin. I'd heard that this park had been built in a move to eclipse Tokyo's Disneyland, and was operated by the South Korean Samsung Group. It was already bigger than Tokyo's Disneyland, but hardly anyone outside South Korea had even heard of it. "Crush Japan" was the ultimate goal for many Korean corporations, a sentiment that drove not just the automobile and home appliances industries, but the entertainment business too. During the Japanese colonial period the Japanese tore right through the the Korean imperial palace, Gyeongbokgung to build their central government building. After independence, South Korea unflinchingly levelled this symbol of their national humiliation. Would the memories of colonialism just disappear? Could hunger for progress only come from deep, unresolved hatred?

My first stop at Everland was the 'American Adventure Zone'. I took a couple of heart-stopping rides, the Pirate Ship and Hurricane, adrenaline-pumping rollercoasters that left me half-paralysed with terror. I purchased the photograph the on-ride camera had taken of me, a snapshot of me looking terrified in my mid-ride frenzy. Then I left American Adventure and made my way to 'Zootopia Safari World'.

A minibus stopped at the bus stop where we waited. The front of it looked like a gaping tiger's mouth, and its carriage was painted with stripes like a tiger's body. It deposited a group of tourists at the pavilion before picking us up and taking us into the park.

Lions and tigers were sitting or standing around lazily in groups of two or three. They cast the occasional haughty look in our direction before twisting their heads away again, as if we silly humans had disturbed their sleep and were not worth a second glance. One lion had clambered onto an abandoned jeep on the dirt track, and was staring down at us as we approached, like a watchtower sentry officer protecting his homeland. As our minibus went past, the lion approached and delivered a roar so frightening that everyone in our bus started shrieking.

Our vehicle drove through an area that had been designed to look like an African safari park. We made a couple of turns, and found ourselves face to face with a number of brown grizzly bears as big as humans. The minibus slowed, and the driver took out some biscuits. The bears wrinkled their sensitive noses and a few of them bounded over, circling our bus and standing on their hind legs. The driver barked some orders, and the bears raised both paws and began to spin around. Everyone on the bus was in fits of laughter, adults and children alike, and our cameras flashed in quick succession. The driver tossed the biscuits towards the bears, who nimbly caught them in their mouths. One frustrated bear who hadn't caught any continued to spin desperately round, round and round. Once the biscuits were finished, our vehicle slowly pulled away, and a few eager young cubs continued to trail after us.

It was dark by the time I got back to the youth hostel. Mr Kim asked me where I'd been. Everland, I told him. Mr Kim's immediate response was that the amusement park was meant for families or couples, had I really gone on my own? Yes, on my own, I replied. Mr Kim seemed to be looking at me with pity, a look all too familiar from back home. It was mostly reserved for single women over thirty, or those who showed no signs of having found a decent man. This look had an element of suspicion, trying to work out if you had a problem that might explain your lack of male companion, but also traces of pity, and a warning to be careful you didn't die old and alone in your apartment!

Two more roommates had joined our dormitory room, Inka from Germany and Yoko from Japan. Plump Inka, was a student in Tokyo. She'd had to leave Japan for Seoul for a couple of days to sort out her visa. Yoko, who had her hair pulled back with a wide black mesh headband, had quit her job as a photographer's assistant to backpack around South Korea.

"Are Taiwanese photographers as foul-mouthed and abusive

as Japanese ones?" Yoko seemed still very disturbed by her nightmare job. We had been sitting around the table under the persimmon tree in the youth hostel courtyard, drinking beer and chatting casually, when Yoko had asked this out of the blue. She seemed to have suffered in her job, and had run away from her boss and her stressful Tokyo life in quite unfortunate circumstances.

"Some photographers have terrible tempers and love bossing people around, while others are more civil and humble the more famous they get—everyone's different," I said. "Did your boss have a bad temper?"

"He was completely insane." Yoko lifted the beer bottle to her mouth and took a gulp. You could hear the anger in her voice.

"So what do you plan to do in the future?" Hans, a lanky middle-aged man from Amsterdam, also new to the youth hostel, joined the conversation.

"I'll decide after my trip. When I've finished travelling in South Korea I might take a boat from Incheon to Qingdao, and take photographs in mainland China. Once I've got the qualifications, I hope to become a photographer. But I need more experience first." Yoko's eyes shone as she discussed her dream.

"I left my job to travel too. I even sold my house, furniture and car," Hans said.

"How long do you intend to travel?" asked Inka. "A few months, half a year."

"Where are you going?" Yuko asked.

"Northeast Asia, Southeast Asia, mainland China and then back to Europe," Hans replied.

"Why did you decide to start in South Korea?" Mr Kim chipped in, sounding eager, perhaps hoping to hear of Hans' fascination with South Korea culture and the far-flung East. But the answer he got was disappointingly banal. "I'm completely new to Asian culture. A novice. Seoul is my first destination because the travel agency had cheap flights here," Hans replied.

This was a practical consideration for any backpacker, and we all burst into laughter. Yoko's tiredness was getting the better of her, and after asking Mr Kim where she could have a sauna, she wandered off in her sandals. As soon as she'd left, Mr Kim's friend appeared, the peroxided guy who loved Teresa Teng.

"Been to many places these past few days?" he asked, sitting down opposite me in Yoko's old seat.

"Quite a few," I said. "Gyeongbokgung, the museums, Gangnam, Korean Folk Village, Everland. I even did a Han River cruise."

"Where did you like best?" he asked, pouring me a small cup of soju.

"The folk village was pretty nice, I spent a whole day there. I got a better understanding about the lives of ordinary people throughout Korean history, especially farmers."

"Do you think what you saw was a true reflection of the lives of Korean people?" he asked.

"It may not all be true, but it's a start, especially for a foreigner like me who doesn't know much about Korean culture," I said. I was starting to sense that something was amiss; even though the guy was speaking gently, he seemed to have a chip on his shoulder.

"It's all an act," he said.

"Actually, the Han River cruise was excellent too. The river has been extremely well-maintained, it's very clean," I said in an attempt to change the topic.

"The US troops were recently discovered to have been pouring toxic waste into our Han River. The river where all our drinking water comes from!" he said.

This had been a big news story in the papers these past few days.

We all sat around the white plastic table looking at each another in mute horror, trying to work out if the youth hostel drinking water could have been contaminated, glad that there were no Americans sitting among us.

I didn't think Mr-peroxide-hair-with-the-silver-framed-glasses actually cared whether there were any Americans with us there under the tree. He began telling us a story from his childhood, his first ever taste of delicious, sweet Coca Cola. "A glass with a straw, and a mysterious coffee-coloured liquid with crystal clear ice cubes. I took a sip, and my God! I'd never tasted anything like it. I thought it was the most incredible drink in the world." We all started chuckling at his description of Coke in all its mystique and glamour, since none of us actually liked the drink, which was nothing but a heap of chemicals dyed to look like syrup. Inka and Hans frowned, wrinkled their noses and shook their heads in bewilderment, smiles on their faces, as they listened to his veneration of Coca Cola.

But Coke itself was not the point of his speech; the story behind Coca Cola was. He came from Gyeongju, the ancient capital which had a long history. He seriously urged us foreigners to take a train southeast to visit this ancient heritage site, and the series of thousand-year-old tombs that stuck out of the ground like hills— "Really worth seeing," he said. "And you absolutely mustn't miss Cheonmachong. And the Cheonma Tapestry excavated from those tombs." He was insistent.

His childhood in this ancient capital had been a traditional one, so a foreign product like Coca Cola had been a novelty. Even the faraway capital, Seoul, had seemed like a huge, distant and unfamiliar city to him back then. One summer he took the train to Seoul with his sister to spend their summer holidays with relatives. They'd frolicked around the city all summer, exploring every single inch of the place. That was when he'd had his first taste of Coke.

A distant relative of his worked in Itaewon, the residential district for US troops and their families. This green leafy Namsan Mountain area right in the middle of Seoul was shrouded in mystery for most Koreans, who weren't allowed inside this secluded enclave within the bustling downtown district. Having this distant relative meant that he'd been allowed to enter this constantly guarded secret place.

He was dumbstruck. This wasn't South Korea. It was heaven. Fireplaces. Big houses. Huge courtyards. Expensive American furniture. Expensive American home appliances. Lives that couldn't have been more different from those of ordinary Koreans. He felt green with envy. And it was within that secluded American community, that dreamy paradise, that this distant relative had poured him a glass of Coca Cola, that delicious drink he'd never forget. How grateful he'd been.

After starting university, he'd gradually begun to understand the nature of this elite place within the bustling city centre. While in Seoul's other districts every inch of land was expensive, the US military leased this land for next to nothing.

"The first time I got a taste of class difference was when I got that delicious mouthful of Coca Cola in the US military residential district; this was the class that profited from our war and caused the split of North and South Korea." He lowered his head as he said this and lifted the Soju to his lips. Tilting back his head, he gulped down the liquid like a man drowning his sorrows.

A sombre mood descended. Under that Persimmon tree, no

one said a word. The hazy yellow moon hung high in the sky, moonlight filtering through the leaves, splitting into fragments and landing on our slightly tipsy faces. A sense of loneliness descended upon the scene and made me feel far from home.

There *were* no Americans among us out there in the garden. James, the only American in the hostel, was inside walking about obliviously, preparing vegetarian food that Mr Kim jokingly described as healthy but disgusting. There was a pile of household items stacked up in the kitchen. James was about to leave after seven years in Korea and kept saying he'd sell them on the internet, although he never did. He walked around barefoot, looking as if he owned the place, cheerfully preparing his dinner.

"Some time ago, there was a barmaid in Itaewon who was raped and killed by those pleasure-seeking American soldiers," the Mr Peroxide said after a pause.

We fell into even deeper silence. Mr Kim, wanting to smooth things over, decided to introduce us formally to this man who had darkened the mood of our conversation so.

"This is Park Chang-chuk," he said. "We were university classmates. We both come from the same hometown, the ancient capital of Gyeongju. He often comes here after work.

"He has a very unique line of work. He's a poet, but spends his days labouring on a construction site."

A shy smile appeared on the face of poet-construction worker Park Chang-chuk. He went inside, saying he was going to put on a beautiful Teresa Teng song for us. Returning to his seat, he told me he was reading a biography of Mao Tse-tung. He was interested in Mao's reunification of China, he explained.

Conflict Nine

My head ached so badly when I got out of bed the next morning I felt as if it had been shackled with lead weights. Chatting under the persimmon tree the night before I'd mixed my drinks: alongside the beers I'd bought for myself, I'd had that small cup of Soju Park Chang-chuk had given me. These two types of alcohol had taken possession of separate regions of my body and begun to fight it out.

I went to the bathroom to take a shower to alleviate my headache, but the only water that flowed out was cold, the water heater giving no sign of life. Standing on tiptoe, I tried to reach up and switch it on, but still no hot water trickled out. I decided to put my clothes back on and go downstairs to get Mr Kim to help me.

Sounds of an argument could be heard from the ground floor. I had the vague feeling that it was Mr Kim and the American guy, James.

"I've told you so many times, this is a communal area. You're not the only one staying here," Mr Kim said.

"Of course, but aren't I a member of the community too? I always pay my rent on time," James argued.

"That doesn't mean you're allowed to dump seven years' worth of belongings here. You've had these things here for a few months now."

"I've left my washing machine, microwave, coffee maker as well as pots and pans here so that everyone can use them, isn't that helpful of me?"

"We've got all those things here already. Yours take up too much space. And the only reason you've got them here is because you can't sell them."

"Okay, okay, you think I'm too messy. I'll take them away then, okay?" James said.

When I reached the bottom of the wooden spiralling staircase, I saw James' chagrined expression. He shrugged and raised his hands innocently, before shuffling reluctantly to the kitchen, presumably to clean up his mess there.

I told Mr Kim about the water heater problem. As he went up the staircase, Mr Kim was still muttering indignantly to me about idling Yankees like James, only out to take advantage of Asian women, that if he wanted to behave outrageously, he could go back to America to do it. Entering the upstairs bathroom, he discovered that another huge heap of personal belongings had been dumped there: the small room was filled with a heap of razors, bottles of mouthwash and shampoo, a mouldy wet towel, a toothbrush and tube of toothpaste. The floor tiles were covered with strands of brown hair, which were clogging the shower too. Mr Kim started shaking his head again, muttering, "It's that James again".

After my shower, chatting with Mr Kim, I learned more about

James. The guy had been living in Asia for the past seven years, making his living by teaching English. This had allowed him to move from country to country. A few years ago he'd married a Korean woman, and had been living in South Korea ever since. Some months ago they'd decided to give up their apartment lease and move back to the States. James' wife went first, leaving him behind to tie up all the loose ends and sell their belongings on the internet. Their house had been returned to the landlord by that point, and seeing as he didn't get on well with his in-laws, James had had nowhere to live. That's when he'd moved into this youth hostel. Several months later, he seemed less concerned with selling their things than bringing girls back to the hostel, Mr Kim said.

Each time his wife phoned from America urging him to hurry up, he'd tell her he was having trouble selling their stuff and sorting things out, and couldn't go back at the moment. I don't think he ever plans to go back. If it weren't for his wife wanting to live in the States to get her Green Card, I don't think he'd ever have thought to go back. Isn't it great swaggering around Asia as if you're the king of the castle? Oh, and are Asian women really this cheap? Mr Kim, who used to study in the States, shook his head and sighed.

I said nothing. Not a word.

I lowered my head and quietly edged past Mr Kim, making my way round the kitchen table.

Judy, who hadn't been back in the dormitory by the time I'd gone to bed last night, had come in and was now slumped in a chair next to the table. She looked gaunt, dark circles under her eyes.

"Are you okay?" I asked. I filled the stainless steel kettle with water and put it on the gas stove, planning to make her a mug of instant cappuccino.

"I phoned him last night," Judy said.

I knew I couldn't just up and leave, so I pulled out the chair opposite her and sat down. I began to listen to Judy's report of last night.

"I knew I shouldn't call him, but I couldn't stand it. I wanted to know how he's doing."

"When the phone started to ring, I got nervous and hung up. But I wanted to hear his voice badly. So I dialled again. There was no answer. I phoned again. Still no answer. Right up into the small hours, no one answered. He never did that while we were living together, no matter how late, he'd always come home. He wouldn't stay out all night. Maybe he has a new girlfriend."

"You still love him, don't you," I said.

"Yes. But I was the one who ended it. I couldn't live with him anymore. That time he beat me like a madman, locked me in the bedroom and wouldn't let me leave. I secretly phoned his friend and asked him to come and save me. I was terrified. I was scared that he'd beat me to death if I stayed in that room. His Chinese friend brought me back to his place where I stayed one night, before my boyfriend persuaded me to come back. "Every family has their issues," he said. As she was telling this part of the story, Judy's eyes widened, as if she couldn't believe that he'd said that.

"I've got a bone to pick with those friends of his too." Judy's voice was filled with rage.

"They came to our apartment for a meal once. He entertained them very well, and after dinner, I sat down with them and when they pulled out their cigarettes, I did the same. I'd jus lifted the cigarette to my mouth, when one of them said the word, 'Whore'. Women who smoked were whores, according to this friend. I began arguing with him, asking why women who smoked were whores? And how dare he come to my house and call me names like that, was that how a guest should treat his host? Later he told me that when they saw a woman smoking in China, they'd just assume she was a whore."

"It's a good thing I don't live in China then," Judy said. "Western women would be labelled as whores very easily over there."

"Chinese men aren't the only ones who think that way. When I was living in Europe, Western men from all over would mistake all the Asian women they saw for prostitutes. This might be more a problem between the sexes," I said.

"So you've lived in Europe? Where?" Judy asked. "Britain and Ireland," I said.

"Ah, that's where my ancestors come from," Judy said, though she didn't seem very interested in this topic, as she went straight back to talking about her Chinese boyfriend.

At that moment the stainless steel kettle started whistling. I switched off the gas and poured the hot water into the mug to make myself a cup of coffee—my daily essential. Judy said she didn't want coffee; she only drank tea.

Conflict Ten

But, … oh, but … Judy said. This Chinese man was an incredible lover.

Sometimes he was as docile and accommodating as a cat, other times he had the rapacious energy of a hungry lion. In actual fact, he was nothing but a crazy perverted monster, Judy giggled. As she said this, Judy gave a charming smile, her eyes sparkling; it was impossible to tell that she harboured any resentment towards her ex-boyfriend.

If falling in love can take you to such high emotional and physical peaks, my past loves must have all been in vain, I thought. They all pale in comparison to this Asian man, Zhou, with his long, slender phoenix eyes.

Zhou. That's what Judy called her Chinese boyfriend. His surname, I assumed.

The first time Zhou seduced me, she went on, we were in our university campus. After class he called me over to the secluded cluster of cherry trees behind the classroom. The sky was filled with cherry blossom, dazzling and enchanting in its beauty. At first, we stood under this blossom with faint smiles on our faces, feeling slightly awkward. Then he plucked a cherry flower from the ground, one that was still fresh and full, and tucked it behind my ear.

"You're exquisite, just like this cherry flower." With his right hand trembling ever so slightly, he began lightly caressing my cheek, tracing his finger over my eyebrows, the tip of my nose, my mouth.

"I want you to be my little Western doll," he said.

I don't think he'd ever touched a Western woman before. He was like a fresh-faced schoolboy when he spoke, an adult's body but a child's heart. He had this real mystique.

I didn't know what tricks he had up his sleeve, but I allowed his hand to explore my body inch by inch, as if he were stroking a sculpture. All the while I was scrutinised him openly. Wanting to see what he was up to.

He started kissing me. From my cheeks, to my ears, and down my neck. He lifted my sweater and unfastened my bra, leaning down to suck my nipple like a greedy baby. He got down on his knees and tugged down my panties from beneath my skirt. It really felt as if he was embracing a sculpture as he hugged my thighs, buried his head beneath my skirt, and began to suck and lick me down there. I was tingling all over, unbearably. I didn't care that we were in a public place—I began to moan under that cherry tree.

"I love the way you taste," he murmured, after he'd finally extracted his head from my skirt. He stuffed my underwear into his coat pocket and said, "Meet me at Yasukuni Shrine at seven o'clock. I'll give your panties back then." Off he went, leaving me in my pleated skirt, with no underwear.

I didn't know where he'd gone. I was utterly captivated. The only think I knew was how much I needed to find my way to Yasukuni Shrine, at the very least to get back my underwear.

A bitter wind blew through Tokyo that dusk, and it filtered through my clothing, and right through to my underwear-less nether region. It was a strange feeling. My inner thighs were completely wet, a mixture of Zhou's saliva and my excitement. The wind embedded itself into my lower body, giving me a cold, hollow sensation. There I was, in a skirt with no underwear beneath it, strolling along the streets of Tokyo, with people bustling about all around me, walking into the Metro station and taking the train to Kudanshita station, and Yasukuni Shrine.

I was insanely turned on as I made my way there. No one could have seen anything amiss from my outward appearance, although with nothing between them my thighs rubbed together, while my aroused lower body squirmed. Catching the gaze of the occasional passer by, I'd wonder gleefully if they knew my sweet and shocking secret. As I got closer to Yasukuni Shrine, I felt my ears getting hotter, my heart starting to pound in my chest, while my wetness began to ooze out in an uncontrolled flow, and run down my thighs.

He was standing by one of the monuments at Yasukuni Shrine waiting for me, a Chinese book in his hand.

By the time I had reached him, he could no longer contain himself. Like a ferocious lion he pushed me down against the cold surface of the monument. With his mouth wide, he sucked at my tongue, and impatiently plunged his fingers into me.

"Oh, you're so wet." He had his eyes half closed as if inebriated, and murmured faint unintelligible words to me. He pulled down the zipper of his trousers, and took out his cock—hot and hard, and thrust it into my wetness.

I was like a slumbering volcano that had lain dormant for too long, rumbling now, ready to erupt. He stood up, gripping me tightly to him, while I clamped my legs around his waist. I heard a plonk as the book he'd been holding dropped to the floor. We rocked violently against each other. It was as if he'd hit a mysterious spot deep inside me, and soon I felt my body being overpowered by spasms. I cried out as I erupted like a volcano.

"All I want to do is make love to you, all I want to do is make love to you," he mumbled again and again as he trembled violently.

We came at the same time. At that moment, a flock of crows circling overhead began vigorously beating their wings, as if disturbed by our convulsions and guttural cries. They let out a chorus of loud, nasty caws, a seeming show of strength against us savage beasts, or perhaps a protest against us invading their long-held territory among the shrines.

"These crows are so irritating!"

"Yes, they are." We smoothed down our clothes and gazed at each other, before bursting into laughter.

"What's that book you're holding?" Dressed once more, we began to stroll to the front of the shrine square.

"Yu Dafu's novel *Sinking*," he replied.

"Who's he?" I asked curiously.

"A famous Chinese writer from the 1930s," he replied. "He studied in Japan as well. He graduated from Tokyo Imperial University's Department of Economics and then taught at Peking University, his alma mater. He denounced Japan during the War of Resistance , even though he'd once studied there. Towards the end of the Second World War, he travelled to Southeast Asia where he worked as literary editor for a Chinese newspaper, living in anonymity. He was later discovered by the Japanese invaders to be proficient in Japanese, and they captured him and made him interpret for them. When the Japanese surrendered at the end of the Second World War, they feared he knew too much, so they took him to the Southeast Asian wilderness and killed him."

"What a pity for a literary genius to die like that," I said. "Are his novels good?"

"They are great. He wrote about the psychological state of Chinese students studying abroad. I can really relate to it," He, gave a slight smile.

"I hope to learn Chinese one day, so I can read his novels with you," I said.

Excited and shy like a child, he lifted me into his arms. One day he'd take me to see Beijing, his hometown, he said.

Thus began our crazy romance.

Conflict Eleven

Judy was smitten with her Chinese boyfriend. Even though he had beaten her, and she knew they couldn't be together, she was in too deeply to extricate herself.

Many years ago that young professor had told me this was called jungle fever and that one day I'd wake up from the delirium of my relationship with a Westerner. He made it sound as though I was suffering from a tropical disease like malaria and needed to be saved and given treatment. That African-American director Spike Lee's movie *Jungle Fever* had been showing in cinemas around that time, and it was all the rage. The movie depicted the relationship between a black man and a white woman, who eventually split and returned to their respective communities. As if placing a curse on me, the young professor told me that sooner or later I would see the light. I was just a university student back then. Fat Luo was my friend, and so was Taomei. We weren't just friends, more like comrades.

We were all literature students at university together. We pored over the modernist works of Lu Xun, Ding Ling, Pai Hsien-yung and Huang Chun-ming. We scrutinised the ancient texts like *Records of the Grand Historian*, the *Book of Songs*, *Poems from the Song Dynasty*, *Yuan Verse* and the *Dream of the Red Chamber*. We perused the translated works of Balzac, James Joyce, Ivan Turgenev, Gabriel García Márquez, Milan Kundera and Yukio Mishima. Once in a while we studied books in their original language such as George Orwell's *Animal Farm*, Hemingway's *The Killers* and Oscar Wilde's *The Happy Prince*.

We lived in a fantasy world of language and words and nursed fervent delusions that one day we too would be like the literary masters we worshipped. We were obsessed with the thought of becoming great writers. We spent our days in raving states of self-pity, believing that our only purpose in life was to create. That world was like a castle built in fairy tales that became tainted, little by little, by the impurities of love and lust, power and fame, which eventually destroyed it. Just like a sandcastle built on the shaky foundations of a beach, crumbling with every lashing wave, until no trace remained.

Our young professor, Gary, was charming and charismatic. He was sharp-tongued and quick-witted and a master of biting sarcasm. When dealing with people with different leanings and different ways of thinking, his general tactic was to mock and suppress. He was very attractive, a rogue who blurred the line between good and bad, a ruffian full of vigour, but with his own code of honour. Because of this he became the superstar professor for every student from the faculty of arts.

But, one day my friend Fat Luo, who had been idolising him

for years and now seemed hell-bent on surpassing him, suddenly said, "He has a huge cock." An expression of huge contempt and disdain flashed across his face as he said it, a look that showed his unbounded envy. "Hmph," he said, with the ardour of a child, or a teenager who wanted to give his old dad a good thrashing. Fat Luo had just spent his long summer break following Gary's instructions. He'd watched the entire thirty-something episodes of a Japanese drama series, so that he could learn about plot transition and narrative pace. He'd also copied out Eileen Chang's novels *The Golden Cangue* and *Eighteen Springs* three times each. He was convinced that as long as he put in the work, he'd eventually eclipse Gary the father figure and gain supremacy in the literary world.

He said he had spent all twenty odd years of his life feeling inferior and humiliated. Primarily it was because he was fat.

"Do you understand how much humiliation a fat person endures?" Fat Luo was driving me around one evening after class, in the second second-hand car his mother had bought him. We were on our way to pick up Taomei. We were going on to a spot near the public hot springs bathhouse left from the Japanese era, carrying Styrofoam boxes of lunch leftovers, to feed the pack of stray dogs that hung out there.

I sat next in the passenger's seat next to him, looking fixedly out the window, trying desperately not to laugh. I was very tempted to respond with: I've never been fat, how would I understand it? The serious and self-righteous way he'd asked gave the beautiful scenery rolling along outside the window an absurd and perverse edge. My reaction might have offended him.

"Don't scoff," he said. Then he began to tell me about his sorrows as a little fatty in elementary school.

There was a beautiful girl in his class called Shan Shan. She had pigtails tied with bows, was a smart talker, and every teacher's pet. She was smug, wily and mean, often using her role as class monitor to tyrannise other children. Fat Luo was a chubby little boy who did badly at school. When he was assigned to sopranos in choir, he became the butt of all the other boys' jokes. Our timid little Fat Luo somehow developed a crush on this bitchy girl. After school, he excitedly told his mother, who worked at the bank and was very wealthy, that he really liked Shan Shan and wanted to marry her when he grew up. He didn't dare say anything to his father, because the whole family was afraid of this dignified old gentleman, a university teacher, including his wealthy mother, who had been his father's student at college.

Like a devoted servant, Fat Luo would help Shan Shan with her calligraphy after school, and copied his homework out for her when she couldn't be bothered to do it herself. He split the daily pocket money from his mother with Shan Shan, so she could buy herself sweets and paper dolls to play with.

He'd never have imagined that one day his beautiful doll would turn into the wicked witch from Snow White, bullying him with her claws out and teeth bared.

Their teacher was handing out exam papers at the front desk one morning. When Fat Luo's name was called, he guilelessly bounded to the front. As he was passing Shan Shan's desk in the front row, she suddenly stuck her leg out in front of him and tripped him up. He landed in a heap on the floor.

Fat Luo rolled around on the floor like a dog, and began to howl in agony. As he struggled to get up, Shan Shan raised her hand to inform the teacher that he had accidentally tripped up and hurt himself, and she would be happy to take him to the sick bay. The teacher praised Shan Shan on being a model pupil, full of compassion for her fellow classmates and an example for everyone else, and permitted her to take him.

The skin had been stripped off Fat Luo's knee, where blood and grime formed a blurry mess. The metallic smell of the blood made him feel sick, and the sting of the purple ointment being rubbed onto his skin made him yelp. Fat tears began to roll down his cheeks.

"Stop crying. Why are you crying, you useless idiot," Shan Shan said impatiently. She held a bottle of Gentian Violet in one hand and wad of cotton in the other.

Fat Luo dried his tears and blew his snotty nose. He limped back to the classroom with gauze bandage around his knee. In that quiet corridor, he asked, "Shan Shan, you did that on purpose, didn't you?"

"What do you mean, did it on purpose?"

"You deliberately stuck out your foot out to trip me up, didn't you?"

"Yeah, I did," Shan Shan said. Our little friend Fat Luo had hoped that Shan Shan would try to hide this fact, at least say it was an accident. He hadn't counted on such a display of integrity from her, not even an attempt at a lie. Fat Luo felt his young soul had been stabbed with a knife, accompanied by the high-pitched sound of something scratching along glass.

"Why did you do that?" He may have been timid, but Fat Luo had his first taste of looking someone in the eyes with vengeance. He looked coldly at Shan Shan.

"I wanted to see what a fat ass looked like falling over," Shan Shan said with indifference.

That was also Fat Luo first taste of cursing women. Slut. Little bitch. Village bicycle. He spoke each word with gusto, with as much force as ejaculation. When school ended, he did a pencil sketch of how he imagined female genitals looked. This is Shan

Shan's rotten cunt, Fat Luo explained. He aimed at the picture with a slingshot, used it for target practice, ripped a hole through it.

Humiliation. Fat Luo said. Do you know what it feels like to be bullied just because you're fat?

Hearing his story made me feel so sad I couldn't speak. "I still have that scar on my knee," he said, pointing at it.

After leaving elementary school, Fat Luo and Shan Shan went off to separate schools, and didn't have any further contact. Until university.

Shan Shan had graduated from the foreign languages department at her university and had become a flight attendant for China Airlines, flying around the world day and night.

Meanwhile our friend Fat Luo, having flunked his high school entrance exams, found himself at cram school. He didn't manage to pass his university entrance exams either, and was held back another two years. So while Shan Shan was stepping out into the world, Fat Luo was still stuck in university.

Humiliation. Fat Luo said. Some time later Shan Shan came across his debut short story in a literary magazine. She leafed through their elementary school yearbook, found his number, and phoned his home to congratulate him.

"So you're something of a writer!" Shan Shan said into the phone. He hadn't seen her for a long time, and Fat Luo's hand was trembling slightly as he clutched the receiver.

"The elementary school girl who was raped in that story of yours sounds somewhat familiar. Should I be collecting some royalties?" Shan Shan asked.

"Ah, yes, ah—" Fat Luo was flattered that beautiful Shan Shan had thought to call him after so many years. But, her question disconcerted him.

"You'd love it if I was raped, wouldn't you?" Shan Shan asked.

"No, no, it's a work of fiction. It's made-up," Fat Luo clarified.

"I'm going to sue you. For slander." It was hard to tell from her tone of voice if she really was angry or just putting it on.

"Sue me? Why would you sue me? The story is made up. Fictitious," Fat Luo was quick to rebut.

Shan Shan gave a frosty, "Huh," and said, "Should I call you a genius or an idiot?"

"Umm …"

"If you're fantasising about me being raped and dying violently in the schoolyard, it must mean you're still a virgin?" Shan Shan added the word, "Pervert" and then hung up the phone.

Humiliation. Fat Luo's hand that had been holding the steering wheel was now clenched into a fist. So many years later, she was still out to humiliate me.

"Calling you a virgin isn't humiliating you," I said in an attempt to console him.

"You don't understand," Fat Luo said.

"So what if you're a virgin? That's nothing to be ashamed of. Are you that worried about what other people think?" I was raising my voice without meaning to. He was getting on my nerves quite frankly, being completely ridiculous. "You've seen a pack of stray dogs? Well, I am the most scab-ridden one," Fat Luo said sorrowfully.

Being called fat has made you into a stray dog? What bullshit logic, I thought to myself. But out of compassion, I reminded myself that I should learn to listen to him. Even though he and Taomei, my other friend, were at severe loggerheads with each other at the time, embroiled in a conflict that had arisen due to the bumping of feet. The only way those two communicated now was through glares.

Listen. I must be gentle and listen. Whether it's to stories about stray dogs or wretched cockroaches being trampled to death, I must learn to patiently listen.

He always got the worst results in his class, he told me. Do you know what it's like to be caned by a teacher in front of forty or fifty classmates? To go to school each day expecting to be caned? Other students had callused hands from doing their homework, while I had a layer of dead skin growing over my palm as the result of these daily canings. Humiliation. The teacher would humiliate him in other ways too. Asking why he was nothing like his father who taught at the teacher's college.

And if he couldn't be like his father, he might at least behave more like his elder brother and sister. Or if that was beyond him, perhaps he could refrain from sleeping in class, snoring with his head bobbing about. His teacher didn't understand how a good family like that had produced such a dud. If his mother hadn't shown up at school each day to give him fruit and snacks, he would have walked out long ago, crossing his name off the class list.

As everyone expected, he failed to get into any high school and his mother was forced to send her timid, stuttering son to that military-style cram school. One dull and isolated year later, he finally got into Chenggong High. It wasn't famous, but it was one of the top five government-run high schools. His mother could finally stop fretting.

She couldn't have anticipated the new nightmare that would soon unfold. In this new school, Fat Luo joined a gang and started getting into gang fights. His mother spent her days in tears. But it was during these bloody, brutal conflicts that Fat Luo finally reclaimed his dignity.

Do you know what it feels like to thrust your fists in somebody's face as they're lying on the ground beneath you? To plunge a knife into someone's body and pull it out red? To watch someone fall to his knees before you, begging for mercy and calling you *Daddy*? You can get addicted to that feeling, he said.

This carried on for several years. Fat Luo squandered a lot of his time at the ice-rink, and carried a switchblade wherever he went. He prowled around in his pack, blocking peoples' paths, and if he didn't like the look of them, calling for his gang to knife them. His mother had been promoted to bank manager by this time. She was convinced that the child she had spent her blood, sweat and tears bringing up, was a lost cause. When she wasn't at work, she'd go to the temple to burn incense and pray for Buddha to bring back her lost son. She vowed that if her prayers were answered and her son saw the error of his ways, she and he would repay the debt by becoming vegetarian for life. Fat Luo had a good friend back then, a well-mannered classmate called Lu Ziyu. He was Fat Luo's only close friend who wasn't in the gang. His mother took Lu Ziyu in as a surrogate son, in the hope that he might have some influence on her son.

Was it the compassionate light of Buddha shining down on them, or Lu Ziyu strong friendship that ultimately led to Fat Luo's reform? At any rate, Fat Luo lost his thirst for blood. He began to feel sick and faint in bloody situations. Eventually the mother of that spoilt boy recovered what she'd lost: the obedient son who used to hug her legs when he was little and say nice things to make her happy, the obedient little boy who used to cling to her. To repay the debt, mother, son and surrogate son all became vegetarian. His mother poured half of her love out onto her surrogate son Lu Ziyu, in gratitude for the positive influence he'd exerted on Fat Luo. "Babykins, be good to Lu Ziyu. He's the reason you got your life back. You owe him half your life.

Whenever you have any tasty snacks, remember to share them with him," his mother said.

Our friend Fat Luo did not seem to grasp the nature of his mother's heartfelt words and it wasn't long before he and Lu Ziyu, who'd been like a brother, fell out over a girl. Their friendship was severed. Fat Luo began to play the victim, acting out a scene in some dramatic plot he'd devised, and walked away from the friendship a martyr.

Humiliation. Humiliation. He used to take a notebook around with him. Like the childhood picture of Shan Shan's cunt he'd once drawn to use as target practice, he now sat in the red notchback that he and Lu Ziyu had once shared, and sketched a picture of two dicks. One was wrinkled, shrivelled and impotent, next to which he wrote *Lu Ziyu*. The other was huge and powerful. He drew a picture of a bodybuilder too, both arms raised, showing off his thickset, Arnold Schwarzenegger muscles. That's me. Me in the future, Fat Luo wrote next to it.

Revenge. Revenge. One day, he would get his revenge. Every single person who'd caused him his devastating humiliation would be made to stand up and take notice. They would be filled with awe and reverence, he said. Revenge. Revenge. Hate was the single driving factor for his creativity, he said. I have to set a target, an enemy to defeat before I can create, he said.

Conflict Twelve

How do you recount a *Rashomon*-type event? How could a friend, once as close as a comrade-in-arms or a brother, turn his back on you? Why do some people want to cast themselves in the tragic role, turning all friends into aggressors overnight, while completely banishing their own deplorable acts from memory? It was down to silence, everyone's shared silence, that allowed the perpetrator to endlessly reiterate his version of events and position himself as the hero of the tragedy. As a result, memory is completely re-written.

From that first knock on my door, my fate in this drama was sealed. I went from bystander to participant. Taomei was the first to arrive. She was like a cornered beast, fuming with rage. She seemed to have lost all thread of logic. "Someone tell him to stop loitering around on my route back home everyday. Tell him to stop calling me three times a day. Stop making me breakfast each morning, stop waiting around in his car for me."

"What are you talking about? I'm confused."

"I'll go mad if I have to carry on like this."

"Who are you talking about?"

"That insane idiot Fat Luo of course!"

This happened in the fourth floor student apartment I was renting. Taomei rang the bell and stepped into my room and started her story by firing out a string of curses. "Screw that motherfucker!" She flung her leather bag and her customary ankle-length woollen coat ferociously down onto my orange carpet in an attempt to vent her anger, and then grabbed a pillow and plonked herself down on the floor.

I was utterly confused, but seeing Taomei's delicate little face flushed with anger, and hearing her swearing like a trooper, I began to chuckle. It felt that no matter how angry she was, Taomei hadn't lost her quirky and dark sense of humour.

I fell headfirst into the quagmire of the whole affair. Our fairy tale world of tight-knit friendship was destroyed.

There were four people involved. Taomei. Miaozi, a painter, who was almost thirty, and lazy—a close friend of Taomei's from out of school. Fat Luo. And Lu Ziyu.

These four often went for rides in the red hatchback Fat Luo's mother gave him, and naturally became a clique. They went everywhere—Datun Mountain, the second highest peak of Taipei's Yangmingshan, fields of taros, their flowers blooming so brightly it just didn't look real, or the grazing cows at Chingtienkang, it was all their playground. During the winter these four would hibernate together in the student dormitories. With the electric heater on, they'd sit on the carpet with a duvet thrown over their legs, playing cards all through the night.

The bumping of feet and the conflict that ensued took place on one such night. So why had Taomei's delicate legs and feet brushed up against those of Fat Luo sitting across from her?

* * *

When her sole inched its way towards my foot, I felt a faint current of warm air against my skin. Her foot was touching mine. I couldn't move. I was frozen in shock at first, Fat Luo said. I pretended nothing was happening and calmly carried on playing cards. But I was increasingly losing my game. I was very aware that it was due to Taomei's legs rubbing against my feet.

At first I thought that it was just because there were four pairs of legs reaching towards the centre of the duvet for warmth, and our feet bumping was because it was cramped. But this appeared not to be so—she started to tickle my soles with her toes. It was a brazen attempt to flirt and turn me on, Fat Luo said.

I really was too inexperienced, I thought to myself. When I finally encountered this unfamiliar female body I'd lusted over night and days, when she finally came to me with her bold message, the terror and anxiety paralysed me, I was at a total loss to know what to do. My card tactics were getting steadily worse. I was out of control, plummeting. Fuck!

Lu Ziyi sensed that I was slightly losing my mind. "What's up with your game, Fatso?" Lu Ziyu knew me better than anyone, and could tell I was flustered. But he didn't know it was because of the earth-shaking activities under the duvet.

Each stroke Taomei made with her feet gave off a powerful electric charge and sent blood coursing its way to my balls.

My dick continued getting harder. Getting bigger. It must have been the size of a giant's. Fuck! My balls felt like they were about to explode. I was completely red, even my ears and my neck. I felt like I was on heat, yeah, like a monkey on heat.

I wanted to shove Taomei to the ground so badly, to rip off her panties and press against her as I plunged my huge, giant dick into her deep, dark hole. I wanted to fuck her senseless, ride her until she was delirious, then come all over her face like in a porno. But I was a coward, fighting hard to quash the tremors in my body. I looked around furtively at everyone, gauging their reactions, trying to behave as if nothing was going on. Thirty-year-old Miaozi oozing womanly charm, nonchalantly dealt out the cards with her customary laziness. She didn't look like she'd have the stamina to keep going with the cards all night, as she kept yawning, but she carried on, so as not to disappoint us youngsters.

Lu Ziyu, on the other hand, was completely focused on the card game, intent on trashing and ridiculing my game. As I was having my serious and discreet sexual awakening, he let out a long fart that only I heard. The dirty bastard!

And Taomei? Taomei, the little beauty giving me my erotic baptism, speaking to me in the language of love, what was she up to?

Her gaze, as undecipherable as that of a phantom or a fox, lingered on Lu Ziyi, which made it hard to see where her attention was. Occasionally her eyes would wander back to her lap, and she'd stare at the cards in her hands.

She did not glance at me once.

So women really could think one thing and do another! Those smooth bare invisible feet, their soles teasing out my manly desire, like a slippery fish swimming about, while under the bright fluorescent light, the little slut making as if she were Joan

83

of Arc! As soon as men are confronted by their own desire, it is authentic, stark-naked, without inhibition. Her feet continued to rub and wriggle against my legs. I was wishing the game would never end, that the night would last forever. Instead everyone ran out of stamina and the game drew to a close. The group dispersed, leaving me there with my poor unappeased dick, in agony due to that huge rush of blood, and my crestfallen face.

What women want is for a man to take charge, isn't that right? Ha, ha, ha. I went home and spent an entire day mulling this over. I thought about it so much that my brain tingled and my skull felt like it was about to split. I finally came up with a plausible explanation: Taomei must be looking for a male aggressor.

I gave my ally Lu Ziyu a blow-by-blow account of the events that night. There was something wrong with the guy, it wasn't just that he wasn't happy for me, he actually accused me of talking crap.

"Did Taomei really do that to you?" Lu Ziyu asked incredulously.

"Don't you believe me?"

"It's not that I don't believe you, I just find it a little strange."

"In what way strange?"

"Has she shown any signs of liking you in the past?"

"Actually, no."

"If she didn't have feelings for you before, why would she suddenly develop them?"

"Precisely! But love is very hard to fathom. Perhaps she's only just recognised my charm. But seriously, I've always thought of Taomei as a little slut."

"Taomei, a little slut? Really?" Lu Ziyu scratched his nose with his index finger, looking doubtful.

"Don't you think she gets this lusty expression in her eyes whenever she looks at men?"

"Really?" Lu Ziyu's voice was getting deeper and deeper.

"Absolutely. I'm telling you, she's like that girl in our class with the huge tits who struts around with them jiggling around on her chests. That chick has the nerve to wear tight-fitting blouses, if that's not deliberate, what is? A slut is a slut, regardless of how she presents herself. Take my word for it, I've got good instinct on this." Fat Luo was on fire, the words bursting out his chest.

"Lu Ziyu was quiet a while. "Do you plan to ask her out?" he mused. "Yes. That's my intention."

"Well, best of luck then," Lu Ziyu said, but there was no trace of happiness for me in his eyes. He actually looked slightly crestfallen. To think that my friend Lu Ziyu, the low-class beggar who'd been living off my family all this time, would even think to try and snatch sweet, delectable little Taomei from me. Fuck! Fuck!

* * *

Who could have known what was to follow. If I hadn't been like a curious cat, and had kept myself distant from it all, I might have avoided the storm. But my love for stories outweighed everything else, and I let curiosity get the better of me.

Then?

Why?

These words were like my mantra as I tried to get to the bottom of things. I regularly got swept up in the storms as a result, and ended up being flung to the ground, giddy and broken. Or when the story concluded and its teller had run out of steam and got back to normal life, it was as if I'd been given food poison, and only through chronic diarrhoea could I purge the waste from my system.

"You're like a rubbish bin. Everybody likes dumping their rubbish on you," a friend told me truthfully one day.

Maybe rubbish bins had their own virtue. All the rubbish I accumulated—all the odds and ends, the recyclables like tinfoil bags, metal cans, plastic bags, or food leftovers and scraps, they would all turn to dust in the end.

Whether I was a curious cat or a rubbish bin—if I could stop people from spiralling into madness, my curiosity and listening skills might actually be of use. Even though they'd nearly tipped my world upside down time and time again.

Alright, back to the world where four people's friendship was about to be destroyed.

Lu Ziyu eventually decided to leave, taking thirty year old Miaozi with him. The two of them moved to Taichung to begin a new life. Shortly afterwards, this older woman and younger man got married. Lu Ziyu continued his studies at a university in Taichung, and lazy Miaozi, who'd never taken a job seriously before, found one in earnest to support Lu Ziyu through university. Our friends Fat Luo and Lu Ziyu made a clean break, severing their brotherhood. Fat Luo, the tragic hero, wrote a novel, *Departure,* to express his tragic and heroic sentiments. "Do you know what resolve feels like, Jiaying?" Fat Luo said. "It's like having your arm cruelly severed from your body. All I can do is watch helplessly through wide-open eyes as the blood gushes out. Severed in two with one stroke of the blade. Forever after I must banish the thought of piecing it back together."

I gazed at his grief-contorted face and wondered why he was making so much of it. Lu Ziyu was the one who had left, hadn't he? But Lu Ziyu kept himself to himself. He left quietly with Miaozi, to begin their new life.

Fat Luo and Taomei remained on the periphery of my life,

staring daggers at each other and bad-mouthing each other.

"That huge pervert is like Hunchback of Notre Dame but instead he thinks he's Peter Pan fluttering around. He goes around day in and day out with that childish attitude, thinking that the rest of us have to suffer his ways. Bull-fucking-shit! He's convinced he's some genius and so the rest of us should tolerate his crap! What a joke. What a truly pathetic guy!" This was Taomei's rant to me. "

"Does she think that the way she behaved that night can be blotted out with a single brush stroke?" Fat Luo ranted. "That she can make it look like nothing ever happened? Can she alter all my memories with one click of her fingers? She was the one who started the whole thing by rubbing her feet against mine. Or did I dream the whole thing up? Maybe she actually has amnesia," Fat Luo said aggrievedly.

I became their battlefield.

"Do you know, I'm not the only one he's been like this with. He's done this to other girls from class in the past too," Taomei said.

She didn't just tell me this; she actually brought Lili, a girl from our class, to my apartment.

Lili had been Fat Luo's study-buddy. When you start out at university, you are randomly assigned to different houses and paired up with a senior student to look after you. Lili and Fat Luo were assigned to the same house, and became the first girl at university he got to know. After going to a couple of house gatherings together, and receiving care and advice from the same seniors, Fat Luo began to shower Lili with gifts. He got her breakfast and gave her flowers. He would call her up at the same time each morning and evening and ask how she was, and sometimes came to pick her up in his car. Lili had just moved from Yilan to Taipei for university, and wasn't yet used to big city ways. She'd never had a boyfriend before and Fat Luo's actions terrified her. Shy and wispy, Lili spoke with trepidation: "I run away whenever I see him now, and keep my distance," she said.

"I don't know if my intuition is right, but he doesn't seem very normal. Everything he does for me just comes across as pitiful. He's like a caretaker lurking around in an elementary school playground, trying to cop a feel of the female student's arses."

We sat in my cramped little apartment, going over the nitty-gritty details of what Fat Luo had done. We dissected his actions the way one would a frog, putting all the dismembered bits of flesh under the microscope for inspection.

Of course, with only girls present, we began to discuss the events of that night, candidly and without reservation.

Taomei had thought that the legs she was probing belonged to Lu Ziyu.

Huh? What was that about? I was becoming increasingly bewildered.

It transpired that Lu Ziyu had been planning to move to a university down south. The four of them had taken a trip to Taichung in that red hatchback to have some fun, while looking for an apartment for Lu Ziyu. During the trip Lu Ziyu finally summoned his courage and told Taomei how he felt about her.

"Will you come and visit me in Taichung?"

"Why should I have to tire myself out to see you in such a far-flung place?" mischievous Taomei said.

"Because I'd like to see Dadu Mountain with you."

"You're crazy. What's so good about Dadu Mountain? I can see Yangmingshan in Taipei whenever I want. And if I really wanted to see Dadu Mountain, I could just go on my own!"

"Taomei—"

"What?"

"I think … Oh … This …" Lu Ziyu stuttered like a student standing before a strict teacher.

"Just spit it out," Taomei barked.

"Taomei. I think, I'm going to think about you a lot when I move to Taichung."

Now it was our friend Taomei's turn to be speechless …

She stood still for a long time before quietly turning and leaving without a word. She kept it secret from their group of four. Back in Taipei she went on as if nothing happened, and told no one about it.

Lu Ziyu was about to leave Taipei, and Taomei started to have a faint sense of grief and longing. In the few days after returning to Taipei she had carefully considered Lu Ziyu's proposition, but she couldn't find it in herself to give him an encouraging response. She thought she was beginning to feel the faint stirrings of love, but faced with Lu Ziyu's burning, searching gaze, she evaded his question, saying neither yes or no.

But she did write a number of saccharine and unintelligible poems, and roamed around for miles like a lost soul. When she reached Pingdengli Farm where dragon juniper and rhododendron seedlings grew, she took off her leather gladiator sandals, and lifting the edges of her bleached denim skirt, traipsed barefoot through the banks between the fields. She stood on tiptoe and started to dance, dancing as if she might just soar off into the sky.

Finally we get to that night in early spring, everyone whiling away the boring evening by playing cards. Taomei decided to give Lu Ziyu a clear answer to his question—by nudging him with the bare feet that had strode through the fields and had been infected with the secrets of the soil.

"How could I have known that it Fat Luo's legs I was touching?"

Taomei voice wavered between aggrieved and angry.

Ah, so that was what happened. Lili and I nursed our porcelain cups of honey tea, and nodded as it all became clear. "And the rest you know already," Taomei said. She was referring to Fat Luo's subsequent harassment and proclamation of love.

The matter concluded when Lu Ziyu departed with Taomei's close friend, Miaozi. Fat Luo and Lu Ziyu's brothership ended. Of the four, only Fat Luo and Taomei were left, having to see each other in class every day despite being at permanent loggerheads.

Conflict Thirteen

Curiosity killed the cat, as the saying goes. It must be my sceptical and inquisitive nature that leads me back again and again. I cannot help but turn my face to meet the pit, to lean out over it, heedless of the warnings of its dangers and horrors. The pit might be lined with explosives, but only when I emerge with my face blackened and soot-covered and my hair scorched down to the roots, do I understand the phrase, "Some stones are best left unturned".

I remember once when I was very young, I came across a fact in the children's encyclopaedia about how cats need their whiskers for balance. How if the whiskers on one side of a cat's face were removed or cut short, it would lose its sense of balance and have trouble walking straight. I must have shared this scientific nugget with my little brother Ah Zhong, who generally had two strings of snot hanging from his nostrils, and was rash and impetuous, and had only recently given up the habit of occasionally eating his own shit.

One day Ah Zhong and I took our mother's fabric scissors and lifted our fat, but fast-footed tabby cat, Pepper and carried him over to the armchair. We took the round dressing table mirror our mother used to apply her makeup and our father for trimming his nose hair, and held it in front of Pepper. We wanted him to get a good look at himself. Imitating the way our father trimmed his nose hair, we snipped off Pepper's whiskers, one by one.

Pepper was extremely vexed at first and struggled against us, letting out a series of desperate meows. Ah Zhong pressed him down onto the armchair and twisted his head towards the mirror, meowing along with him. Pepper started to watch himself in the mirror transfixed; he even reached out a paw to try and catch his reflection. That was great for us, he became pliant and let us to snip away the whiskers on one side of his face.

Pepper did lose his sense of balance, as the encyclopaedia said he would. He began knocking into things as he walked around. When he tried to leap from the living room sofa to the top of the television, as he used to, he tumbled with a thud onto the terrazzo floor, and let out a series of forlorn and distressed mews.

My brother and I were wracked with a profound sense of guilt, but we had no way of replacing his whiskers. Pepper's behaviour became increasingly erratic, until even our mother, who hated small animals and used to threaten to kick the cat out the house, tuned into Pepper's strange behaviour and the shifty look in our eyes. We soon confessed to what we'd done and were given a good thrashing with the cane. We were then made to kneel down before the wall balancing a washbasin on our heads as a punishment. My brother mumbled, between convulsions of sobs, that he felt so bad about what we'd done, but that it had all been my fault really.

Curiosity had set this all in motion. As the saying goes, Who will not be ruled by the rudder must be ruled by the rock.

I remember another time, when a neighbour of ours, a Hakka man known for being thrifty and hardworking, gave us a black and white spotted dog. The dog was two or three months old and we named her Jia Jia. I often stroked Jia Jia's tiny head, or scratched her furry neck, and imitating the tone of adults I'd say, "Good girl, Jia Jia, I'll get you some milk to drink in a bit." Before long I was completely besotted with the young dog and saw myself as her mother.

Nothing was more exhilarating than going to the seaside for a swim in the summer. I still recall that sweltering humid afternoon. My siblings were about to launch into the sea on their inflatable boat, while I held Jia Jia against my chest, feeling excited, singing the words, "We're going for a swim, we're going for a swim. Mama will teach you how to swim!" to her in a strange chirpy voice. Jia Jia shook her little head, naturally not having a clue what I was saying.

When we arrived at the beach, I set Jia Jia down next to a boulder, about half the size of a person. I left her there while I dove into the water with my siblings. *Front-crawl, breaststroke, front-crawl.* We were having so much fun that a water fight soon broke out. Our mother stayed paddling near the shore, in water no deeper than her knees, despite us shouting our throats hoarse that she should join us. The nasty thought of dunking our mother in the water had probably crossed all our minds, but none of us would dare to actually do it, because she'd probably kill us.

After swimming back and forth a few times, I slopped my

way back to the shore, planning to take Jia Jia in my arms for a swim. But Jia Jia was hiding under the boulder. She was nothing like Ding Ding and Meili, the hunting dogs we'd had in the past, who used to fly through the sisal bushes and their lightning rod pines every time we brought them to the beach. They didn't care about being pricked. They'd spurt ahead like tornados, galloping like crazy, and dive into the sea, before emerging like proud sea serpents showing off their swimming prowess. Jia Jia was another story. She cowered under this bolder shivering like a complete coward.

"Don't be frightened, Jia Jia, swimming is fun." I stroked her head in an attempt to reassure her, before lifted her into my arms and carrying her into the water.

I tried to recall the way my father had taught me to swim. How he'd supported me under my belly with his hands, so that my body floated above water and my limbs could glide freely through the water around me.

I stood in the water with Jia Jia in my arms, smooth slippery pebbles underfoot, as an endless onslaught of waves crashing against us. When a wave approached, I'd start treading water, and, ride the crest of the waves with Jia Jia in my arms. My siblings were now engaged in a mighty swimming competition, to which my father had naturally been appointed Judge. Jia Jia and I had been forgotten out here between the ocean and the sky, bobbing up and down with the waves. I tried to replicate the way my father had taught me to swim so I could teach Jia Jia. I placed my hands under her belly, so that her legs and head remained above the water. Jia Jia thrashed about frantically, looking flustered. Her fur was drenched and clung to her pointed and now tiny-looking head. She didn't look like a dog anymore, more an emaciated lamb.

I started to tire and couldn't carry on any longer, so I took Jia Jia back to the shore and wiped her with a bath towel. But Jia Jia didn't stop trembling. She fixed me with her bright glassy eyes, her expression strange and sorrowful. I placed her by the boulder once more, and stroked her head, saying, "What do you think? Isn't swimming fun? Be a good girl and stay here." I turned and headed back into the embrace of the ocean.

When we all finally left the water and were getting ready to pack up our things to go home, we were shocked to discover that Jia Jia was dead. Jia Jia was dead. She had died there without a sound.

I was overcome with shock and horror. Before it had sunken in, my brother Ah Zhong pointed at Jia Jia's cold stiff little body. "It was you," he accused. "You killed Jia Jia."

I was dumbfounded. It was still confused how it had happened. I really didn't know.

"Jia Jia really couldn't swim, but you insisted on taking her swimming." My whole family turned to stare at me. With Jia Jia's body lying prone on the ground, I expected my mother to stomp over and give me two slaps across the face. But she didn't. Instead, in an unpleasant tone of voice she told my brother and me, "Both of you. Take Jia Jia's body and bury it."

Ah Zhong wrapped Jia Jia's ice-cold body in a towel. Walking behind a line of people, we crossed through the sisal, and along the road that led back home.

I trailed behind my brother the whole way, like a faltering child who'd done something wrong.

My brother and I chose a sturdy looking Casuarina tree, and we dug a hole in the ground under it. We lowered Jia Jia into the hole, her puppy-like body, perished before it had had its chance to fully develop.

We scooped up the soil with our hands and used it to cover Jia Jia's body, peaceful as if sleeping. I searched frantically for the tears that should have come by now, but I didn't shed a drop.

My brother stuck a withered Casuarina branch into Jia Jia's tiny grave and in an adult-like tone ordered,

"Get down to your knees, and kowtow to Jia Jia."

I knelt down, and with my hands by my sides, I lowered my head to the ground three times. I straightened the Casuarina branch that symbolised Jia Jia's gravestone, and then headed silently through the Casuarina trees in the direction of the fading sunset glow towards home.

After this I began to wet the bed at night. I was often gripped by the sensation of being adrift in a vast cold ocean, icy waves lashing around me. I'd wake with a start to discover the duvet and bed sheets were soaked through.

My curiosity had killed Jia Jia, and caused grievous harm to Pepper.

But that didn't curb my curiosity. I continued to act out the same absurd drama, which only grew more absurd.

If I hadn't played the listener with Taomei and Fat Luo's foot bumping incident. If I'd been like Taomei and called Fat Luo a pervert, kept my distance from him, all the sorry incidents that followed might not have come to pass.

But what's the point of saying this now?

A dog does not change its habit of eating shit. And I'm afraid that dog is me.

Conflict Fourteen

Zhou and I began our crazy love affair. He was a gentle, sensitive, considerate but varied lover, Judy said.

Sometimes he was caring like a father, attending to my every need.

Other times he lorded over me like a feudal king, as though I was his territory.

"Get a new pair of shoes. Don't wear sandals that show your toes, they're ugly. Get a pair of proper shoes, I'll buy them for you."

He could be incredibly critical. He'd find fault with my choice of clothes, as if it were completely up to him what I wore.

One day I was about to go out wearing a loose, backless dress. When it was boiling hot in Australia, my friends and I wore dresses like this all the time. I even went to a nude beach in Queensland once. No one thought revealing a bit of skin was a big deal—no one except Zhou, who flew into a rage.

"Things are different now you're with me. Which man likes other men looking at his woman?" he bellowed.

I was completely bewildered. It was like we were speaking radically different languages and coming at the issue from completely different logics.

"What are you talking about?" I said.

"Don't you know what most men will think about when they see you wearing that? Can't you learn to protect yourself? Aren't you afraid of being violated? You're so unbelievably naïve."

"Tokyo is filled with women dressed like this, you're making a mountain out of a molehill!" I said.

"They're not my girlfriend, so it's their problem. They're nothing to do with me. You're my girlfriend so it's different."

"Because I'm your girlfriend you think you've got the right to control what I wear? You don't think it's those revolting perverts who should be taken to task? The rapists punished rather than the women just trying to keep themselves cool in hot weather?"

"You're talking about theory, but I'm telling you the reality," Zhou said. He went on to say how he loved me more than he loved himself. He said that he was prepared to give up everything he had for me. That if he was so poor he only had one dollar, he'd give that dollar to me. That was how much he loved me.

He had a very unique way of expressing his love.

In the beginning of our frenzied love affair, he developed this weird infatuation with Yasukuni Shrine, that odd place we'd first had sex. Going there gave him a rush and turned him on like crazy. It felt like we were having a wild orgy in a graveyard, with a bunch of dead souls.

On the way into Yasukuni Shrine you walked past a huge, rectangular square, with a bronze statue of a Tokugawa shogunate warrior erected in the middle. This statue was enormous, the height of five or six people stacked on top of each other. To the back right, there was a war museum. And at the far end of the square were the tablets of martyrs who had died for their country, symbolising "*Yamato-damashii*"—the Japanese spirit.

Zhou didn't have class one afternoon, and we made an impromptu plan to visit the war museum. We arrived to see an actual, real-life battlefield tank guarding the entrance.

As we were entering the museum, we passed several Japanese men on their way out. They all looked around seventy and were wearing dark suits. "Those men might have killed people in China and Korea when they were younger," Zhou whispered to me.

On the right hand side of the museum's ground floor we saw photographs of the Japanese royal family and handsome portraits of them in their military garb. Glass cases displayed hand-written books royal family members had read as youngsters. I asked Zhou about the books, which were written entirely in Chinese characters. "They're the ancient Chinese literary and historical classics," he explained. "Look at what they're wearing," I joked to Zhou, "They're dressed just like Europeans. They've even styled their beards like Europeans did back then. But the books they read were all classical Chinese texts. How the hell did a race that steals everything from other cultures manage to become one of the world's top economic powers?" We both laughed.

The museum was cold and gloomy. There was a huge painting of a war scene hanging on a white wall. It showed a heroic Kamikaze pilot carrying out a suicide attack against an American aircraft carrier, blasting it to bits. Next to the oil painting was an enormous Pacific War battle map. There were several books within the low glass case, including the Dissenting Judgment of Justice Pal, clearing the Japanese of war crimes, next to which were laid out pitiful letters written by soldiers before they set off for their missions.

Also on display were the uniforms of soldiers who had died in the war. These clothes were dry and flaky and bullet-riddled, and smelt of smoke and the past. Before leaving the museum, Zhou took me over to look through the feedback book on the table. We flicked through it, and on each page saw the words: "The Japanese spirit will not die!" "Long live the soul of Japan!" These messages were written by students visiting the museum, judging by the handwriting. Zhou read through them all, and then sat down and in huge letters, wrote the word "SHAME". He took my hand and we silently departed.

As we were leaving, an old man, the caretaker probably, gawked openly at us. Zhou told me he was probably wondering what the hell a white chick and a Chinese guy were doing together in this place. Our eyes met and once again we started to chuckle.

We'd always wait until dusk fell before stealing into the shrine. As soon as we made our way through the square, Zhou's blood would start pumping, and there'd be a bulge in his jeans. Sometimes as we were walking he'd grab my hand and show me how stiff he was.

"Aren't I hard?" he'd murmur huskily.

"You're *so* hard," I'd say, feeling a bit like Sally from *When Harry Met Sally* faking her orgasm in the restaurant.

We fucked in the square beneath the tree that had been planted to symbolise the perished souls of the Pacific War. We fucked on the tank in front of the museum that had been hauled back from the battlefields of Manchuria. We even sneaked inside the solemn shrine, past the "Entry Prohibited" sign, and in a dark corner, by a white screen printed with chrysanthemums, we fucked each other's brains out. Just as he was about to come, Zhou would pull out his cock and shoot his spunk all over the tree and the soil, or the disused tank or the white screen printed with chrysanthemums.

We were like two dogs in heat, yes, just like two dogs in heat. I found the thrill of danger, and of doing something so wrong, utterly exhilarating.

He was frenzied, passionate, gentle and caring all at once. These extremes made up his strange, complex contradiction of a personality. Naturally there were times when I had misgivings about the way he was with me, even his gentle, caring side felt more like how a father might act towards a little girl—even though we were roughly the same age.

He'd often bathe me, like a father with his young daughter. He'd lather my body inch by inch in soap, rubbing it over my back, my chest, my arms, my inner thighs, my buttocks and the soles of feet. Tenderly he'd wash my hair, squeeze all the white foam from it, and then gently tell me to close my eyes, that he was going to rinse my hair now … He even shaved my armpits for me, with the endless love and affection of a father.

"Lift your arms," he commanded in that low and soothing tone. He was squatting by the side of the bath, while I stood up naked in the tub. Obediently I raised my arms, and let him transform my armpits into smooth bare plains …

* * *

Judy and I were lying in our dormitory beds. The moonlight streamed in through the windows as she unhurriedly recounted her story.

But as I lay there, Judy's words seemed to drift further and further away from me, like a witch on a broomstick riding off into a dark and lonely planet. As I listened, my mind wandered. I was thinking, wasn't my father the man washing his little girl in the bath? Had I been three or four back then, or even seven or eight? As I child I was constantly clinging to my father's leg or hanging off his shoulders. Even going to sleep, I'd have my arms wrapped around his belly.

I didn't like it when my mother washed me. Impatient and quick-tempered, she didn't care if water got in my ears when she rinsed my hair. And if I howled because water went in my ears, she'd pinch my thighs or ears until I stopped.

But my father was different. My father would cradle my small body as if he were holding a treasure in his arms, and set me down gently onto the large metal basin.

"Cover your right ear, I'm going to rinse your right side now." I heard his instructions and tilted myself back like on a seesaw, cupping a palm over my ear and turning to meet the splash of water from the pail. Then he'd do the same for my left …

"Are you even listening to me?" Judy asked from the bed opposite. She seemed to have sensed from my lack of movement that my mind had wandered.

"Yes, I'm listening," I lied, dragging my thoughts back to her.

"Don't you think he sounds strange?" Judy said.

"Zhou?"

"Of course."

"You mean because he's both aggressive and gentle, or because he gets off on having sex at Yasukuni Shrine?"

"The latter," Judy said. "He burst into tears after we had sex once."

* * *

102

He whimpered and sobbed like a helpless child, Judy said. Only minutes before he'd been on top of me, sweat pouring down his back, pounding me vigorously.

"I want to fuck you. I want to fuck you," he said. "Do you feel good?"

"Yeah," I said.

"Do you like it when I fuck you from behind?"

"Yeah."

"Say it louder so everyone can hear. Say that you love it when I fuck you, say that you love being with me."

"I love it when you fuck me. I love being with you."

"Did you come?"

"Yeah. "

"Do you want me to make you come more?"

"Yeah."

"Beg me for more."

"I'm begging you, make me come more."

"Say you can't live without me."

"I can't live without you."

"Say you love this Chinaman."

"I love this Chinaman."

"Say you worship me."

"I worship you." I was like a dog on all fours at that point, my body arched like a bow. I turned around to see him standing behind my arse, his legs he wide apart. He looked intoxicated, like he'd taken some psychoactive drug. I saw the lines of his muscles go taut as he withdrew his throbbing cock and shot his thick liquid all over the white screen swaying in the wind, tiny droplets spurting out over the chrysanthemums.

Spent, he collapsed on top of me. He gave a long sigh, and started mumbling.

"I'm like that fool Ah Q from Lu Xun's work, thinking he's won when he hasn't!" He laid his head against my bare breasts like an innocent child who needed mothering. He shut his eyes and fell silent. I'd assumed he was tired and had drifted off, but all of a sudden I heard sniffling. I intuitively reached out and touched the corner of his eyes. My fingers came away wet; he was weeping.

"The bloodthirsty murderers who butchered my people are still buried and worshipped at this shrine," Zhou said.

Was he talking about the Second World War—that was well in the past now, wasn't it? What was this constant need to carry the weight of the past, to obsess and agonise over it? Weren't we living in the time of globalisation and the internet now? Australia was involved in the Second World War too. Our young, energetic men were sent by the distant British Empire to fight the Japanese on the frontlines. Countless young lives were lost on the battlefield, treated like cannon fodder. Should we too be harbouring this historical hatred in our hearts?

I expressed this opinion to Zhou, but all he said was, "You're a Westerner, you'll never understand." And that was it. He seemed to be lost in an elegy, an elegy composed of his family's war memories.

I was raised by my grandparents, Zhou told me. When my grandfather was a child, the Japanese were already occupying northeast China and had moved into the northern plains. After they attacked Marco Polo Bridge, full-blown war broke out. They took over the whole of my family's province, Hebei. My grandfather's uncle was a Qing dynasty military commander, and at over six foot two, he was strong and sturdy. With one swing of his blade he'd have people cowering with fear. While he was studying at school as a child, my grandfather also learnt swordsmanship from his uncle. When the Japanese invaded, the Big Sword Unit, a secret society of fighters, formed pockets of resistance all over the province. To defend their homeland, civilians with nothing more than knives took to the streets to battle against strong, fierce, heavily armed Japanese troops. They took many of these Japanese unaware, creeping up on them and decapitating them. But the occupiers were obviously not going to give way to the Big Sword Unit and they did a blanket search of the area. Anyone suspected of being a fighter was killed without hesitation. They were publically beheaded, and sometimes their entire families were executed, too, to serve as a warning not to harbour suspected Big Sword Unit members.

Because his uncle was commander of the Big Sword Unit, my grandfather's entire family was put to death. My grandfather only survived because the family had panicked and sent him off to stay with an old family friend. But on the day of the execution, he still came to the town centre, and blended into the crowd to watch. The friend covered his mouth firmly as he watched his father, mother and the uncle he had worshipped being tied up tightly like pigs, made to kneel down before the crowd with guns against their heads, and then shot point-blank, blood and brains spraying everywhere.

My grandfather was trembling violently. Even his thick blue woollen sweater couldn't conceal his shaking body. They had come to collect the bodies, but if anyone were to find out who they were, the bodies would be taken away from them, and they too would be captured and executed. This was the warning this family friend gave my grandfather, his hands still covering his mouth.

In the dark of this cold winter night of heavy snow, my grandfather collected up the bodies strewn in the square. Their ears, arms and thighs had already been chewed by wild dogs. My grandfather used a handcart to drag the bodies of his parents and uncle back home. When the snow stopped, he buried the three of them.

My grandfather spent his whole life full of anger and hatred. He despised the fact that despite his energy and youth, his family had forbidden him from joining the Big Sword Unit. Someone had to carry on the ancestral line, that was the reason they gave him. So he carried on living, but what for? To bury the dead? When the Japanese surrendered, my grandfather took to the streets with a group of his friends and beat up every Japanese person they saw. After storing it up for so many years, they finally got to release their hatred and anger.

My grandfather and grandmother met in Beijing after the war ended. They fell in love and got married. My grandmother was born in Nanjing. She was only twelve when the Japanese invaded. During the Nanjing massacre, she and her entire family hid in the storehouse, but the bloodthirsty Japanese soon discovered them. She was stripped naked in front of her whole family and raped by four or five soldiers. Each time she fainted she was beaten back to consciousness. With eyes like a dead fish, she was forced to watch as her father, mother and siblings were tortured to death. The Japanese taunted her that she'd been spared for her beauty. Her beauty had saved her. She passed out, and woke, who knows how many days later, to find herself in the city brothel.

She went to toilet, and finding the window unlocked, took her chance and managed to slip out unnoticed. She caught the train and fled north, making the tough journey to the meeting point of the communist guerrillas. Once there, she snipped off her two long braids, and learnt how to use a sword and gun.

I can't even bear to think about how much depravity my elegant grandmother was subjected to. How her family were forced to watch as they took turns raping her—only twelve years old, a mere child, Zhou said.

* * *

Hadn't my father and uncle lived through a similar time, I thought? My father had been a student at the Yunnan Teaching College when the Japanese invaded Nanjing. He and his family assumed that long before he had graduated the Kuomintang would have defeated the Japanese and sent them packing, back to their little country only half the size of Yunnan province. He would be a teacher by then, and would travel to the hill tribes on the plateau to teach. Instead, the Kuomintang troops stationed in Shanghai were defeated, and three months later things in China went drastically downhill. The Japanese marched in and quickly captured Nanjing, the city the Kuomintang had made their capital.

We heard my father's grisly stories so many times, the events that led him to abandon his teaching plans and decide to fight instead. "Japanese soldiers tossed babies into the air and then held bayonets up and skewered their bellies. Blood and intestines flew everywhere. The soldiers holding the bayonets would have faint smiles of pride on their faces."

Or he'd say: "When the Japanese invaded Nanjing, they burnt and looted the city and slaughtered countless people. They raped all women no matter their age, sixty year olds or children were all fair game to them."

As a child I listened to these stories with wide-eyed fascination. They felt like they belonged to some far off world—like Arabian Nights. He told them with little emotion or colour or any sense that they had really happened. They seemed more like the stories adults told to scare you, of child-eating monsters lurking in the dark.

Were people slaughtered in the same way pigs and dogs are? I asked, holding my father's hand. I was barely up to his waist back then, I was like a little doll that tottered after him. But I had already developed my appetite for asking questions.

"It was much worse," my father said.

Pigs being slaughtered. I imagined the shrill shrieks of the pigs I always heard early morning, drifting over from afar. It was always like that in the slaughterhouse, the pigs struggling and howling in the face of death. I wasn't sure how those pigs were killed; all I knew was their anguished screams, as if they were begging for their lives. As a child the sound always filled me with horror and fear. It was like a sharp object scraping across glass, and it would stop my breath.

"Want big delicious apples? Go to northeast China! That's what the Japanese taught their children," my father said.

"So when they grew up and wanted to eat big apples, they went to northeast China?" I asked, only half believing him.

"Yes," he said without hesitation. "It was written in the children's textbooks."

I was too young to understand my father's world, or the world of war. It didn't make sense, just like ethnic hatred didn't make sense. All I knew was that all the middle-aged bachelor friends my father was always surrounded by had once fought the Japanese. Whenever Japan was mentioned, they'd give a disdainful, "Little Japan. Pirates. Descendants of pirates."

It was towards the end of the Second World War that my father joined to fight the Japanese. He was just a student and had never even touched a gun, but he signed up to military school all the same. After a brief military training he was sent off to the battlefields of Burma.

"We rode horses into battle!" My father always sounded so proud when he said this. But wasn't the real reason they'd rode horses because they lacked the sophisticated battle tanks and jeeps of the Japanese?

"The Japanese had already invaded Yunnan via Burma, and China was close to ruin," my father said. The new soldiers were released from military school before their full training was up and sent out into the battlefields. Never having fought before, they were hugely unprepared, but they managed to drive the Japanese back into Burma. "We didn't have tanks or jeeps, but we led our horses along the mountain paths. We were the children of the plateau, and knew the terrain like it was the backs of our hands. We knew how to make ourselves invisible there. The Japanese might have had the sophisticated weaponry, but they couldn't get us, they couldn't take the mountain paths. They were badly defeated and driven back to northern Burma, where the Wa people helped us fight them, because their villages had been destroyed by the Japanese—burnt and looted and razed to the ground."

So the Japanese really were pirates! I said to my father. I had been listening curiously, as if to a bedtime story.

"Burma was a British colony back then. It didn't belong to the Burmese people."

So where were the British when the war broke out?

"They were utterly defeated! What good is it having the most sophisticated weaponry, when you have your entire family there with you, needing your protection? Of course the British were defeated."

My father didn't sound like the same boy who'd been full of glee and pride showing off his new Oxford shoes to his friends at the football pitch. Instead, his voice carried disdain.

"Those incompetent British," my father said.

My mother had not even been born when my father was off fighting. She came along shortly after the Second World War. Her father had also been fighting the Japanese for many years, engaged in numerous battles, big and small, and it was with a sense of victory, and weary elation, that he had returned home to Fujian.

He then married his childhood sweetheart, a girl from the same village, a beautiful and graceful woman who worked as a teacher in the village school. But their honeymoon was cut short when the news came that my grandfather's army unit were being transferred to another province. The civil war between the Kuomintang and Communists had been stopping and starting, but it was still going on. My grandfather took my grandmother with him, though she was already huge with my mother.

It has often occurred to me that my mother's feeling of displacement started before she was even born, all that moving from place to place without ever settling. This must have contributed to the way she used to scream hysterically at us children, a means of venting her frustration and anguish.

"But I didn't start the war," I'd yell in frustration, too, sometimes. Particularly when my furious, weeping mother hit her head repeatedly against the wall, yelling, "What kind of world is this?" Later my grandmother had another child, a boy.

When I was a child my mother often told me how my grandmother had given birth to my maternal uncle beneath a giant rock, as in those days there had been no way of getting to a hospital. My uncle was born into calamity, shots of distant gunfire welcoming him into the world.

Without her husband by her side, my young grandmother was all on her own caring for the weeping toddler who would become my mother, while also cradling a new-born in her arms. The baby would stare through blinking and bewildered eyes at the absurd world before him. The three of them fled from place to place like a pack of mongrels running for their lives.

And my grandfather, where was he at this point? After defeating the Japanese, this Kuomintang commander was now engaged in a front line battle with the Chinese Communists—a group of farmer-fighters, even more ill-equipped than them. And yet the Kuomintang was gradually forced into retreat and many were escaping in boats to Taiwan.

My young grandmother had no food and was producing no milk to feed her baby, so she bit her own finger and nourished him with her blood. It still wasn't enough to save the little boy whose entire life had been eclipsed by the war. Sometimes I wonder if it's a good thing my uncle died, or he would have been destined for an unhappy childhood too. The shadow of the war would always be looming over him. He too would have developed my mother's manic temperament. He'd never have been able to erase the image of his father sitting defeated in the living room, his face red and unhappy, drowning his sorrows, glass by glass, whispering authoritatively in a strange dialect: "Watch out for spies and traitors. It was because of poor intelligence that we lost the war. We were taken in too easily. Those Communists can't be trusted. We must catch all spies and traitors."

My grandmother had been too weak to cope with the grief of her son's death, and she passed away soon after him. Before she died, she delivered my mother to a Kuomintang military base.

My mother was only three, and did not understand a thing. Death was a completely foreign concept. She didn't even get the chance to say goodbye to her mother before she died, she was too busy stretching her hand out for Kuomintang rations, and running up to gun-wielding soldiers, throwing her arms around their legs and crying out, "Daddy! Daddy!"

She was far too young to remember her father's face. The only memory she had of him was how he'd once taught her how to use a gun to fight the "big baddies". She remembered how to make the sound of gunshots—Bang, bang. Bang, bang.

It was the time of the great retreat. My mother was passed from hand to hand in the dilapidated old military base. In the end a lieutenant who'd served under my grandfather stuffed her in a suitcase and took her on a boat to Taiwan to meet my grandfather's unit.

When my grandfather saw my mother again, there was no trace of smile on his face.

All he said was, "They're all dead, why are you still alive?"

I don't believe there was any malice in those words. He hadn't been able to come to terms with the loss of his wife and son. It was said out of anguish at his loss. Or perhaps marvelling at the tenacity of life—that this little three-year-old girl had managed to survive against all the odds. But it was my mother's first real memory, and although she was only three when she heard those words, she never forgot them. From that day on, she was convinced that her survival mocked and wronged those who had died, while placing a burden on those still alive. This belief was further reinforced when my grandfather married again in Taiwan. The story of her young mother who had perished in the chaos of war became a beautiful myth that floated over the island of Taiwan, sometimes drifting across the Taiwan Straits to her hometown in Fujian.

My mother did not adjust well to Taiwan. In Taipei it rained endlessly, and everything grew damp and mouldy. People got rashes all over their bodies. Strangely enough, despite having moved about constantly since her birth, from military base to military base, from her birthplace in Jiangsu to all the way down south, being separated from her whole family in the middle of all this, my mother had never suffered any major illness. But as soon as she arrived in Taiwan she fell ill.

My grandfather was constantly getting ready for a counter attack against the mainland, and had no time to take care of my mother. He left her in the care of some friends, a couple from his hometown village who'd also fled the war.

My grandfather would visit my mother during his time off work, often taking her to Neihu cemetery. He'd carry her or take her patiently by the hand, and they would make their way past all the tombstones, in search of his dead wife's grave. In an act of kindness, a fellow Fujian also fleeing the war had brought my grandmother's cremated remains to Taiwan and had them buried in the ramshackle makeshift graves at Neihu.

My grandfather would search through every inch of tall grass, looking for a sign of her burial site. The friend from Fujian who had carried her ashes had been a devout Buddhist. He had passed away in Taiwan before having the chance to tell my grandfather where his wife was buried. But my grandfather never gave up hope. He and my mother would leap over the higglty-pigglty grave markers, scanning each one for my grandmother's name.

But they never did find it. Her father would sit on one of the grassy hills overlooking the land, looking weary and defeated. He'd pull out a clear bottle of liquor and take swigs from it and sorrowfully warn my young mother, who only half-understood his words, to, "Never ever marry a soldier. They can't even protect their wives and children."

When my mother grew up, she paid no heed to his warning.

My grandfather's new wife, my step-grandmother, was a full-fledged beauty with a peach face and eyes that were big, round and dark. "My hometown Quanzhou is a big harbour. We've had a flourishing international trading port there for hundreds of years now. We're different to your grandfather, who comes from the mountains." My step-grandmother was a soft-spoken woman of few words. She seemed very gentle, except for her smugness.

She did not get along well with my mother. At the beginning they didn't even know about each other. It was only on their wedding day that my step-grandmother learned the truth from my grandfather—that he'd been married on the mainland, and had a daughter only a decade her junior. When my Grandfather revealed all this on their wedding night, my step-grandmother was dumbfounded. She couldn't speak. Less than a few hours before they had been drinking merrily with their wedding guests. Now she felt as if her world had been flipped on its head. My grandfather sat on the marriage bed, his face full of grief and defeat, looking as if he were about to cry. My step-grandmother was silent for a very long time, her face deathly white. When she finally spoke, her voice was cold as ice, "Why didn't you tell me before?"

My grandfather, who'd always been a confident, straightforward man, found he couldn't look her in the eye. "I was afraid that if I told you, you wouldn't agree to marry me," he said, bowing his head like an ashamed child. When my step-grandmother didn't answer, my grandfather panicked, and began to cry. In frustration he blurted out, "It's not my fault, it's not my fault. It was all because of the war."

Not long after, my mother moved from my grandfather's friends' house to live with the newlyweds. But she felt unwanted in their house. She stubbornly refused to call her step-mother "mother" and settled instead for "aunt". My grandfather lost his temper once and raised his hand to slap my mother. But my mother's confident response was, "How can you claim you respect my mother? How can you claim you respect my dead mother?"

My grandfather didn't answer, but he withdrew his fist. My step-grandmother started to forbid my mother from sitting at the dining table during mealtimes. My mother thought it was a one off at first, but it gradually turned into the norm. If my mother refused to follow orders and do the chores as she was told, she would be denied dinner, and as a result, often went hungry. In order to get food, she took on all the household chores. She'd walk two kilometres to fetch the water and two kilometres to carry it back, a journey she repeated several times a day. She'd light the fire to cook with and boil water for the family to bathe. During the winter, she would have to plunge her hands in icy water to wash everyone's clothes. My step-grandmother was only ten years older than her and started giving birth to child after child. The house was soon full of her children—my mother's step-brothers and sisters—all of them much younger than my mother, who was put in charge of caring for them too. She cared for every single one of my maternal uncles and aunts.

After preparing dinner one evening, my mother curled herself up in the bamboo bed by the kitchen to take a rest. She suddenly heard voices in the courtyard and her ears pricked up. It was my step-grandmother saying, "Are you talking about our little house maid? She's been living with us for a while now, but she's still terrible at housework ..."

My mother never forgot those words. Little house maid. So she was nothing more than a maid to them. No wonder she had to eat her siblings' leftovers. No wonder she was given such an endless stream of chores. No wonder she only had hand-me-downs to wear. She swore to herself that one day she would leave home. She had to grow up quickly and leave this place. She stopped going home at lunchtime, preferring to take afternoon naps in the school corridors instead. A soft southern breeze blew as she inhabited the hazy world between sleep and waking life. She visualised herself at seventeen, meeting her handsome Prince Charming who would whisk her away on his white horse … She prayed that this would come to pass. She anticipated his arrival, this man who would whisk her away from her sorry existence.

That person appeared. It was my guerrilla-fighting father.

My mother was only seventeen when she met my father, but she looked less like a girl, more a sad, old housewife. There was a glimmer of grief and sorrow in her eyes that told the story of how she'd been homeless since the age of three.

My mother had finished school and started making plans to leave the home that had never been a home. She got a government job, and then a friend introduced her to my guerrilla-fighting father. My father had spent many years leading his troops of guerrillas in the mountains by then, and had made a total of 165 parachute jumps.

He was in his thirties, a fellow with good posture, a handsome gaze and polished leather shoes. My mother had heard stories from colleagues and friends about these strong, courageous fighters roaming unseen around foreign borders, and she had read in the papers how they'd infiltrated the mainland and travelled five hundred kilometres inland—and had defeated the Burmese army twice. Their reputation had spread so far and wide that eventually even the Kuomintang government had become fearful. They were afraid these guerrillas might become mutinous and decide to establish their own independent nation, perhaps rebuilding the ancient Dali Kingdom in Yunnan. The whole thing escalated into an international incident, and the guerrilla troops were forced to withdraw back to Taiwan. My mother met him like a little girl meeting her hero. She wore a tight-fitting cheongsam dress, and her hair pinned decoratively up. Her gaze darted between her friend and my father. He looked so different to the way she'd expected the commander of a pack of coarse, boorish guerrilla fighters to look. My father's hair was combed back and shiny and he was wearing suspenders, a diagonal striped tie and a peaked cap—a far cry from her imagined bearded fighter in combat gear with a gun slung over his shoulder.

My mother listened curiously to my father's fighting tales. Then she told him her own story, about being a refugee and orphan since the age of three, before finally drifting to the shores of Taiwan. She spoke in a low voice, her shoulders wracked with sobs. My father gently stroked her shoulder. Don't be frightened, he told her, I'm here. No Communist, or foreign invader will ever hurt you again. With tears shining in her eyes, my mother gazed up at my father. She wasn't sure what he'd said, but it had sounded like the promise of a man. Was he promising to protect her for the rest of her life? There were tears at the corner of my father's eyes too. All invaders must die. All their imported ideologies and systems would be destroyed, my father said.

It was only after living with my father for some twenty years that my mother finally realised that the man she'd shared a bed with for so long had not spoke those words or shed those tears because he was moved by her story. There was only one thing my father was interested in, and that was national salvation, national salvation, national salvation.

When my parents got engaged, my father came bearing ham and sausages for my grandfather. My grandfather chased him out the house with a broom and hurled the sausages onto the streets. "Don't you even think of marrying my daughter," he bellowed.

"You didn't love or care about me when I was living with you, why do you care who I marry?" my mother responded, equally livid.

"Since you were a child I've told you never to marry a military man. Why didn't you listen? And he's so much older than you, how can I accept him?"

"Just because you left my mother to die, doesn't mean that all military men are bad news," my mother spat out boldly.

My grandfather looked devastated, but he said nothing. It was like stamping on someone's injured foot. He curled up on the bamboo chair, where he remained for a long time. Finally, sounding very alone, he said, "It's not my fault. It's not my fault. It was all because of the war!"

Some twenty years later, it had become my father and my turn to walk among these higglety-piggelty tombstones. My father, former deputy guerrilla troop commander, said, "Those who fought with me are my brothers in life and death. We looked after each other in life, and we continue to look after each other in death."

Conflict Fifteen

My mother's old high school teacher was my high school teacher too. While handing out our exam papers, this teacher was suddenly reminded of something and said, "Your mother wrote wonderful essays when she was a student! They were the best in the school."

Her words filled me with suspicion and a certain amount of derision. The idea my mother the cry-baby, a woman so hysterical she could have played the female lead in a primetime soap opera, could be any good at writing. How could it be?

I was the one who'd been lavished with praise for my literary talent, the one who harboured ambitions of becoming a writer —not my mother. All she was capable of was howling at us and chasing us round the house with her cane shrieking, "If you run away don't you dare ever show your face in this house again." She was like a fishwife, running through the streets yelling abuse, thinking that the whole world was against her. My mother, so absurd she'd hit her own head against the wall when she was angry or depressed—how could it be? It sounded like a joke.

I was still suspicious about all this as we were sitting at the table eating dinner, and so I probed into the matter, my words to her laced with the usual amount of hostility. "Your old high school teacher Mrs Zhang told me you used to write great essays."

"Oh. That was such a long time ago, do they still remember that!" My mother was surprised and flattered, and her face instantly transformed from a tired old housewife's into a little girl's. She seemed bashful even.

"What did you write about?" I asked.

"Just some stories about my family. People found them quite moving, some even cried," she said, sounding self-conscious. She didn't look anything like a housewife anymore.

"I can hardly believe that they'd still remember something like that twenty years later." She seemed to have lost herself in the memory and her speech became slower and more graceful.

I was still sceptical. An essay so moving that people still remembered it twenty years on? It was odd. I ran to ask my father.

"Father, mother's high school teacher told me she was a good writer!" I expected my father to respond in a jokey tone of voice, and a comment to the effect of, I'm sure your teacher was just exaggerating. To my surprise, his response was an earnest one. Absolutely, he said, your mother's writing was very good. Before we got married, your mother and I lived apart, one in the north and the other in the east. She used to send me letters everyday, pages and pages of them. I always found them very moving. That's why I decided to marry her.

My mother's letters had been so good they'd convinced him to marry her? Astounding!

"Where are those letters now?" I asked, wanting proof of my

mother's alleged literary prowess.

"They got lost when we moved house," my father replied mildly.

Was my ambition to become a writer just fate helping my mother to achieve her unfulfilled dream? It was absurd, especially considering how much I despised my mother. So much so that when I was five years old, begrudgingly dressed in the pyjamas she'd sewn for me, holding the doll with the eyes that opened and shut, and rocking back and forth on a wooden rocking horse, I told my neighbourhood friend, "I'm going to marry my daddy when I grow up."

With her long hair curled into princess locks, this neighbourhood girl snickered and said, "Li Jiaying says she wants to marry her daddy when she grows up."

"What are you laughing at?"

"You can't marry your daddy when you grow up!"

"Why not?"

"Because your daddy is married to your mummy!" She laughed some more.

"But if my mummy goes away, then I'll be able to marry my daddy."

More laughter. "Li Jiaying, you're so stupid. You can't marry your daddy."

"Why can't I marry my daddy?"

"Because he's your daddy."

"But when I grow up I can."

"When you grow up your daddy will be old."

"But he'll still be handsome."

"You still can't marry your daddy."

"Yes, I can."

"No, you can't."

"Yes, I can."

"No, you can't."

"You dare say that one more time."

"You can't marry your daddy."

Bam. I leapt off the wooden horse and sprang at my playmate with her princess locks. We began to tussle. In the process, she might have bitten my cheek, while I might have snatched a fistful of her hair and knocked her to the floor. All we could hear were the sounds of our scuffling and howling as we tore at each other's clothes and tried to bite each other the way dogs did. This continued until both sets of parents swarmed in to pull us apart, slapping us both across the face.

Then it was just the sound of crying and finger-pointing.

For a long time I thought that the only reason I couldn't marry my father was because my mother was around.

"You're too old to still be sitting on your father's lap!" my mother would yell at me whenever she saw me there with my arms wrapped coquettishly round his neck.

Each time we children sat on my father's back pretending he was a horse, patting his rump and telling him to giddy up, our exhilarating battle game would be interrupted by mother's furious shrieks. "What sort of behaviour is this? Get down and do your homework!"

I despised my mother. I refused to wear those pyjamas she'd sewn for me and I refused to wear the sweater she'd knitted. "It's so ugly. Everyone will laugh at me," I'd say, fixing her with bright round eyes that brimmed with hate. As long as I was forced to wear her handmade clothes, I'd feel as though the whole world was watching me. It made me so miserable I sometimes couldn't walk straight.

I despised my mother. I'm not sure how, but I came across a Western film one day about a beautiful, alluring blonde maiden dressed in a long white Greek-style tunic. A man knocked on the door and went in, wielding a sword with a sharp slender blade. He ripped the clothes from the woman's chest, and with one slash, cut off her breast. The scene had me completely bewildered. I had no idea how it had been filmed. There was a shot showing the splatter of blood, and then the woman's mouth flying open before she'd even realised what had happened. She continued to stand there with her mouth agape, mirroring my own horrified expression—my mouth like a ruptured peach on my face.

"Why can't that happen to my mother?" I secretly asked myself —even though it had only a few years since I'd been weaned. It was around the time my mother had started booting me out of their bed, forcing me to join my big sister in her bedroom. Unable to sleep, I'd creep quietly back to my parents' king-sized bed and crawl in between them as they slept. Out of habit, I'd put my arms around my father's belly and finally drift off to sleep. When my mother turned to hug my father, she'd find that I'd slipped into their bed again, and nudge me to edge of the bed with her leg.

"Go and sleep in the other room," she'd bark, her voice raspy and sleepy, but still as commanding as ever. My father would generally pretend to be asleep throughout this, not wanting to get involved. But if my mother pulled me by my ears or kicked me so hard under the sheets that I started crying, my father would suddenly pipe in with,

"Do you really need to do that to her? She's just a child." His words just inflamed my mother further. "You cunning scoundrel with your guerrilla tactics," she'd bellow. "I see through your act. You'll always be a wolf in sheep's clothing."

I'd be chased from their bed in tears, and make my grudging way back into my sister's room, where she lay sleeping like a baby. I'd shove her to the other side of the bed and turn to face the wall, clutching the blanket, my body all bundled up. In the darkness I'd conjure up the image of that woman with the sliced-off breast and picture the same fate being inflicted upon my mother. I'd see her standing there with her mouth wide open, shocked into silence. I'd mirror her expression, my mouth just as wide, staring her down as she suffered. She wouldn't be able to pinch my nose again after that, nor to force me to swallow down that horrid, bitter medicine she spent so many hours preparing to treat my chronic lung infection. She'd no longer have the power to throw away my paper dolls and the marbles I'd won at marble club in games against boys.

I wanted her to disappear from our home. If magic existed, I would use it to make her disappear. I wished for her to be taken away on Aladdin's magic carpet, to disappear into the night, and never come back. Only then would we be free, free to do all do the things we wanted.

My father went round to his guerrilla brother's place one night, and because it was raining and the road was wet and slippery, he didn't come back home that night. A typhoon was closing in, with wind and rain hurling against the windows, tap tap tap. The wind was out in force, a number of telegraph poles had been blown over, and there was a power cut in our house. We were all praying desperately for father's swift return, but he didn't show up. All us children sensed the mounting unease.

My mother told my brother to light some candles, and then hurriedly nailed wooden boards to every window and door. She called us children around her in a circle and hugged us tightly to her, pressing her forehead to ours.

"Your father doesn't want us anymore," my mother said in a deep, tight-lipped voice, so different from her usual high-pitched tone. It was as though she'd had no choice but tell us this inexorable truth. I heard her begin to cry, followed by the sound of my siblings crying. It was as if we were performing some ritual, and in this odd atmosphere, tears began to roll down my cheeks too. It wasn't my father's failure to come home that surprised me; it was finding my mother suddenly transformed into this person filled with warmth, who knew how to hug her children. I felt disturbed and alarmed by the warm proximity of her arms. Whenever I was forced to hold hands with her to cross the road, I'd refuse anything more than a finger hooked through hers. These couple of fingers might have symbolised my mother leading me across the road, but they represented the resistance I had towards her.

During that stormy night, the only sounds the wind, the rain and our crying, my little brother suddenly came out with the repugnant words, "Don't worry, Mama, I'll take care of you." As if our father really was gone for good.

By the following afternoon, the wind and rain had subsided, and my father swaggered home, completely unaware that he was walking straight into the mouth of a volcano. My mother was sitting cross-legged in the living room, deadly still, like a Bodhisattva statue. The look on her face was ghastly, zombie-like, a look of death.

"Last night after dinner Old Wang said they needed another player for their game of mahjong and begged me to stay," my father said in his usual relaxed and gruff manner. "It was terrible weather and raining so heavily I thought it would be wiser to leave after the storm. So I decided to stay and play mahjong with them … why do you look so unhappy?"

"Is your stupid game more important to you than your family? How could you just abandon your family when you knew there was a typhoon on the way? The only people you really give a damn about are your fellow guerrilla fighters, aren't they? You should have just stayed away. Do you actually care what happens to your family?"

"I didn't want to stay away. It was a big storm was and it wouldn't have been safe to take the mountain path. I'm back now the storm's over, aren't I?"

"I think we'd be better off if you had died, you heartless man. Mahjong. Do you think you're still the same rich boy you were back at home, throwing money around like it's sand? We don't have enough money to spare for you to waste on your games. There are so many mouths for you to feed, don't you know? And you've got enough money left for mahjong. I've earned myself eight lifetimes of bad luck marrying you. Are you out to destroy the family's fortune? Playing mahjong. I was blind to have married you. You told me you buried a stash of gold bars back when you were fighting. So where is this buried gold? Don't spend all this family's fortune before you find it."

My mother carried on cursing him without pause for breath, leaving my father no chance to get a word in. He just stood there, like a tortoise with its limbs and head retracted, silently absorbing my mother's torrent of abuse. I stood at the side watching as the hands of the clock ticked by, praying for this storm to soon be over.

We thought the next day might bring the calm after the storm, just like the blue skies following a typhoon, but we were very much mistaken.

Our mother, heavily pregnant with my sister, actually walked all the way to the house of my father's friend, Old Wang, where she launched into another tirade. What sort of friend are you? Don't you know he's got a wife and kids to feed? Do you think nothing has changed since your old guerrilla days, that you can do as you please, with no regard for the consequences? Are you aware that you're leading your friend astray? If you see yourself as a friend, then spare a thought for his wife and children. Does the thought of tearing a family apart make you happy? Haven't you gone through enough years of war to know what that's like?

All my father's retired guerrilla pals ran out from their mahjong den to find out what the hell was going on. They began to murmur in astonishment. Who'd have thought that my father, with his fearsome reputation and so strong in battle, would have ended up with a tigress for a wife? In the future, when my father was itching for another game of mahjong his friends would persuade him to leave. "You'd better get home. Or your wife will tear the place down."

But the matter did not end there. When my mother returned home, she pulled out the dusty leather suitcase from the top of the cupboard, the suitcase that hadn't been touched since they moved to Taitung, and began stuffing her clothes into it.

"What are you doing?" My father stood before the suitcase, at a complete loss.

"You obviously don't want this family. Why do you care what I'm doing?" my mother said, continuing to stuff her clothes into the suitcase.

"It's not as big a deal as you're making it. I've never not wanted this family. I just played mahjong and didn't come back for one night," my father said, grief-stricken.

"You still have the gall to defend yourself! Leaving everything for me to deal with. And your excuse is that you were busy playing mahjong. Don't you know that it's dangerous to leave your wife and kids at home when there's a typhoon?"

"I didn't know it would arrive so fast! It won't happen again."

"Again? You think there'll be an 'again?' Do you think playing mahjong is something to be proud of?" With her suitcase packed, my mother headed for the door.

"I didn't say it was something to be proud of. It was just a few games with some friends. Don't do this! The children are so small." My father leapt over to the door, blocking her exit.

This only increased my mother's fury. "So you've realised the children are still small. I think the only ones that actually matter to you are your guerrilla friends!" She shook off my father's hand and grabbed her suitcase. Tears trickled down her face as she huffed, "Don't block the door," and stalked out.

My father panicked for a moment. Don't leave! Don't leave! he yelled to our mother, while rounding up us three children and telling us to do likewise. Like a dog, My little brother Ah Zhong whipped past our father and up to our mother. He barely reached her waist, but grabbed onto her skirt, and howled, tears and snot running down his cheeks, "Mama don't go! Don't go!"

My older sister crouched behind my father, her shoulders heaving as she cried and cried. My father can't have seen me, hiding behind my sister, my arms folded against my chest, gazing sullenly, and thinking to myself, can't we just let this weepy detestable woman go? If she left it would be my turn to be the mother.

As my brother continued to cry out, Mama don't go! Don't go!, my father was struck by a sudden flash of inspiration. He shoved me and my sister towards our mother saying, "Kneel down. Kneel down. Kneel before your mother." Before we could make sense of it, we were down on our knees. "Say, 'Mama, don't go,' " my father said as if he were a conductor. "Mama don't go," my sister and I repeated in unison.

My mother broke down into shrill tears. "I am so ill-fated to have married this man and borne so many of his children!"

My mother didn't leave after all. I looked up at my parents in bewilderment from on my knees. Wasn't this all my father's fault? So why were we the ones kneeling?

"Get up. Get up," my father said and reached to take the suitcase from my mother's hand.

The next day, things had returned to normal with my parents. They walked barefooted on the concrete floor, hand in hand, back to being in love, singing the *Clay Figures* and *The Moon Reflects my Heart*. They didn't look in the slightest bit as if they had just had a huge argument and nearly separated.

Conflict Sixteen

So much Love between you and me, It
starts off hot as fire, deep as the sea, The
steadiest rocks crumble away too, Love
will never cease.
But from a fistful of soil, I'll make a figure of you …
(*Clay Figures*)

Teresa Teng's singing seemed to reverberate through this foreign place I had found myself in. I struggled to pull myself out of my youth hostel bed. Leaning against the bedpost, I glanced over at the window by Judy's bed. The curtains had been drawn revealing a bright, sunny sky. Judy's bed was empty, and it was still made. It looked unusually tidy, and there was no sign that Judy been back last night.

I gazed out the window and let Teresa Teng's soft, sweet voice wash over me. When I'd been struggling to open my eyes, I'd thought for a moment that I was back in my childhood home, with its huge courtyard surrounded by Casuarina trees. My parents had taken off their shoes and were walking barefoot around the concrete square, hand in hand. Their voices were cloying as they sang the words to this Chinese oldie, *Clay Figures* .

But it wasn't my father and mother singing. I was in Seoul, capital of South Korea. I was on foreign land. It took me a while to return from my reverie and re-orientate myself, and work out that the music was probably drifting up from the ground floor, put on by that poet-worker Park, who liked Teresa Teng, but not her French boyfriend. Why wasn't he at the construction site today? As far as I knew it wasn't a public holiday.

I made my way to the bathroom to clean my teeth and have a wash, and saw that the clutter had been cleared away. Not only had those many items been removed, the bathroom looked much cleaner too. Mr Kim and James the American must have finally reached a compromise, but who knew how long it would last?

As I made my way down the spiral staircase, I heard humming. A woman humming along to Teresa Teng, without singing the words. The downstairs hall was deserted, no sign of Park or Mr Kim. The song was definitely coming from the ground floor CD player, but the woman's voice was coming from the kitchen.

I followed the voice into the kitchen, where I found a willowy blonde woman dressed in a floral cotton dress. She was leaning against the kitchen counter, humming as she did the dishes, her backside swaying to the music, as if there was no one else there.

When had this beautiful golden-haired girl arrived? Just from the view of her back, I could tell she was charismatic and vivacious.

I decided to be friendly to this new dorm mate and make the first move.

"Morning," I greeted.

"Oh, Jiaying, it's you," the blonde girl answered, turning around.

God. I felt a huge jolt of surprise. I stood frozen to the spot just staring at her.

"Did I scare you?" she asked.

"Um. No. Uh… I'm just a bit surprised, that's all. Did you have a makeover?" I stuttered.

"Is that why you didn't recognise me?" She giggled. "Interesting, interesting." More giggles.

"Are you wearing a wig?"

"No. I dyed my hair and got it restyled," she replied.

It was Judy. Judy post-makeover, like a whole other, much younger person. That sloppy, unkempt woman now looked like a stylish, attractive girl. Her hair had been feathered, and a choppy fringe covered her forehead. Her mouth curled up into a faint smile, and with the feathered golden hair that turned up at the edges, she looked just like Meg Ryan in *You've Got Mail*, impish and alluring.

I told her she looked very different. Which pleased her. She made me a cup of coffee, and told me to sit down. She obviously had something she was bursting to tell me. Her eyes shone with excitement.

I sat down at the dining table by the window. There was a pile of Korean language books and notebooks on Judy's chair. Was she learning Korean? Something had given her a new lease of life and burst of energy at any rate.

"Do you want to hear a secret?" Judy lowered her voice, trying to play up the mystery. "I met this really cute guy."

"Oh?" All I could manage was this awkward reply. She seemed to be moving things along too fast. It was only ten days or so since she had been beside herself, grabbing me to talk endlessly about her Chinese boyfriend in Tokyo. Zhou, who her life had revolved around, and had completely broken her heart. But now she seemed completely healed, and was launching herself towards a new romance.

"Where's he from?" I asked, assuming it would be another Asian guy.

"He's Korean. He used to be a member of the national Taekwondo team," Judy said with pride. "He had to quit after an injury though." She sounded sad about this. The Teresa Teng CD stopped.

"Did you meet him here?" I asked curiously.

"Yes, in a bar in Itaewon," Judy replied. "You should have seen the way he was dancing. He was killer. His body is super hot. I swear every girl was looking at him. Do you know the South Korean dance music duo, Clon? He's got a body type just like one of them, and they dance the same way too," she added, sounding a little boastful.

"Clon? Are you talking about the bald one or the one with long hair?" I asked.

"The bald one, of course!" Judy said emphatically. "*Funky tonight … la la la la la …*" She sat down next to me and began swaying her shoulders and bobbing her head as she hummed the Clon tune. She looked as if she might have been drinking.

"He asked me out for a meal next Tuesday," she said with excitement. "I have to learn some Korean quick. I'm wondering if I should quit my course in Tokyo and just move to Seoul. Learning Korean's not a bad idea, is it? And living costs here are much cheaper." Her head was swimming with ideas, and she leapt from one future plan to another.

I didn't know whether to be happy or sad for her. She was just a naïve little girl, with overly beautiful visions for the future.

When I left the kitchen, she was still fumbling over Korean words in her language book, repeating them over and over, with a determined look on her face, as if the reward for all her effort might be true love.

I went back up to the dormitory and got ready to go out. I could still hear Judy's clumsy pronunciation of Korean words. When I'd got out of bed, I hadn't made any plans for the day, but after my conversation with Judy, I decided I had to visit Itaewon now, before I left for Europe. I had only seen on this bar district when all the revellers were there at night, and had no idea what it looked like by day.

I took the subway and headed for Itaewon. Shops lined the streets, selling things like mounted paintings, pandering to the tourists, although almost every shop I saw was empty.

Itaewon was a must-see for tourists according to my guidebook, which said that the leather clothes and goods being peddled were a real steal. The American military base in the area gave the streets an interesting feel. But Mr Park from the youth hostel thought this area symbolised national humiliation, a representation of class difference between the different races.

I walked around to Itaewon with my guidebook in my hand, looking like an eager tourist. The air was very dry and I pulled a bottle of mineral water from my backpack, and stood by the roadside to take a long, satisfying gulp. Just as I was tossing the empty bottle into the recycling bin, a police car zipped past, its sirens blaring. It made me feel tense and uneasy, like I'd seen a bad omen.

Itaewon by night had given me the impression of a pitiful Asian prostitute, one who'd stepped right out of *The World of Suzie Wong*. Heavily made up, with its neon lights and air of debauchery, it was trying to project a Western image, give off a Western feel. I saw a prostitute, her body pressed up against the door as she smiled, slick and seductive, waiting for foreign customers to part with their cash so that her body could be fed, her soul saved.

One night I'd wandered into an Itaewon restaurant called *California*. The flashing neon sign had promised authentic Californian and Mexican cuisine. The only customer in the huge restaurant apart from me had been an enormous beer-bellied American. From the way he was dressed, I could tell he was an American soldier stationed here. As I walked past his table, I saw him gorging on his food. Every so often he'd summon the waitress and request something else. He looked like a man with a huge appetite who thought that the waitresses were only here to serve him. The dishes I ordered were completely inauthentic, but glancing at the restaurant's only other customer, this fat entitled man, I found myself forgiving the chefs and waitresses for not being able to cook American or Mexican food. They hadn't been born knowing how to cook this stuff, they'd just tried to learn it, albeit not very well.

I continued my walk around the bustling Itaewon streets. Another police car blared past. I watched it speed away, and wondered if something had happened, a robbery perhaps, or a car accident. Like a snoop, I quickened my pace and hurried ahead to take a look.

Just round the corner from the wealthy residential area of the American soldiers, I heard the high-pitched cries of a crowd. Lots of people were gathered by the sounds of it. Their cries rose up one after another, like waves rolling endlessly across the surface of the sea ...

That's when I saw the barricades set up across the street. And barbed wire fencing towering above the hot asphalt pavement, which in the eighties had been a common sight on the streets of Taipei, too, like an iron-fist clamping down on the rising fury.

It was a protest. Tens of thousands of Koreans had gathered on the streets of Itaewon next to the American military base. I was worming my way round the back of the crowds, past the War Memorial of Korea, when I heard a cry of, "American imperialists —*get out!*"

"We want peace, not war. Evil American imperialists, get out! Long live the reunited North and South Korea!"

"A life for a life. Surrender the American culprits, and subject them to prosecution under local law!"

"The Han River is the life water for all Koreans. Westerners must not be allowed to contaminate it. Respect Koreans—Asians are people too!"

"Leave our country and give us back our land!"

"We are not a colony and never will be again. Stand up, Koreans!"

"We refuse to be second-class citizens in our own country!"

Rage. Humiliation. A sense of injustice. The driving forces behind racial conflict. The conflict of economic and class inequalities. The conflict between powerful and weak nations. The conflict of uneven distribution of resources. The conflict between the arrogant and self-centred, and the inferior and small. Like a bomb without a timer, it was ready to explode …

I walked cautiously after the crowd, seeing banner after banner of Korean and English slogans, while the chanted slogans began to sound like a deafening roar. Someone in the crowd hoisted up a Stars and Stripes flag and set fire to that icon of the USA with a lighter. The tongues of flame spread quickly in the dry air, and soon the flag was engulfed. The crowd whooped and cheered, as the fire starter threw the burning flag to the ground, and encouraged the crowd to stamp on it.

Someone held up a banner and some caricature puppets and put on a puppet show. A war-profiteering American arms dealer puppet with a whip in this hand was putting pressure on the White House: "Understand how it was you came into power. It's our money that got you voted in. Supply arms and ammo to third world countries, let them take themselves out and destroy each other over ideology, or whatever the hell the reason they're fighting, so that our arms trade flourishes and creates endless job opportunities. Money first, money talks, the world value system is constructed on money," the arms dealer shouted as he whipped an American President wearing a business suit. "Foster local governments that will listen to us and buy our weapons, buy our weapons! Use your influence to get these countries to buy our weapons. That's the only way we can continue being the world superpower." The arms dealer puppet began to laugh raucously, and gave the American President puppet another lash of the whip.

The next group of actors who came to the stage represented the Korean people. They were clad in the traditional white hemp Korean national costume, the *Hanbok*. They stood on a line that symbolised the 38th parallel, the separation between North and South, weeping for their loved ones they'd been separated from for over fifty years.

"We cannot bear to be separated any longer. Our loved ones are priceless. We can't let foreigners continue to profit from our country's division. We Koreans must stand as one! We must find a reason to live!" They began to give a *Nongak* performance, traditional Korean rural music and dance.

Next a clown dressed as a slimy Japanese politician appeared, and hissed, "North and South Korea must not be allowed to reunify. Their unity threatens our national power and the competitive power of our products. If they do, we will be forced to return to the Stone Age, wearing caveman clothes and bowing down to Koreans." The crowd erupted into laughter, and the short man playing the Japanese politician was pushed back into the crowd. As soon as the plays ended, the chanting started up again. There were lots of university students and intellectuals in the crowd, and among them, a horde of people in alternative, bright-coloured costumes caught my eye. They held placards that said they were filmmakers. A middle-aged man, who looked like a director, broke away from their group. He took hold of the microphone and began to speak. Someone translated for him:

"We are against globalisation. What is globalisation, really, but *Americanisation*? Globalisation is the tool of Western people and wealthy nations, in which the rich become richer, and the poor become poorer. We are proud that we are not like the Americans. We are proud that our culture and traditions are different. We refuse to assimilate. We have our own language and sense of humour, our pride and the legacy of our Korean nation. We wish to pass this down through the generations. We reject vulgar Hollywood culture. We want to direct our own films, tell our own stories, sing and dance in our own ways. We want to believe in ourselves, believe that we too can create world-class films, and have a first class culture that takes the world by storm. We wish to break away from a fate chained to someone else's culture and products. We wish to forge our very own path. Because we are different to the rest of the world, and we are proud to be different." There was another huge round of applause, and this bald middle-aged man returned to the crowd.

A furore suddenly broke out within the crowd, and people began to shout what sounded like a name, over and over again, before erupting into an earth-shattering crescendo of applause. I saw a familiar figure rise from the crowd, and make his way to the front. He reached out to take the microphone and the foreign and local reporters who'd been standing some way off, suddenly rushed over. They surrounded him, their cameras flashing, and his face disappeared beneath the sea of people.

Who was he? Where had I seen him before? Despite being over a hundred metres away, I felt a strong sense of familiarity towards this figure whose appearance had stirred up such a thunderous response from the crowd.

I grabbed the arm of a foreign journalist. "Do you know who that man who just went on the stage is?" I asked.

"Don't you know?" The journalist gave me a withering look. "He was the leader of South Korea's student movement a few decades ago. He strongly supported the reunification of the Koreas. Once he even led a group of students across the border into the North, and when he returned he was arrested and imprisoned for a number of years. After Kim Dae-jung came into power he was finally granted amnesty and released."

When he'd finished his explanation, the journalist glided, shark-like, towards the front of the crowds to get his news story.

Who was this guy? I stood on tiptoe, trying to get a better look at his face. Where had I seen him before? My line of vision was completely obscured by the bulky foreign journalist.

Who was he? Just who was he? My curiosity compelled me to follow the path that the journalist had just opened up in the crowd, and squeeze my way through to the front of the stage. I finally got a clear view of the man standing in front of the throng of people, holding the microphone and speaking in Korean, holding their rapt attention.

My god. It was Park. Park Chang-chuk, the poet-worker I'd chatted to in the youth hostel. Park Chang-chuk, who liked Teresa Teng, but not her French boyfriend.

So he'd been the leader of a turbulent and radical student movement. He'd broken the law by crossing into North Korea. He'd even spent time in jail …

I was looking up at him along with everyone else in the crowd. At first he spoke unhurriedly, like an amicable philosopher, although I couldn't understand because it was in Korean. As he continued his tone grew increasingly impassioned, his gestures more dramatic. His voice buzzed in my ear and though I didn't understand a word of it, I was thinking it was probably a good thing I never got the chance to tell him that, like Teresa Teng, I too had once had a Western boyfriend … Had I done, I might have become yet one more enemy for him to crusade against.

Whether he was speaking unhurriedly and affably, or sounding fervent, the crowd before him were unequivocal in their response. Thunderous applause broke out periodically. Until a commotion stirred the crowd …

"You! Yes, I'm talking about you! You don't even speak Korean? Do you know what's going on here? Or do you plan on returning to America to spread your lies and false reporting? What *truth* will you take home with you? Funny isn't it, how one turns a blind eye to truth when matters of national interest are concerned. Look around you at these Koreans. Go back and tell your government and your people why they've outstayed their welcome."

Park Chang-chuk had switched to English, and was pointing at an American-looking news reporter in the crowd as he shouted. The American reporter towered a head above everyone else, and seemed to disagree completely with what Park was saying. I didn't catch what he was muttering, but I saw the indignant expression on his face. As he was pushing his way out of the crowd, he turned towards Park Chang-chuk, lifted his right hand and gave him the finger.

Park Chang-chuk clearly noticed, as he leapt down from the stage, seized the man by the collar and started to wrangle with him. The crowd closed in on them, and a skirmish soon broke out. Amidst the riot, I heard the shrill sounds of a police whistle being blown and saw numerous policemen dashing towards the brawl, raising their batons and bringing them down on the writhing crowd.

Policemen in riot gear stood at the sides holding megaphones. They seemed to be calling for the crowd to keep calm and not resort to violence. But to no effect.

The mob was becoming violent. Angry shouting, shrill whistling, the sound of scuffling and the piercing cries of someone who lay bleeding on the ground.

"We do not want imperialist lackeys!"

"A century of tragedy for the Asian people, being subjugated to the incessant plundering from greedy Westerners. Rise, Asian people, reclaim the ownership of your land, become your own masters!"

Within all this chaos and terror, someone grabbed the microphone from a policeman's hand, and shouted for the police to surrender and join their side. But the police ignored these passionate cries, and continued to rain blows mercilessly on protestors with their batons. People were getting trampled. Blood was seeping soundlessly into the roads, its salty stench rising up from the hot asphalt.

I scrambled away from the frantic mob, and stood a few hundred metres off, taking in everything that was going on. Within the chaos I saw someone being dragged out and handcuffed, and hauled into the police car like a convict.

It was Park Chang-chuk. As they were dragging him in, Park turned around helplessly and our eyes met. He looked straight at me.

Helplessness. Anguish. Indescribable grief. He seemed to be saying to me, "The injustice of it all—surely you understand?"

I did understand, actually. When Lawrence and I were on the verge of breaking up, shuttling between Europe and Asia every year, all our cultural and historic differences exploded. I was a black-haired, yellow-skinned Asian, while he was a blonde haired, blue eyed European. You'd think that love could overcome age, borders, skin colour, race, and culture, but you never learn how to face the issues of colonial history with an open heart, or the injustice that continues to take place, the favouring of the privileged, and the persecution of the weak by the strong. You become a troublemaker, someone who speaks incessantly about injustice. But no one pays any attention to what you're saying. Soon you find yourself getting paranoid. Perhaps what you really needed was a visit to the mental hospital for some electric shock treatment.

Conflict Seventeen

After the Korean War my uncle returned to Taiwan. But like the war, his life had run its course too.

He was an old man now, an emaciated old man. Every injustice and cruelty of the war had been sealed into his heart with ice on the 38th parallel, the border that divided North and South Korea.

He had once fought for the US army. He was one of the few Taiwanese recruited by the US Military Assistance Advisory Group in Taiwan. He received US military-style training. He spoke American English and was paid in American dollars. "He was paid about ten times what you'd get from the Kuomintang." My father said, envy in his voice.

He put his life on the line for the Americans. Under Douglas MacArthur's command, he fought on foreign soil. Of all those Taiwanese spies sent by the US military to the frontlines, he was the only one who made it home alive. But his spirit perished on that foreign soil.

He came back the husk of a man, his walk slow and stooped. He looked as if he'd had the life sucked out of him. He looked like a dried corpse walking beneath the orange streetlights at dusk, navigating a space that was not his. You could never have imagined that he'd once been a hoodlum. Or that he'd acted as master of ceremony for a wedding when he was only nine years old, standing in for my grandfather who was always away on business. All the adult wedding guests were made to listen to this young boy making the speech. My uncle had once lived for fame and glory.

My grandfather did business with Englishmen in Burma and spent months on end away from home. Each time he went off he'd take hundreds of mules and people carrying guns and goods. They'd travel for weeks, walking over mountains and crossing borders to sell their goods.

My grandfather often brought back exotic treasures, some from Great Britain across the ocean. As well as the customary rolls of textiles like cotton and yarn, he'd sometimes bring home things like pretty English white lace umbrellas for the women of the family. My grandmother and aunts would wear their little Mandarin gowns, and parade with these English umbrellas up and down the bustling streets in the town centre to get people's attention.

Once my grandfather's entourage of mules came back with a white wash-basin that was given to him by the English businessmen. This basin had violets engraved on its shiny white ceramic, and there was a pipe attached. My grandfather placed this gift from far away in the bathroom of their old courtyard house. No one apart from his own family members knew what on earth it was.

My mischievous uncle played a prank on everyone within a

hundred mile radius of their courtyard house.

"It's a Western potty," he told everyone. "Those Westerners are so tall and big that their potties are wider than our waists. Filthy rich Westerners make a huge fuss over what they pee into. Every single one of their potties has to be engraved."

My uncle got better and better at exaggerating stories. At the time there was a rumour passing around the Dai people, who lived in the plateau valley, about these strange objects the like of which they'd never before seen, that let out a thundering boom and looked like iron crows flying around the sky. "You see those iron crows flying up there?" my uncle told everyone. "The white devils made them. They invented trains too that make the earth shake when they move. And they've installed them all with exquisitely crafted potties."

My old grandmother found it very puzzling that the townspeople kept flocking over to look at their bathroom. Even the local school-teacher made a visit. Finally she heard the street gossip—my young uncle had tricked the entire neighbourhood into thinking they had an exquisitely carved Western potty. He was even collecting money from curious parties wanting to take a look. My old grandmother stormed home when she heard this and gave my uncle a good beating. For three days and nights he was made to kneel at the front door of their courtyard house, facing the streets, with a board around his neck on which were written the words: "I did wrong".

That was my mischievous and playful uncle before the war.

But it was a changed man who returned home from the battlefields. A large portion of his stomach had to be removed. When you were a spy, you had to be constantly on guard, my father explained. My uncle developed chronic gastritis as a result of all the stress. He signed an indenture with the American government, an oath to keep their government secrets for the rest of his life.

"At least he made it home alive," my father said. "It was the one fortunate thing we had among a series of misfortunes." Sometimes my father would say something sarcastic like, "Aren't those Americans clever? Our lives had absolutely no value compared to theirs. They'd never take a bullet or barter with their own lives, they just got others to do it for them. They're just as wicked as the Japanese or the British."

When my uncle was almost forty, he was matched with a girl he'd never met, and the two of them quickly tied the knot. But during the frost and snow of war, my uncle had forgotten how to love.

Working as a spy, my uncle had met a singer who performed in a traditional Korean restaurant he used to visit. Wearing traditional Korean court costume, this singer would perch on the raised stage and perform ancient Korean songs for the customers.

"Her skin was fairer than Korea's drifting snow. No one could have seen her and not fall under her spell, I was seized by a sudden impulse," was how my uncle once described meeting Seol-hee.

When he was off-duty, my uncle would go the restaurant near Gyeongbokgung Palace to hear Seol-hee sing. She sang like an oriole in a ravine, trilling in this ancient language he didn't understand. He thought it must be ancient love poetry, subtle and sorrowful in equal measures. He listened to her voice in a trance, vaguely forgetting the sounds of gunfire and explosions raging on in the near distance. He was reminded of a line of classic Chinese poetry by Du Mu:

"The song girl understands not the destruction of the nation,
From the other side of the river she still sings her palace songs."

The nearby Gyeongbokgung Palace was no longer the stronghold of the bygone dynasty from which her songs hailed. The flames of war threatened to destroy the ancient capital of Seoul at any time. Despite all this, my uncle drank in her voice and became inebriated by it. A series of images rose up in his mind, and it felt like watching a silent film.

He was sitting astride a handsome horse twice his height. Drums and gongs were being beaten, and the whole village was crowded around him—at the wedding he had hosted. Under their gaze my uncle picked up the speech my grandfather had written, and began to read it out loud. His voice was still a child's, his words choppy and unpractised, but a round of applause galvanised him. "Superb!" the crowd roared.

It was just as he had started high school that, in the middle of the night, my father had shaken him awake. "We've just heard that the Communists are closing in. Let's fight and save our country." My uncle was dragged out of bed by my father, still half-asleep. In a haze, they sneaked out of the house and into the dark night. In the confusion he had put on the wrong shoes. As dawn broke and daylight shone onto where they had gathered, he discovered he was wearing mismatched leather Oxfords. A tall burly guy with a thick beard pointed in his face and sneered, "Oh my! Look at our little lords coming to war dressed in fine leather shoes! Can you actually fight? Do you know what war is? Better not run home crying to your mummies!".

My uncle, not yet fully grown, had nevertheless been in countless fights. He swung his fist at the man who'd made this comment, who was a different ethnic group to him, a Hui, from an unfamiliar religion and culture. This big Hui swung a fist back at my uncle and knocked him to the ground. They were getting ready to really go for each other, when my father dragged them roughly apart. "If you're real men, save your energy for fighting our enemy," my father berated them, panting with exhaustion.

More and more people joined the group—the Lolo, the Dai, the Hui, the Han. It looked as if it had been arranged long before. All these people of different ethnicities, speaking their different languages had gathered. My father stood before them all and addressed them in a booming voice: "This has been our home for as long as we can remember, but our land and our resources are under threat from all directions. The British came from Burma and stole the minerals from our plateau. The French came from Annam, glaring like greedy tigers and building their railroads here. The Japanese came from the north and south, killing our people and razing our houses to the ground. When the Japanese retreated, we thought peace had dawned at last, but then the Russians and old Mao arrived with their Communist ideals, closing in on this land we call home. Our homes are gone, and our motherland stands on the brink of destruction, but we have joined forces today on the plateau and we will allow no one to take away what belongs to us. No one will intrude upon our motherland. As long as we have one breath left inside us, we will use it to stand up and fight!" The crowd cheered wildly.

My father lifted his heavy cotton jacket, revealing the green military uniform beneath. My uncle was shocked to see several shiny strips of gold strapped across it—the gold bars my old grandmother had kept hidden in the rice jar, which my father had obviously stolen.

"Brothers, these are the gold bars I've brought from my own home. They will be used to pay for your provisions. Don't be afraid, you won't go hungry, there is enough to go round." My father's words stirred up another roar of applause from the crowd.

Another scene surfaced in my uncle's mind as he listened to Seol-hee singing. They were standing on a mountain range on the disputed Sino-Burmese border. My father was leading the crowd, when he saw the national flag being hoisted up slowly. Tears were streaming down his face. My uncle assumed that it wouldn't be too long before they could return home. This optimism he later recognised as naivety, a fantasy that grew ever more distant with the passage of time. Their returning home was unlikely, for as well as battling against Communist troops they were also engaged in furious fighting with the Burmese National Army. In a rare lull in the fighting, my father led the weary fighters over a mountain from which the Burmese had just retreated from. They stuck their national flag—grimy and crumpled—into the ground. This flag contained the blue of the sky, the white of the sun and the red of the earth—and as it was hoisted up, my father led them in singing the national anthem. As he was singing, my father's voice faltered. Whether they were missing their homes and families, or sorrowful for the brothers they'd lost, the others followed suit, and soon everyone was weeping. My uncle glared vehemently at my father. "Look what you've done!" he thought angrily.

He always blamed my father for taking him off in the middle of the night; that was the reason he couldn't go home. He thought if that hadn't happened, he'd still be lord of the house, just like before. It was many years later he realised that staying at home wouldn't have been a good thing either. Once the Communists took over China, they confiscated most of their family land and property, and during the Cultural Revolution his family was classified under the five black categories and died cruel deaths during the Red Guard struggle sessions.

Seol-hee's voice was a tranquiliser. My uncle sat transfixed as he watched her sing. The alien world outside, with its sub-zero temperatures and falling snow, was momentarily left behind.

He once got into a brawl with several American soldiers over

Seol-hee. They were from the base. Initially they had just been drinking and eating at the restaurant. But then one of them, who looked slightly drunk, got up and swaggered towards her, cowboy-style, encouraged by the hoots and cheers of his army mates.

"Hey there, baby, what are you doing tonight? Feel lonely sleeping by yourself?" The American soldier stood in front of her, leering. Seol-hee looked the other way and ignored him. She did not stop singing or strumming away at her gayageum.

The group of soldiers sitting around the table behind started whistling. They began clapping and hooting, egging him on.

When he realised Seol-hee was ignoring him, the American took some banknotes from his pocket and dangled them in front of her face. "Hey, baby, check out these American dollars. They're yours if you're willing to spend the night with me."

"With all due respect, sir," Seol-hee stopped her performance, "I'm a performer in this restaurant. Performers in Korea sell their crafts, not their bodies. You might not have any interest in my music, but other people do, so please kindly respect the other guests here."

"Whoa whoa whoa, this Korean bitch is even spicier than kimchi," the American soldier said. "You better get this straight. You're lucky I'm into you. I've come a long way to save your little country. Do you think you'd be sitting here singing your little songs if we hadn't? You'd be dead by now, like the rest of your people. Ungrateful bitch. You should be glad I haven't made you get down on your knees and lick my toes." The drunk American soldier had his finger an inch from Seol-hee's face as he taunted her.

Seol-hee put down the gayageum, raised a hand and slapped him hard across the cheek.

The American soldier was stunned. He was completely taken aback for a moment, unable to process what had just happened. All he knew was this red hotness he felt in his cheek. And then he saw his army mates howling with laughter.

"The guy's six foot tall and he can't even keep an Asian chick in check," one of them sneered.

His army mates teasing, and the slap across the face, had enraged the soldier. He turned and seized Seol-hee by the arm, and pushed her to the floor. He shoved his alcohol-infused mouth right up in Seol-hee's face, and forced his lips against hers. Seol-hee twisted and struggled to get away. All this time the other American soldiers were standing by laughing raucously, hooting and cheering him on.

My uncle had been sitting to the side, watching the scene in silent fury. But he couldn't hold back any longer. He crossed the room in a single stride and gave the American soldier a violent kick.

"Stop acting like a dog here," my uncle said. "Go back to your own country. Behave like a dog all you want there."

The American soldier turned to see who had kicked him, saw my uncle and spat. "Fu Manchu. You have no right to speak here. I'm warning, stay out of this or I'll make you regret it."

The blood rushed to my uncle's head. He suddenly recalled all the fights he'd got into back home before anyone had even heard of Bruce Lee. He was transformed into a wild beast, yelling and screaming, swing his fists and kicking out with his legs. He was like a fighter from the Boxer Rebellion showing off his might. He felt as though his body was about to combust as he fought against those lightweight American soldiers. But some of them jumped him from behind, and soon had him on the floor under their feet.

"Fu Manchu, you can barely protect your own country and

here you are trying to be a hero for someone else's woman. Get it straight, if it hadn't been for us Americans, your little Taiwan would have sunk into the Pacific Ocean long ago. Look at yourself in the mirror. Who's the hand that feeds you? You're taking American currency, not useless Taiwanese money. Do you get where you stand?"

The American soldiers who'd beaten up my uncle spat at him and at Seol-hee too. Then they swaggered out of the restaurant.

"A fortune born out of misfortune" is an ancient Chinese proverb. Now the phrase crossed the border into another country and culture, and became a universal and timeless truth. My uncle was living proof of it, for after being beaten up by the Americans, beautiful Seol-hee fell in love with him. And being bruised and bloody no longer mattered.

At the military base he exchanged his American dollars for bananas shipped from Taiwan, which he gave to Seol-hee, who had never eaten a banana before. The two of them strolled along the bank of the Han River, peeling bananas, rare fruits in Korea. Seol-hee slid the banana into her mouth, smiling as she declared it the most delicious fruit she'd ever tasted.

"There are banana trees everywhere in Taiwan. There are so many of them, humans don't bother eating them anymore, only monkeys do," my uncle said. He seemed to have returned to exaggerating stories again, just like in his youth when he'd fooled his entire town into believing that a wash-basin was a potty.

They held hands as they strolled along the bank, and looked across to the wide river to the other bank so far away you'd need a boat to get to it. Whenever their eyes met they'd duck their heads to hide shy smiles. Seol-hee pointed at the calm, remote Han River as she told my uncle about her hometown to the north, Kangwon province, and how when she was little she used to go looking for wild ginseng in the mountains.

"Ginseng bulbs are like tiny little people who have their feet planted in the soil. They're so agile they can run from hill to hill!" Seol-hee said with innocent sincerity.

"Can't you catch them?" my uncle asked just as sincerely.

"I'm afraid not," Seol-hee replied. "If you managed to catch one bulb of ginseng, you could sell it for so much you'd be able to buy yourself a house."

"Oh!" my uncle said, sounding like an astonished little boy.

My uncle had never been in love before. He told Seol-hee earnestly that once the war was over, he'd take her walking in mountains that were full of wild pine trees, and they could look for this elusive wild ginseng.

Seol-hee started to chuckle. "But you're a foreigner!"

My uncle scratched his head, confused. "What's wrong with that?" he asked.

"Ginseng don't let foreigners catch them," she teased.

"And why not?"

"When they hear foreign footsteps in the night they run far, far away."

"Oh," my uncle said, even more astonished.

"And, and ..." Seol-hee went on. "If you come to our village, you'd scare all the villagers. They'd be looking at you wide-eyed, with their hoes over their shoulders, like a bunch of curious puppies."

"And why's that?"

"Because they'd think Yuan Shi-kai had come from Seoul!"

"Oh my!" My uncle was so surprised his jaw dropped.

"And," Seol-hee continued, "Ginseng bulbs are just like humans. They're terrified of gunfire. So they've probably hidden themselves down in the centre of the earth."

Now, my uncle was quiet.

He'd never told Seol-hee he was an intelligence officer who'd trained with the US military. All this time she'd thought he was just a Kuomintang officer sent by Chiang Kai-shek to counterattack Mao's troops. Even when my uncle left Korea, only a rare few knew his secret.

My uncle never forgot the innocent promise he'd made to Seol-hee. When he was off duty, he went around with her. They visited all of Soeul's famous attractions—Gyeongbokgung Palace and Bukhansan. Once Seol-hee remarked that my uncle was different from Koreans, the descendants of nomads, who were big and burly, and slurped down wine and gobbled meat. My slender uncle, strolling by the Han River with Seol-Hee, suddenly whipped off the boots he'd got from the US military base, dove into the river and swam all the way to the other side.

"It's not time for the winter swimming competitions yet, surely?"

"Didn't they cancel the swimming competitions? We're in the middle of a war."

"Is that man trying to kill himself by jumping into the river?" A bunch of middle-aged women, who'd been squatting by the river washing clothes, set down the bundles in their hands and began an animated discussion about my uncle's actions.

"He looks good. He's a fast swimmer." A middle-aged woman with white cloth around her hair stood up and surveyed the figure in the water who was fast approaching the other shore.

"Must chill you to the bone to swim in this sort of weather." There was an outpouring of praise from the people standing around, and Seol-hee's panicky expression suddenly transformed into one of pride. This man is amazing, Seol-hee murmured to herself, her eyes shining.

When my uncle swam back to where she stood, and dragged his wet body out of the water, the middle-aged women were all staring at him in admiration. But Seol-hee spun on her heels and stalked off.

"Why do you need to be such a show-off? Aren't you afraid of the cold?" she said with a pout, but there was a hint of pride in her voice too.

Sure enough, as my uncle chased after Seol-hee, he started to sneeze and shiver.

The crowd watched the two of them walk away from Han River, one in front and the other behind, one dry and the other drenched to the bone.

Past their shoulders in the distant horizon, plumes of black smoke curled up languidly into the darkening sky, like a demon draped in the cloak of death. This was the constant reminder of the war that raged on, a commonplace sight back then, something you'd see every few days.

* * *

Back in Taiwan, my uncle kept everyone at arm's length. He existed in silence, letting no one near, not even his wife. The world blotted him out, just as he had blotted it out. His was a strange world, carried by its own rhythm. Like a dry corpse in a greenhouse, the lines of his flesh clearly visible, but no sense of his soul.

The memory I've always had of him from childhood was his tightly furrowed brows. They were always knitted together, as if there were matters weighing heavily on his heart, as if he only lived in his own dark mind, an impassable fortress that no one else could penetrate.

My uncle came to visit us once when I was very young. I sat on the stool in the living room, quietly nibbling at the suncakes he'd brought us from Taichung, and stealing an occasional glance at him. He was an uncle who lived far away, and who we didn't often see.

His face was half turned away. In the bright-lit living room, he lazily combed his thick hair. I sat to the side of this scene, like a new-born kitten, brimming with curiosity, observing his every move, scrutinising his every actions. We did not exchange a word. He continued to comb his hair, paying me no mind. But he didn't send me away. It was as if I were invisible.

White flakes fell from his hair and from the comb. They scattered and fluttered down, illuminated by the plane of light shining in through the window. I watched these flakes spin and dance in the light, as if they had no care in the world. I think what I was seeing was snowflakes, snowflakes falling in Korea. My uncle hurrying through the border that divided North and South Korea, running for his life, trampling across the frozen bodies of dead soldiers, half visible through the snow. The snowflakes fell non-stop around him, forming a lonely and strangely poetic scene. The image remained clear and crystallised in my deepest memory. It was only when I was older that I realised it hadn't been snowflakes but dandruff that had led me to imagine the Korean girl, Seol-hee. Many years later I found out that she looked like popular actress Lee Young-ae who played a writer in the Korean drama *Fireworks*. She looked like an angel but had a character of steel.

Like a child abandoned by her mother, I went to live with this uncle who had miraculously survived the war. It was a few years after my little cousin died, though I had never met him. I was a rebellious teenager by then, with no outlet to express my angst, I had resentment and hostility written all over my face. I rebelled fiercely against everything my mother did or wanted me to do. As a result I was sent to a Catholic boarding school managed by a Swiss pastor. Everyday I knelt before the altar, facing Jesus on the cross, singing halleluiah with the white-robed foreign nuns, and learning how to behave like a young European lady. My mother didn't mind forking out the money if it guaranteed that I was being disciplined by the nuns at this strict school. Yet when no one was looking I'd still find a way to clamber over fences in my skirt. I was caught each and every time by the thin blue-eyed Germanic nuns. Or I'd escape to a classroom to read or write essays that no one understood, but were later discovered by the cleaning lady, who took them straight to the nuns and pastor.

Of course Jesus never pardoned my sins. And after I carried on skipping classes and refusing to read my textbooks, I was eventually sent to live with my eccentric uncle. Perhaps my mother thought I could learn a thing or two from a man who had been a delinquent in his teenage years too. At that time, I carried around the thick volume of Lin Yutang's *The Life and Times of Su Tungpo* everywhere I went. I saw myself as having a similar fate as Su Tungpo, both of us had been exiled. Another person I thought about often was the Amis boy who had deep-set eyes and long, dark lashes and gave off a leafy scent intermingled with the tangy odour of the Pacific Ocean. A few times I caught him walking deliberately past my classroom. Whenever our eyes met he'd duck his head, flash a shy smile and scurry away. Once, after he learnt how to ride a motorcycle, he stole his father's Wolf-125 and took it for a spin. He was underage and didn't have a driver's license, and risking being caught by the cops. He asked my classmates where I lived. I heard him rattling his way unsteadily up to the gate outside my house, fenced in by trees and facing the Pacific

Ocean. By then I was nearly as tall as my mother, with a short-cropped bowl haircut. When I heard him coming I hid behind a Casuarina tree as big as a fully-grown man. I poked my head out from behind the tree and eyed him suspiciously. "What're you doing here?"

A shy, foolish grin appeared on his face. He didn't say a word. His gaze flitted from where I was, still hidden obstinately behind that tree trunk, to the clutch of his motorcycle. A deep look flitted across his eyes, like clear ripples on the top of the deep blue ocean.

Then he handed me a sky-blue letter, which gave off a rich floral scent. Still he said nothing. He stepped on the clutch and flew off like a gust of wind.

With the letter in my hands, I walked nervously back to the house, my head lowered. I didn't know that my mother had been making dinner in the kitchen and had witnessed this whole scene from the window. As soon as I stepped through the door, she pounced on me like a tiger, blocking my path.

"Give it to me," she said fiercely.

I feigned innocence, hiding the letter behind my back.

"I said, give it to me!" she boomed, her voice as loud as a tiger's roar.

I crushed the letter in my palm, balled it up and held it tightly in my fist, refusing to give it up.

There was a resounding slap as my mother whacked me across the cheek. My hand instinctively darted out to shield my burning face, where it was niftily caught by my mother. She wrenched the letter out of my grip, ripped it to shreds and threw the tattered pieces to the ground.

"If you're not interested in school, why don't you just work in a factory? Be a factory woman! Dating, huh? Dating! I'd like to see you try!" she fumed.

"He's an aboriginal. An aboriginal, do you understand?" she shouted, "Go to your room and do your homework now!"

I locked myself up in my room that night, refusing to eat or shower. I expressed everything I was feeling in my diary. Hot furious tears spilled down my cheeks, coming down thick and fast onto the paper. I poured my heart into these words, tears and ink mingling in a blurry mess. It was impossible that my mother was my real mother; only a stepmother would treat anyone this way. I must have been picked up from a rubbish dump. Where was my real mother? She must have been beautiful, gentle and kind, but had gotten into some sort of personal trouble that had led her to abandon me like that. I imagined that one day she would come back for me. Who was she? Perhaps my mother was that beautiful angel Seol-hee, I fantasised.

In huge bold letters I jotted down the following words: "Shameless! You're a shameless bully! If you poke your nose into my diary, you're a bitch." Of course I knew exactly who I was referring to. If you peek into my diary, you're a big dumb bitch!

I was a strange, rebellious teenage girl who nobody understood. And as a result I was sent to live with my uncle, a lonely middle-aged man who was dealing with the death of his son and the departure of his wife. My uncle was a man of few words. I didn't speak much either. Side by side, we coexisted in an atmosphere of listless silence.

* * *

My little cousin drowned in a nearby creek. The water was shallow, only thigh high. So how could he have been washed away? His name was a taboo in the dark halls of that underworld-like house. There were no photographs of my little cousin on display in my uncle's house. My cousin's short little life was a vanished memory. Just like his mother, who abandoned the shattered family.

My uncle had been gradually swept to the side of the industrial, money-hungry city. He bought himself a sheep and moved to the suburbs. The sheep became his family. My uncle would drift around with his sheep, all alone at the edge of the city. He didn't have to worry about the toxic gases punctuating the sky or being drowned out in the din of cars and people. Every day without fail, he'd take his sheep to the river where my little cousin had drowned. Haltingly, a slow figure backlit by the setting sun, dragging a long shadow behind him, he'd amble on. Sometimes I would walk slowly behind him. The embankment was only wide enough for one full-grown person to walk, and weeds grew alongside it. Mosquitoes darted against my legs like kamikaze fighters. Sometimes I'd stoop down to swat them. Apart from the slapping of my hands, all was quiet as we walked.

The creek water used to be so clear that you could see the bottom, with fish and shrimp darting about playfully in the waters. My little cousin used to love coming here. But the creek had become a trail of toxic water darkened from the curling smoke from the nearby factories. It had become so toxic it could choke you, killing the fish and shrimp in its waters, and inadvertently causing the death of my little cousin too.

Death had always just brushed by my uncle's shoulder. His opium addiction, in the miasma of Indo-China, did not take his life. Out of all the intelligence officers sent to the frontlines of the Korean War, he was the only one who made it back alive. But all the people he might have begun a new life with had perished in the war.

Seol-hee died as the Korean War was ending. My little cousin perished in a creek near my uncle's home.

When Seol-hee passed away, my uncle was spurred on by an iron will to live. He never forgot the promise he'd made to her as he fled step by step to the south, over ice and frost, over destroyed tanks, frozen bones and bodies. On his last mission, he wrote a letter to my father, saying he would make it back alive. He said that he would bring the beautiful Korean girl Seol-hee with him back to Taiwan, and after the war ended, he would marry her.

He never did manage to get that last glimpse of Seol-hee.

After he returned to Seoul, he went to the restaurant where she performed. The boss, a Mongolian with strong features and a sharp nose, mumbled the simple words, "Something's happened to her." He would not elaborate.

My uncle found out what had happened from a waiter there. The American soldiers my uncle had gotten into that brawl with, had gone back there when my uncle was away on mission. They'd harassed her in the restaurant, and then blocked her as she'd been making her way home and gang-raped her.

They left her emotionally and physically shattered. Seol-Hee resigned from her job in Seoul and returned to her old home in Kangwon province. "Who will accept me after this?" She felt utterly ashamed, even though none of it had been her fault. To make matters worse, she was pregnant. She had no idea which of the American soldiers' child it was.

"How can I give birth to this bastard half-breed child?" she asked a childhood friend. "He will not have a happy life. He will be cursed. He should not be born. He has the blood of demons running through his veins. He should be put to death. If I don't do it, he will be murdered by the mobs." In the end, she chose to take her own life. As dawn was breaking, she walked to an old pine tree facing the East China Sea, and attached a piece of white cloth to it. Wearing the yellow-blue traditional costume she had loved to wear while she was performing her songs, she fastened the cloth around her neck and bravely hanged herself. This act, of choosing death over humiliation, was a demonstration of her strong unyielding character. The child inside her body perished along with her.

That was the last they'd heard of Seol-hee, the waiter told him. The villagers had been contemptuous of her at first, calling her dirty, a disgrace. But after she died, the whole village attended her funeral. They called her the East China Sea's woman of chastity and virtue. At least she didn't die in vain, the waiter said.

"Those Yankees will pay for what they've done!" There was a savage, vengeful look on my uncle's face as he said this, his hands forging fists, and the veins popping up in his neck.

"You can't. They're Americans," the waiter said, looking at him seriously.

Ahhhh. My uncle was like a wolf, rolling around in the snow howling in pain.

Ahhhh. My uncle's grief-stricken cry ripped through the chilly Korean sky.

That anguished cry had barely faded from memory when he lost yet another loved one, my young cousin, his son, who drowned in that nearby river.

Conflict Eighteen

"Hey gorgeous, why are you ignoring my letters? Why can't you even look me in the eye? I'm just as good as those men of yours. Wait and see, one day I'll be a literary god. Everyone will bow down to me. I'll be thirty by then, a bright shining literary star. But you'll be old, and nobody will want you anymore. I'll still want you though—I'll marry you and take you home. Just you wait and see."

"By the way, I've started smearing ginger on my chest so it'll be thick with hair soon. Your Western boyfriend won't be the only one with chest hair! I'll end this letter by saying goodbye—for now. This future literary god has some essays to write." "I won't let you lump me with those slobbering men that surround you! Don't you dare take me for some lovesick fool. Do you know how seriously I nurture the tender garden of my heart? Jiaying, all women pale in comparison to you. Do you know how pure my feelings for you are? But all I can do is watch you from afar."

"Do you remember the night we all went Pingdengli Farm and ate one of their wild chickens? When the meal was over, we played a game of cards. I watched you make your way over to us from the distance and my heart was filled with deep sorrow."

"I know we will always be friends. I will repay what you've done for me. When the whole world called me a liar, you were the only one who believed me. You have my word, Jiaying—one day I will repay you."

For a long time I received letters like that. Sometimes it was one a day, sometimes two or three. Sometimes they were stuffed between the metal flaps of my university department mailbox, sometimes slid under my student dormitory door. They were a shadowy presence in my life, springing up like bamboo shoots or dense clumps of fungus after the rain. After breakfast I'd be getting ready to leave the apartment when I'd discover one of these letters my doorstep, written in squiggly worm-like writing. Sometimes I'd head out for an impromptu midnight stroll, and discover one stuffed under the door. They were long and rambling, a furious monologue. All from that wretched guy Taomei had such problems with—Fat Luo.

Fat Luo's infatuation with Taomei had subsided, but had transferred itself to me instead. *What was I to do*? I didn't know. I was poor old Fat Luo's only friend. He was a feeble cockroach who had been stomped on so hard by mankind that he was a grimy mess of innards on the floor. I couldn't bear the thought of stepping on him again. But Taomei was my friend too. She was like an infuriated cat watching from the side, occasionally darting out a paw to play with her prey, keeping him only just alive.

"Jiaying, this is our little secret. Guard it in your heart forever. *I LOVE YOU.* I will be your blood brother, even if it means dealing with the agony of watching you from afar. It's a deal. Let's do a pinkie shake on it."

"Why are you brushing me off, Jiaying? Have you no affection for this land we live in? Is that why you look down on Asian men —and Taiwanese men in particular? Is that why you're dating your Western guy? They've got bigger dicks, their countries are superpowers, they're wealthier, stronger and better looking than us. Is that why you ignore my letters? Do you know how it breaks my heart to see you with that Western guy? It feels like having a knife plunged through my heart! It's like when all those superpowers forced their way into the Forbidden City, plundered our treasures and razed the Old Summer Palace to the ground. But this time the treasure these Western powers have taken is you! Why do you insist on your misguided course? Return to your people! We are the ones who will give you true happiness. Mark my words: when you grow weary, I will be the only one by your side. Oh fuck, my hands are trembling as I write these words."

This putrid lovesickness permeated the air, and I couldn't waft it away no matter how hard I tried.

Fat Luo began waiting for me outside my student dormitories in his red hatchback. I decided to confront him. I wanted to tell him that I valued his friendship, but that any sort of romance between us was out of the question.

We drove to the public hot springs bathhouse, near the bus terminus, to feed the stray dogs. Dogs with scabs, dogs with missing limbs, dogs with cataracts, dogs whose ears had been bitten off in fights—they would all scurry up to us begging for food. Without looking at each other, Fat Luo and I scooped the food from our Styrofoam boxes and fed it to the dogs.

"Don't do this, Fat Luo," I said awkwardly.

Fat Luo kept his stony silence, and just watched the dogs.

"Aren't we good friends?" I asked.

"Why have you got to draw such a distinct line between us!" Fat Luo's voice was raised in anger. He'd been bottling this up for a while.

"Aren't we good friends? Blood brothers?" I said.

Fat Luo was too angry to respond. He was like a little boy throwing a tantrum after being ignored by his mother.

"I feel like Van Gogh. I've sliced off my ear and given you the bloody remains, but you still refuse to accept me." He sounded grief-stricken.

"I'm not the prostitute Van Gogh fell in love with. I'm not some sort of imaginary Muse-like deity!" I said. Fat Luo was delusional, spouting this confused nonsense.

"Fat Luo, you're met my boyfriend. He thinks you're his friend. You know I'm in a difficult situation because my family is against our relationship. Why are you adding fuel to the fire?"

Fat Luo turned up his collar and lit a cigarette. Fixing me a look like a sorrowful old hound, he tilted back his funnel-shaped chin and gave a helpless, "You just don't understand men."

"Maybe I don't. All I know is that Lawrence and I are in love, and it has nothing to do with nationality, race or class. Love can transcend all boundaries, just like literature, music or art."

"So naïve," Fat Luo sighed, sounding and looking like an old man this time.

More and more strays were gathering at the hilltop, attracted by the smell of our food. Some were panting, huge tongues lolling out as they snatched up scraps from our hands. They had savage, hungry looks on their faces, as though they'd never eaten a good meal in their lives. Some were weak and trembling from the cold, shuffling back and forth, scrunching up fallen leaves with their paws.

"Even stray dogs have a fighting instinct, don't they? If needs be, even the weakest will lash out to seize its prey. It might be frightened by his own nerve, but deep down it knows its actions are driven by survival instincts. It doesn't matter how vile its behaviour is, the most important thing is that it captures his prey," Fat Luo said.

"You're living by the philosophy of dogs, not humans. Humans can choose to live with dignity."

"That's where you're wrong. Humans are just as wretched as dogs."

"Wretched people view the world through wretched eyes and see everything in the world as wretched," I said.

Fat Luo flared up. "How dare you insinuate that I'm wretched."

"I'm not insinuating, I'm telling you," I shot back.

"How dare you have the gall to look down on me," Fat Luo continued,

"I don't. I value your talent, which is why I'm still talking to you and not calling you names like other people," I lectured, sounding very self-righteous, like a mistress or a mother.

"I'm warning you! You will regret your attitude. When I'm famous, all the girls will worship me. People will *beg* me to write for them!" Fat Luo said smugly, a little boy once more.

"And you'll be happy to take advantage of them?"

"They'll come willingly."

"If you weren't so wretched and vile, people might actually like you," I said.

Fat Luo sighed, but said nothing.

After they'd finished the food, the strays started to relax. They began wagging their tails, and from their eyes it looked like they were smiling. They'd even stopped baring their teeth.

* * *

A massive billboard loomed over the city. The man on it had his head slightly tilted, but his gaze was direct, looking down on the pedestrians as they hurried up and down the street. "*You're behind the times if you don't know Gary*", was written in large print. It was a giant poster advertising the publication of Gary's new book.

Passersby would occasionally look up at the billboard, but most of them walked on without a second glance. "Another impoverished writer!" most were probably thinking. Sometimes there was a trace of disdain in their eyes, as if to say, "Must a writer put himself out there like a film star?"

Gary, my university professor. He was the son of an old veteran who had opened a grocery shop after the war. Gary was always disappointed with the way people treated him, but even more, he was disappointed by the way society treated contemporary writers. "Did none of you buy my books? We're doomed, we're all doomed." Slightly drunk after dinner, he peeled off his denim shirt to reveal an old veteran shirt full of holes. He spoke like a poet disillusioned with the world, with the authority of a much older man, gesticulating with his thumb as he gave all us students a heavy dressing down. None of his books had sold well. He castigated writers whose books sold better, scoffing at their success and calling their books *kitschy*, the word popularised by Milan Kundera. "Those kitschy so and sos! Superficial idiots with no technical grounding. To think that people are actually emptying their pockets for that crap. God help us."

Not long after, his latest book secured a spot in the bestsellers list, and soon it had leapt to the top. He pressured a good friend from his book's publishing house, to get all its employees out there, visiting the chain bookshops and convincing them to bulk buy it. Consumer behaviour can be very irrational, and the public are generally blind and unquestioning, spurred on by the herd mentality, he explained. Finally, after mobilising money and manpower, he got what he wanted. He had proven his worth. Although he was keenly aware that most buyers of his book were just sheep, and had no real interest in his work.

After weeks in the bestseller charts, the book and its writer— whose face was displayed on the billboard posters overlooking the city—won many adoring fans. Overnight, Gary became a literary icon, admired by many young writers aspiring to be just like him. His face became such a common sight that people outside the literary scene assumed he was an actor in a martial arts film.

In this media-obsessed city, everyone got their fifteen minutes of fame. As Gary's literary status grew, so too did his ego. He seemed to have acquired a new pair of balls. He zipped up and down the narrow roads in his white German car, an Opel, driving like a hurricane, as if he were the king. He may have changed on the surface but deep down, he was still the same guy. A thug who wouldn't think twice before grabbing a rolling pin from his house and running into the streets to fight anyone who dared to get in the way of his car. His old father, bent and grey, with a head of white hair, had to hold back his temper every time his good-for-nothing son got into yet another brawl. He'd screw up his fists and shout, "Virtue! Think about virtue! If you continue to act in such an uncivilised way, fate will not be kind to you!" There was sorrow in his eyes when he said this, for he had been an older man when his son was born, and had brought him up hand-to-mouth from his meagre grocery shop earnings.

"I've spoilt him, that's why he's become like this," he'd say. He had no idea that his son saw him as nothing but a dumb old man. Dumb, just like the rest of the world too.

Dumb was Gary's favourite word. He used it to put down others, chanting it like a mantra. Dumb, dumb, dumb. Who in the world could possibly be cleverer than him?

We'd heard rumours of how many women he was with when his book was at the top of the bestsellers chart. Among them was a porn star, a radio DJ whose father was an important politician, a fashion designer, a singer-songwriter, a TV presenter ... "These sluts all want a go with me!" he told us in private once. "These women are all fools. Women are like public transport, they show up every thirty minutes." The biggest kick he got out of writing was the extra attention from women he could prey on. One day, he summoned thick-headed Fat Luo to him. With his mouth up against Fat Luo's ear, he quietly told him that Tomas in the *Unbearable Lightness of Being* was no big deal—all he did was order women to undress. Gary just needed to click his fingers, and women opened their legs for him. That put him about three rungs up from Tomas.

"Dumb women. This world is filled with dumb women," Gary said, and his words became like a mantra to Fat Luo.

While Gary was telling Fat Luo all this, we wondered if he'd forgotten he had a kind, gentle girl called Weng waiting for him at home. Didn't her feelings matter?

* * *

"Li Jiaying is a lazy student," Gary said, referring to my habit of skipping class. Gary was pretty laid back when it came to his classes and didn't really care if students showed up or not. But one day he flared up.

"Get Li Jiaying to come to class," he ordered Taomei, his most ardent devotee, in front of the whole class.

I started dragging myself in reluctantly, but spent most of the time staring into space. I had absolutely no interest in what he had to say, be it deconstruction, semiotics, or metafiction. Gary floated in my mind like a heavy nightmarish mass. How can I even begin to express how oppressed he made me feel. There weren't really the words …

Each lesson was an ostentatious display of his knowledge. He was a performer, whose intellect, personality, and soul had been splintered into many fragments, all which served to add to his celebrity. The knowledge he presented to us in the classroom may have originated from the West, but he was unrelenting in warning me to stay away from my Western boyfriend, as if Lawrence had been afflicted with some horrific Western illness. My professor was a thug through and through, and had the whole department at his beck and call, including my friends Taomei and Fat Luo.

Fat Luo was always the first to arrive in the classroom. He'd pick the best seat—right in front of Gary's desk—and wait in nervous anticipation for Gary's arrival. Often he'd be so nervous he'd get a pain in his stomach. He was terrified of being looked down on by Gary.

Fat Luo was infatuated with Eileen Chang back then. He spent the first part of his summer holiday watching every single episode of a highly regarded Japanese drama series, before beginning another project—copying out Eileen Chang's book *Eighteen Springs* a few times over by hand. He did this to sharpen his writing technique and expand his vocabulary. He regarded Gary's lessons with awe and anxiety, while referring to all our other teachers as bullshit. He called one teacher, a lead figure in the feminist writer movement who happened to be single, "A sad old slut who's been left on the shelf. She comes to class looking like she's been rolling in a haystack. From where I sit in class I can even see her underwear. Shameless good-for-nothing. A forty-year old maid who can't get a decent man to marry her. Ha ha!" A white-haired professor who taught poetry and verse was called a "she-beast". Before examinations, Fat Luo would devote hours and hours to copying poetry out onto pieces of paper. He'd write these poems down in tiny ant-like handwriting and roll them up in the transparent glass case of his ballpoint pen and then look at them during the exams. His talent for cheating surprised us, as he never showed much aptitude for day-to-day tasks. He was never found out, not once. He urged the rest of us to do the same. "Who cares about the process? It's the results that count. You've got to have a few tricks up your sleeve if you want to survive in this world." He told us once, in all seriousness, that he was trying to gain weight so that he didn't have to do his compulsory military service. He told us that the military was for simpletons. How could a literary genius like him be expected to serve—it would be a total waste of his talent. And not seeing his mother for days on end, no women for long periods of time—it would be too hard to deal with, he said.

Taomei was completely infatuated with Gary. He was suave and talented. She saw him as a god. We soon discovered there was more to the matter. Gary's hand, which flew with such speed across the blackboard, had started stroking Taomei's cheeks. His fingers, long, slender and refined as a piano player's—and completely at odds with his personality would, after hazy nights out drinking, slip themselves under Taomei's skirt. Fat Luo was the one who discovered this. Look over there, his eyes were saying. I turned and saw this older man with a fresh-faced, wide-eyed girl, smiling teasingly at each other, desire lighting up their eyes.

It all began in a big rented house with a Japanese-style bathhouse. There were five of us: wide-eyed Taomei; Hui who seemed to suffer from autism, and would talk incessantly to her friends about her dreams; soft-spoken, upright Ying who looked like a Buddhist statue, who along with her boyfriend struck us as the model-couple; PhD student Ting who had great literary astuteness, but the voice of a little girl; and then me, quirky with sloppy habits.

We were all friends and got on well, so we decided to split the rent on this place and become housemates. We meant to look out for each other, but instead it became the place that our friendship fell apart.

The house was at the foot of the mountain and big enough to accommodate all five of us. It had a long, narrow garden and that huge bathhouse, which smelled faintly of sulphur. It was one house among several that had been rented out to students, and had a view overlooking Qianshan Park on the left and Mount Shamao on the right. Sometimes the five of us would stand, gazing out at the view. Fat Luo and the guys in our class lived in the top floor of a block behind us, in a tiny apartment with rooms that had been partitioned like matchboxes to accommodate all of them, and no living room or kitchen.

It was a self-sufficient mountain retreat concealed from the rest of civilisation. All year round white mists of sulphur drifted up from the drain, a constant reminder of the invisible, restless energy that lay beneath the earth on which we had made our home. On this volcanic terrain, as we sought out mutual warmth and companionship, a conflict erupted.

"Doesn't Fat Luo seem pretty despicable?" Ting, the Women's Studies PhD student, pondered during dinner one day, her brow furrowed.

The rest of us looked at each another. We had no wish to discuss this topic. Taomei looked like she was about to say something, but

I shot her a glance and she swallowed her words.

"He comes to our place everyday and has a good look around, and brings us breakfast and lunch. Don't you find it weird? Who made him our caretaker? I have absolutely no interest in having him 'look after' us," Ting said, disgruntled.

While the rest of us engaged in a heated discussion over what Ting had said, Ying only smiled. She did not butt in or add her piece. As Ting continued to rant to us about her discomfort at Fat Luo's actions, Ying merely nodded and smiled as she listened. "Wanmei told me Fat Luo used to ring her up in the middle of the night for no reason, and ask if things were going okay with her boyfriend. Wanmei found it quite disturbing. Sometimes her boyfriend would be right next to her when the phone rang and he'd get quite angry when she told him about it. He even threatened to give Fat Luo a good beating! But Fat Luo thought nothing of it." Ting's brow was knitted tightly—she clearly found the matter bewildering. Taomei and I exchanged a smile. "Wanmei is probably not the first girl to have been harassed by Fat Luo, and neither will she be the last," Taomei chuckled. "It seems as if Fat Luo has been harassing several girls at once!" Ting's eyes widened in realisation. "So I'm right. He is a letch. A lonely old pervert."

After dinner, Ying's boyfriend arrived and she left the table first and retreated to her room with him. He was a few years older than us, a computer engineer senior and had come to university after completing his military service. He was over six feet tall and we often teased Ying that they both towered so high above the rest of us, their future kids would probably be giants. Ying's boyfriend came by at our apartment every evening and spent the night with her. We all assumed they would be getting married soon. Indeed, that was the impression they gave. Ying's fiancé always appeared after dinner. After greeting us they'd disappear into Ying's room, closing the door, drawing the blinds and retreating into their own little world. We never knew what happened behind those closed doors, for Ying was lost in her own happiness. Every morning was the same: Ying's fiancé would leave with a polite goodbye, quietly shutting the door behind him. They were like a married couple, silent and stable.

When we didn't have class, the five of us would stay huddled in the big house, chatting as we went about our tasks. Sometimes we'd visit the guys in the opposite apartment. Sifeng loved the saxophone and Nietzsche, and sounded like a medieval monk when he spoke. Jack acted cool and wrote poems that sounded as if they'd been composed by an ancient swordsman. And then there was Fat Luo. Every corner of Fat Luo's room was filled with mess. It looked like a pigsty, with half-eaten cans of meat on the desk and mould growing over the carpet. Fat Luo, who never stopped eating from day to night, so he could gain enough weight to avoid military service.

Gary would visit our apartment too. He'd discuss literature and aspirations. We'd climb the mountain to eat wild chicken at a restaurant called Chicken Town, take a dip in one of the hot springs resorts, or play cards. Often at home a shrill ring tone would pierce through the night, startling us girls out of bed. It was Gary, on a high after completing some manuscript or other. He'd want all of us to take turns in talking to him, bleary-eyed and half-asleep, me included. We'd stagger to the receiver muddled and confused, barely able to understand what our professor on the other end was saying. The last person to take the phone would always be Gary's favourite, Taomei. We were too busy hurrying back to bed to pay attention to what they talked about, but we'd rise the next morning to discover that Taomei had spent the whole night with her ear pressed against the receiver. Getting out of bed to wash, we'd see her looking exhausted, with dark circles round her eyes, stumbling back to her room to sleep.

Gary's visits to our house started becoming more frequent. Sometimes after our meals at *Chicken Town*, feeling euphoric, we'd all launch into a raucous game of battle horse in the fields. Gary had usually downed a few bottles of beer by then. He'd choose Taomei as his partner, and squat down, pretending to be a battle horse for Taomei to clamber astride. Though we were all desperate to win, we were still wary of Gary's professor status, and avoided attacking him outright. This made Gary and Taomei invincible. Utterly defeated, the rest of us would keel over on the cold earth. We'd discover our knees and hands covered in dirt, and groan. Gary, on the other hand, would be euphoric, picking Taomei up and spinning her around. Taomei giggled in delight in Gary's grasp, her skinny legs flapping like a fish tail. Then Gary, tipsy and in high spirits, would plant his lips onto Taomei's cheeks, as they continued to spin around the field. It was the same in our card games. Gary would hold his deck of cards in one hand, while the other stroked Taomei's cheeks, Taomei lapping it up like a cat. Taomei returned the odd looks we shot her with ones of lovesick euphoria.

The telephone continued to ring in the middle of the night. Taomei continued cooing into it as if she were rocking an infant to sleep, until the morning birds woke us with their chorus.

Gary became a constant presence in our home. Sometimes he showed up straight after lessons, and after a hearty meal or a glass of wine, we'd play some game or other. Once Taomei asked if we'd like to bathe with Gary. There was a chorus of objections at first, but Taomei suggested we wear swimsuits. After much wheedling, we finally agreed. Taomei filled our enormous tub with water from the hot springs, until every corner of the bathroom was filled with mist. The dim yellow lights were replaced by flickering candles. The combination of vapour and sulphur caused a strange atmosphere to descend.

We filed into the bathroom and slipped into the tub. As soon as Gary entered we scooted to the sides to make room, sure to keep enough distance. He began to remove his clothes. He hadn't brought his swimming trunks so we'd assumed he'd keep his underwear on. None of us had any idea that he would strip down completely. We looked him up and down, stunned. The only source of light was from the weakly flickering candle, but it was evident to us that years of heavy drinking had taken its toll on Gary's physique, from his extended belly to his sagging skin. Gary's penis dangled limply and pitifully between his legs, and looked devoid of any strength and power. We were regarding his figure with frightened and bewildered eyes, wondering what to make of this matter, when Taomei said, "You intellectuals are such degenerates". Gary burst out laughing and without another word, leapt into the water.

When Taomei saw the rest of us frozen stiff like a zombie army, yet to recover from the shock of seeing our professor naked, she was seized by a sudden impulse. "The water is so nice and hot, let's all take off our clothes. I'll put out the candles so it's too dark to see anything."

Gary said nothing. Like an old man from a manga comic, he folded his towel and placed it on his sweating brow. He tilted his head back and his mouth fell open. He was clearly having a good time.

Taomei stepped out of the tub in her swimsuit and extinguished the candles by the window. She stripped off like Gary just had. No one else followed her lead. We continued chatting in the dark until the water around us cooled.

Not long after that, Gary had two brand new bicycles delivered to our place. Fizzing with excitement Taomei told us this was Gary's present to us girls. We'd all heard about how generous Gary was to his students, but we'd assumed this meant leaving us money to buy groceries. This gesture took us by surprise.

"Gary and Taomei are definitely dating. That shameless guy!" Fat Luo said viciously one day when Taomei wasn't home. He had come on his daily food delivery round and was visibly seething.

Were Taomei and Gary really dating? I didn't know.

One day Gary came over and as usual, we ate and drank with him. Perhaps he'd drunk too much, for as we sat around listening to him, Gary's voice suddenly started to sound old and feeble, completely different to his usual arrogant, rambunctious tone of voice. He began to tell us the sorrowful tale of his first love, a classmate from the Chinese Literature department, who had left him, poor and penniless, to go and teach in Hualian. She had broken his heart.

But there was another girl who had broken his heart even worse, he told us. He had fallen in love with an older woman, but as if in a dream, the girl he'd believed to be the love of his life, had heartlessly betrayed him. He had replayed the scene in his mind over and over again, always wondering if it had really been him standing in the doorway the day it happened.

He had gone to her place as usual. But pushing open the door, he discovered her in the throes of passion with another man, on the very bed where they usually made love. He watched the face of the girl he loved contorted in pleasure-pain as she came. Who was that man lying on top of her? Who could elicit such moans? He must be seeing himself, he thought. The sight, he said, ripped apart his flesh and spirit. He saw himself on the bed, flesh and bone, a tangle of limbs, yet his spirit remained standing at the door, taking in the sight before him. Surely he must be looking at himself. But why did he have such light brown hair?

No. That man, thrusting madly into the girl he loved, was a white man. A warm-blooded, handsome white man.

"Standing in that doorway, I felt like a cockerel who'd had its head chopped off. I'd had all the breath knocked out of me. I felt utterly defeated. I don't even remember leaving."

So Gary had his vulnerable side too. He spoke slowly, his voice charged with rare emotion. We said nothing. We just sat there listening with bated breath, not daring to move.

Even now, Gary still remembered the burning love he had for this woman who had left him, who immigrated to California with the Western guy. Gary poured his agony into writing a song about two lovers who were torn apart after one of them had to move to California. This song was awarded the *Song of the Year* prize, although no amount of accolades could make up for his anguish and humiliation.

Gary had one too many beers that night. We made up our spare room for him so that he could stay the night. The display of sorrow and heartbreak made Gary seemed smaller, more pitiful and sympathetic in our eyes. But as we huddled around discussing the room arrangements for that night, his old arrogance resurfaced. "Taomei will sleep in my room tonight," he said in his usual commanding tone, as if he were back in the classroom and no one better challenge him.

None of us dared make a sound. We glanced at Taomei, the same thought flashing across our minds. No, Taomei, no.

"Okay!" Taomei said without hesitation.

So Taomei went into Gary's room. And everything changed.

Conflict Nineteen

"Taomei's a public toilet. A slut. A whore," Fat Luo said with fury. He went through every insult he could think of.

"She thinks that by fooling around with her professor she'll manage to climb the social ladder. She thinks she can use her looks to actually get ahead of us with her writing. Fuck her! Literature is a serious endeavour.

"If being a good writer is all about sucking the right cocks, why do we hold the craft in such high regard?" Fat Luo couldn't hold back the fury in his voice.

"Fat Luo, you have no proof—don't be so quick to jump to conclusions, okay?" I said once, as we sat on his balcony, drinking tea and looking out at the mountains. Fat Luo was having another rant about Taomei. You couldn't have guessed he'd once thought so much of her.

"The truth is right in front of our faces. Do you see the touchy-feely way they are with each other? It's disgusting. An unmarried couple sleeping in the same room—that's all the proof you need," Fat Luo said. His other housemates were showering or listening to music in their rooms. It was just the two of us having this conversation.

"Don't jump to conclusions about things you haven't seen with your own eyes," I said.

"Don't be so fucking naïve. A man and woman sleeping in the same room—what else do you think they're doing?" Fat Luo said.

"I only trust what I see with my own eyes," I said.

"Foolish empiricist," Fat Luo said.

We decided to confront Taomei, to find out once and for all.

She was standing in the passage in front of our house one evening, her hands pressed against a stone pillar, gazing leisurely out at the scenery. This was when Fat Luo and I showed up and started talking to her. We moved straight in for the kill.

"Everyone seems to think you're dating Gary, Taomei," I probed, keeping my words slow and measured.

Taomei stared back at us wide-eyed. She seemed to be giving our odd question some thought.

She didn't answer.

"You're dating him, aren't you!" Fat Luo said.

Still nothing. Taomei stared back at us, a strange look in her eyes.

"Admit it, you're dating Gary, aren't you?" Fat Luo repeated.

"Yes. I'm in love with him. It's my choice, nothing to do with you," Taomei replied.

I thought Taomei would deny the accusation, and so I was left stunned by her response.

Though she had said yes, I was still sceptical. Perhaps what Fat Luo said was true—I was really an empiricist at heart!

The phone continued to ring nonstop in the middle of the

night. But now it was a woman on the end of the line, Gary's girlfriend Weng.

Weng's phone calls had a subduing effect on Taomei. Each time she got a call from Weng, Taomei's voice would sound low and strained, very different to the relaxed way she laughed and chatted with Gary. Weng generally seemed to be the one doing the talking, while Taomei just listened.

The first few times Weng called we were curious, and asked Taomei why our professor's girlfriend was calling the house.

"She wanted to know how we're doing, I guess!" was Taomei's breezy response.

One day when the five of us were eating dinner, Taomei suddenly mumbled, "Weng is quite an incredible woman." She dropped her head and she carried on eating.

Some time later Fat Luo wrote a novella about Taomei. He entered it into an annual writing competition organised by the local newspaper and was awarded first prize. In the story, Taomei was depicted as a pathological liar who used her beauty to entrap men, enticing them into bed, before ditching them and moving on to her next victim.

"That slag, she's like a public toilet. Hiding her sordid deeds behind the mask of literature. Luckily I saw her for the dirty whore she really is. I rejected her when she tried to get me to sleep with her," Fat Luo wrote. He lashed out at Taomei in a satirical manner, comical, mocking, exaggerated and savagely chauvinistic. His novel depicted Taomei as a depraved, disgusting woman, but between the lines I saw his volcanic fury, and his severe inferiority complex. These powered his systematic destruction of her whole reputation, under the banner of creative freedom. But I said nothing. I felt small and insignificant. Perhaps somewhere deep inside, I too disapproved of Gary and Taomei's relationship. Perhaps it was Gary's despicable actions I was really against. Perhaps it was this inner helplessness that meant that I did nothing when it was discovered that my housemates' underwear had been going missing.

On the day the literary prize-winners were announced, a large red banner was plastered across the billboard. In calligraphic print were written the words: The star of the literary department and The star of the Chinese department. Fat Luo became an overnight sensation. He treated the entire department, teachers and students, to a meal, paid for with his prize money. Like a king hoisted on the shoulders of his people, Fat Luo got a first taste of what it felt like to be adored by the masses.

Meanwhile Taomei found herself being shunned. She was given a wide berth, and was met with hostile glares, whispers and glances.

No one knew what had gone on between Taomei and Gary in that room. No one questioned the truth of Fat Luo's claims. A strange atmosphere descended over the writing department. People adopted Fat Luo's derisive manner and sneered at Taomei every chance they got. As Fat Luo emerged triumphant, she was sentenced to death.

I didn't reach out to her, even though I was one of the few who knew the truth. We ate and basked in Fat Luo's glory while I feigned innocence every time Taomei sent a powerless look my way. I knew the degradation Fat Luo had subjected Taomei to— the prey he'd once relentlessly pursued. To prove his worth and garner everyone's attention, to walk away with the prize money and the accolade, Fat Luo had done everything in his power— even debasing a girl he had once cherished and loved. It was all just a joke, Fat Luo insisted.

Fame mattered, power mattered, creative works mattered.

But a woman who'd once rejected him didn't matter—she was no different from a hooker. It was all a joke, his story. He had succeeded in getting people talking, and made a handsome sum. Why not? It was fiction, only a fool would take it as truth, Fat Luo reasoned.

Taomei became a shadow of her former self. Once confident and vivacious, she'd speak up against people who got on her nerves without a second thought. Now she spoke less and less and walked around with sorrowful eyes. She retreated into herself, becoming increasingly like a withered shell, pushed into a grey, unlit corner …

The incident of the missing underwear happened some time before Fat Luo won the prize. The general attitude towards Taomei had not been hostile at that point; we were all still on friendly terms.

When we discovered our underwear was missing, we were united in our outrage. "When I catch that pervert, I'm going to beat him into a bloody pulp!" we sat around the dinner table raging.

"I'm going to castrate him and make him watch as I feed his penis to the dogs," Taomei said.

Even though we were unified in our revulsion, there was a grim atmosphere in the house. We placed a couple of garments on the clothes rack as bait, and decided to take turns keeping guard. But as night fell, we started to get scared. What if he planned to rape us? Ting asked, distraught. We wouldn't be a match for his strength.

Anyone who does a thing as contemptible as this has to be a coward, Taomei said. He's so cowardly he has to resort to stealing girls' underwear. I'm sure I could lure him out, Taomei said cheekily, anyone willing to join me? But none of us were. In the end we decided to start drying the clothes in our rooms instead, to prevent a repeat occurrence.

The guys from next-door came to see what had happened, and expressed their concern. They offered to patrol the area and catch the culprit for us.

"We're here—you have nothing to be afraid of. If that pervert shows his face again, just scream. One of us will come and beat him to a pulp." Fat Luo lifted his arms round his head like a bodybuilder and clenched his fist.

"Don't be scared, I'll protect you!" Fat Luo said, and pummelled his chest fiercely, like Tarzan.

The pervert didn't make another show. Perhaps by being on high alert we had frightened him off, or maybe he'd stolen enough underwear to keep him going. Whatever the reason, the incident slowly faded from our minds.

One day I made an impromptu visit Fat Luo at his apartment. I wanted to check out his progress on the novella he was submitting for the writing competition. I was going to offer to look through what he'd written if he needed someone.

I stood in the balcony facing his room and knocked on the windowpanes, hoping he would hear me and come out. The lights were on, but there was no response. So I went in through the main door, walked down the corridor and stopped before Fat Luo's wooden door. I tapped on it several times. The door was slightly ajar. Music was playing in the room. It was soundtrack from Wim Wenders' *Until the End of the World*—a film we had all been bowled over by.

I knocked on the door several more times, but got no answer. I thought perhaps Fat Luo had gone out or was taking a shower. I decided to wait for him in his room, thinking that while I was there I might as well give his draft a look over.

Dirty and messy. Fat Luo's room was in its usual messy state. Piles of books had fallen off the bookshelf and onto the dark blue carpet. There was a plate of mouldy toast on his table and a cup of water that had clearly been there for days. Dirty clothes were strewn all over the carpet, giving off a pungent odour. I was brushing aside some of the mess to make enough room to sit down when a cockroach scurried out from beneath some books and papers. I picked up a book and hurled it at the cockroach. I missed, and the cockroach darted beneath the table before scuttling behind the plastic wardrobe.

I saw the cockroach antennae waving from behind the wardrobe. I crept over to the corner of the room, padding as silently as a cat. *You won't get away, you disgusting creature*, I said to myself. Looking down at the gap between wardrobe and the wall, something caught my eye. Pink. Cream. Yellow. Jet black. It looked like bundled up clothes, female underwear to be exact. The cream-coloured item with the lace pattern work looked particularly familiar.

I squatted down, shoved my hand behind the wardrobe and tugged at the bundle of garments. God, it was all the underwear we'd had stolen.

Bras, knickers, silk stockings. I picked them up item by item with trembling hands. No doubt about it, these were the undergarments that had been taken from our place. What was going on?

Was the underwear-stealing pervert Fat Luo? Was it really him? What was going on?

I caught a sour fishy smell and looked down to notice that every piece of our clothing was stained with a dry yellow substance. I looked at the cream garment I was holding, which had a huge blotch of it in the gusset. I held it up to my nose and took a sniff.

It hit me like a ten-ton truck. I thought I was going to be sick. It was semen, sour semen.

I threw the garments on the carpet and ran for the door. My stomach heaved, and I puked my entire lunch onto his balcony.

Vile. Completely vile.

There was no question that Fat Luo was the culprit. He had jerked off all over our underwear.

I revealed this shocking piece of information to no one. None of our housemates, not even Taomei. Was I protecting Fat Luo? Maybe a little, but not entirely. Perhaps what I really feared was the mass hysteria that would result if people found out.

Not telling the others was a mistake. The illusion of peace had been shattered. We all left the fairytale castle we'd created together. All of us, except Ying. Good girl Ying, who we found out later had deceived us all, but no one more than her loyal fiancé.

The first to leave was Taomei. Isolated and shunned by everyone, how could she not go? She slowly faded from our social group. Gary eventually broke up with his girlfriend, Weng, but he didn't stop his womanising. When his mother found out about the breakup, she was so furious she chased her nearly forty-year old son out of the house. "That girl was perfect—what is wrong with you?" she shouted after him.

Gary deserted Taomei in the end. He turned forty, and married his office secretary, a girl even younger than Taomei. She was petite and androgynous-looking, with narrow eyes and dark-rimmed glasses, unlike any of the tall and feminine women he'd previously dated.

Perhaps Gary was growing old and weary. Perhaps he needed a younger womb to carry on his lineage.

This girl quickly bore him a son, who was given celebrity status, like his dad. Gary brought his son out for public appearances, acting out the good husband and father. Gary and his son even appeared on the cover of a mothers' magazine.

Taomei kept moving house. After a few months she'd fall out with her neighbours and have to move on. Someone was out to get her, she said. They kept kicking up a ruckus outside her window in the middle of the night.

Bitch. Whore.

Public toilet.

Rotten deceptive slag.

No matter where she moved, they would follow her, she said. Of course, she never showed weakness by shouting back at them. But she heard these voices every day without fail, in the dead of night, right outside her window.

They're just jealous of me. Of the way I look and the attention I get. They're brimming with envy, Taomei said.

Those voices in her head became Taomei's constant companion. They became the door to a strange world that none of us could access or understand. Taomei had left us for real this time.

I had lost her. I believed she must be lonely. And I became lonely too.

Taomei disappeared. That girl who used to read magazines on the sly in 7-Eleven with me, who used to tease guys by slapping their arses and running away.

She was gone. And I was the friend who'd stood by and let it happen. When she'd needed my help, I'd done nothing.

* * *

When had Fat Luo and Ying started to become intimate? No one knew for certain. In the early hours, after Ying's fiancé had left with his briefcase, Fat Luo would sneak into her room. The strange thing was that Ying, placid as a Buddhist statue, was a completely willing participant.

The first time we saw him hovering around Ying's room looking shifty, we hoped he'd soon leave. But he stayed in there with her for a long time, just like a tortoise, contracted in its shell. What were they up to in there?

If some of the girls had got up early and were already eating breakfast, Fat Luo wouldn't be able to come in. He'd stand outside Ying's window instead as they murmured to each other in hushed voices. Anyone who walked down the corridor would find Fat Luo lurking there, looking as panic-stricken as a burglar caught in the act. Fat Luo would react by hurling himself into the rhododendron bushes, keeping his head down and tucked between his knees, like an ostrich burying its head in the sand. What was he hiding from? Why was he afraid of being seen? We'd already seen him, so what was the point? We all found it pretty astonishing.

The behaviour was repeated every morning without fail.

Ying's fiancé was the only one left in the dark about this. Each morning he'd leave Ying's warm bed, freshen up and leave the house with a smile. That was when Fat Luo would sneak in. Ying would be there on the bed still as a corpse as Fat Luo drew near. He'd remove her underwear and sink down in between her legs —where her fiancé had been only hours before. Ying would close her eyes and lie there without moving. She'd forget everything, including her tyrannical father, who they all knew had a mistress, and yet still came home and savagely beat her mother each night. She'd forget how her father used to force her and her siblings to come and watch as he bashed their mother against the wall like a ragdoll. She'd forget the way her mother's pitiful howls gave way to deathly silence, and the image of her sprawled on the ground like a corpse. When she closed her eyes, Ying could no longer see the old unmarried janitor, with his deformed toes, who used to violate her behind the schoolyard. When she closed her eyes, she no longer had to think about what a bad person she was, how she didn't live up to the untarnished image they all had of her. No longer had to think that she had grown tired of her picture-perfect relationship and longed for the taste of new lovers, but also couldn't bear to break up with him.

Meanwhile Fat Luo was in seventh heaven. He had finally found a woman who would open her legs for him and take him into her wet warmth. He was no longer the stray dog with wretched eyes wandering around from place to place foraging for scraps. That warm pussy was the home he'd been looking for all this time. He latched onto it greedily, like a wide-eyed suckling infant. It became his sustenance, the source of his virility.

We lived in a constant state of fear. Afraid that Ying's fiancé would find out what was going on, and the whole thing would blow up and cause chaos. Some of us could not bear to see Ying's loyal fiancé being treated like this, and found it very strange, especially as the person she was choosing to cheat on him with was Fat Luo.

But what did this have to do with anyone but the three of them? Why were we getting more riled up than the involved parties?

Perhaps it was because we all felt that living under one roof, there were certain moral obligations that had to be met, and anything that fell outside that line should be challenged. Or perhaps it was the disgraceful nature of it, like two dogs mating, and should be conducted anywhere other than the perfect fairytale castle we'd created. If they wanted to carry on like this somewhere else that was up to them, but we wouldn't accept it under our roof. More than any of this, the reason we were angry was because it involved

Fat Luo, and we were distrustful of everything that involved Fat Luo.

We whispered, we raged, and we gossiped. Our collective rage and self-righteousness multiplied and proliferated in every direction ...

I thought that since Fat Luo and I were close, it was my duty as his friend to talk some sense into him.

I went over to his one day and told him that his behaviour had gotten everyone riled up.

We stood on his balcony, Fat Luo wearing a pair of black denim shorts that showed his dark leg hair. He remained silent, as if having anticipated something like this. This relationship was important to him, he explained, and he would not hesitate to cut ties with anyone who tried to interfere.

But Ying's engaged! I said. At least spare a thought for her poor fiancé! I don't know why you always have to go for girls who are attached. If you had any self-respect you'd just stop. I must have sounded quite aggressive when I said this, because I couldn't help thinking about all those times that Fat Luo had harassed girls, and how I'd been protecting him by keeping his underwear-stealing to myself.

I don't know if Fat Luo took my words to heart, but he fell into a heavy silence. He said nothing, just opened his mouth revealing yellow teeth, then closed it again, and sighed.

The words tumbled out before I could stop them. I called him a fool, venting all my anger and frustration on him, thinking I could right his wrongs, acting like a foolish, well-meaning saint.

I used the example of French writer, André Gide, who we'd studied at university together. Gide's *The Immoralist* has as its protagonist a depraved writer who pursues his own literary ambitions at the expense of all those closest to him. He would put every sordid deed he described in his literary works to the test, even if it meant engaging in acts of debauchery in real life, even if it meant hurting everyone around him. Gide enjoyed the loving care of his wife, while carrying on a wanton affair with a very young boy, which he turned into a novel. He trampled on the happiness of all those around him in order to reach self-fulfilment. He was obsessively selfish and depraved. He believed he could wash his hands clean by transforming his vile actions into works of art, and by so doing he would be reborn into a state of purity. After reading his finished works, readers worshipped him. Yet no one would ever remember his wife, who had been the ultimate sacrifice for his work. His wife had stood by him and cared for him like a loyal friend through thick and thin. Because mere mortals were nothing compared to the sacrosanctity of literature.

I admire your work, but I look down on you, I said. You're like Gide—in love with your own depravity and tragedy, continually repeating the same actions, unable to stop. But sadly you're not Gide. As your friend, I can't stand by and watch you make a fool of yourself.

I thought I was helping him with these words of warning. I never considered the weight of my words, never thought that they may have been too harsh or critical. But this very warning message meant that, returning to Taiwan from my travels sometime later, I discovered that the island no longer welcomed me.

Fat Luo remained silent. A long while later he opened his mouth and said something that remained with me for many years. It was something I didn't quite understand. All he said was, "Li Jiaying. Have I ever mattered to you?"

It was my turn to be lost for words. What had that got to do with anything I'd just said?

Something bad happened to Ying that night. She came out of Fat Luo's room, her face ashen and her breathing rapid, clutching at her collar. She looked as if she were about to collapse. Our other housemate Hui called an ambulance and Ying was taken down the mountain to the hospital.

Some claimed that Ying had tried to kill herself by swallowing detergent. Others, that she suffered from epilepsy and had had a fit.

I didn't want to know what had happened. I just packed my bags and walked away from our place, that seemingly indestructible fairytale castle, and that seemingly indestructible friendship group.

The other housemates left soon after, one after another. True to his words, Fat Luo cut ties with us to pursue the love he had finally found. He moved into that empty, desolate house that we had once all shared. After cohabiting with Ying for some time, they got married and Ying became pregnant. When Fat Luo's new book was published, a happy family photo of the three of them appeared in the newspaper. No one could see that behind the blissful family facade was a man who'd had his heart broken—Ying's fiancé, who never found out the truth.

Where did he go? No one ever knew.

Conflict Twenty

Past experiences shape who you are today. Memories cling like phantoms, vines that wrap around the body, vanquished only by death. Some people spend their whole life playing tug-of-war with memories. No matter how many thousands of times the earth spins, those persistent memories are impossible to shake off.

Can humans exist without memories? I don't know. Perhaps a world without memories would be bitter and cold.

Seol-hee lived on in my uncle's memory. His fiery heart, which had once blazed with such passion, was now sealed beneath the ice of the battlefield. The memory of Seol-hee became a gulf between him and his new wife. My uncle sought companionship from his memories, a burden that grew heavier after my little cousin's death.

I remember that hot summer afternoon. My uncle arrived at

our home after a five-hour bus journey, just like he'd promised in his letter. Despite his tightly-knitted brow, and his sense of detachment, us children were always eager to be around him. We wanted to see what presents he might have brought us, whether there were suncakes for us in his bags.

A calligraphy brush. An ink slab. A Parker fountain pen. And suncakes. We were delighted. But our pleasure didn't last long, as our mother quickly shooed us outside. What was it that us children weren't allowed to hear? Puzzled, we crept under the ledge of the green window screen, and tried to catch a drift of their conversation. We saw our parents sitting with our uncle on the sofa, speaking in hushed voices. The content of their conversation was muffled and indistinct. They were drinking tea for most of the time. Father one gulp, mother one gulp, then it was uncle's turn. Few words passed between them. So why hadn't we been allowed to join them? There was a peculiar sombreness on their faces, as if the world were ending.

After our uncle and father left the dinner table that evening, our mother told us the truth. She spoke in a feeble voice, as if to herself, and didn't look us in the eye.

"Your little cousin is dead. He drowned in a stream," she said. He had been dead and buried for a month already.

So their silence and sadness had been because of the death of a child. That was what had made them all silent so suddenly.

* * *

I spent my rebellious teenage years living at my uncle's, a place filled with grief and sorrow.

My uncle never discussed my cousin's death with me. I'd never even seen him sweeping the tomb. Perhaps he went without telling me. I didn't even know where my cousin was buried.

In the courtyard of my uncle's two-storey house, there was an old pedicab fitted with a carousel for children to play on. About once a month he'd polish the pedicab until it shone like new. He'd set the motor humming, and set off looking like a kindly Santa Claus, one of the rare times I saw him smile.

Standing in the courtyard, the scent of magnolias wafting over, I'd ask where he was going.

"To the park." A grin and he was off, a thin trail of smoke wafting up comically from the back of the pedicab, before he disappeared at the end of the narrow alley.

He left me with so many questions. My uncle was not in need of money. His retirement fund could last him several lifetimes. So why did he still need this other business?

At dusk, throngs of parents and their children filled the city park. Kids skipped along holding candy-floss, their tongues occasionally darting out for a lick. Others bounded playfully between the flowers and bushes with plastic windmills in their hands. My uncle's pedicab was parked under the banyan tree in the corner of the park. The carousel cheerfully spun as lively music rang out from the loudspeaker. Drawing near, you could see children perch on top of the wooden horses, joyful smiles on their faces, their laughter filling their air. My uncle would be standing to the side, grinning like a fool.

Each time he went out, there would be a couple of children who would pass the pedicab and stop dead in their tracks. If their parents or grandparents didn't allow them a go, they'd hurl themselves to the ground and make a big commotion. Whenever this happened, my uncle would peer down at them like a kindly, funny old man.

"Let the child have a ride—it'll be on me," he'd say to the

parents, in a relaxed voice.

Hearing this, the parents would hastily plonk their children onto a wooden horse. They'd shoot my uncle the occasional suspicious glance, as if to say strange old man. Strange old man manning his own carousel under a banyan tree.

I never saw my uncle make more than a few pennies from his carousel. But every month without fail, he'd drive his pedicab to the park—as if it were official business.

"Did you like riding carousels when you were young?" my uncle's neighbour asked out of the blue as I was watering the garden after dinner one day.

"I don't remember," I replied. "I might have tried once in the playground, but I can't remember what it felt like."

"Your little cousin loved carousels. He was always badgering your uncle to take him to the park for a ride on one. He'd sometimes kick up a huge fuss. Your uncle even smacked him a few times for it," the neighbour said, peering over from the other side of the fence.

"After he died, your uncle went to the park and bought the carousel from the vendor. It's such a shame his little boy will never have a chance to ride on it." The neighbour sighed and shook his head.

I stood in the courtyard, gazing at my uncle through the green window screen. He was bent over the newspaper in the dark hall with his reading glasses on. A lump rose in my throat. He must be grieving terribly for my little cousin.

* * *

My uncle lived in the prison of his memory, while my parents lived in the terror of war, being on the run, their families destroyed and everything lost.

After escaping to Taiwan, my mother found herself climbing over the higgelty-piggelty tombstones with my grandfather in search of her mother's grave. Twenty years later, I bounced alongside my father on those same tombstones, scouring them one by one for my father's lost wartime comrades.

"Though our beautiful homeland remains, we shed gallant tears for our impossible return."

"The Donghe River reflects the true human spirit. Warm spring currents course through the Erjia Mountain villa."

"With principles and dignity as lofty as the mountains. Undaunted and unafraid, a harmonious light shines over this charmed land. Emerald mountains and clear waters will protect this splendid village."

"I grew up beside the Gan River in my hometown Jiangxi. My wish to return is unfulfilled, its waters I never again shall see."

I was like a puppy, bounding along after my father. We walked into some tall grasses, and as I was still small, barely reaching his chest, the weeds loomed over me like giants, nearly swallowing me up. I would stomp along the dirt trails, keeping up with my father, while pausing every so often to take a look at a tomb engraving.

"A candlelight illuminates our paths, give no heed to the flickering of your own life. Though the tides may spin and roar, you are a lighthouse showing us the way, standing firm against wind and

rain. *Today you may vanish, like a flower next to a fence, but tomorrow you will rise up again in full glory on the other side of the fence. This world is the place where you have taken root, in an endless cycle of life and regeneration.*
The Donghe River will praise your glory,
The Erjia Mountain will chant your name from afar,
We, who have dedicated our lives to the nation without ever asking for reward, will always remain by your side."

"Mr Li Yingchun hails from Qiongying village, Yunnan Province. He had a peaceful and healthy family life. He benefitted from the excellent teachings of his father Li Gongmao and mother Guo, as well as the positive influence of school and society. He was a man of principles, and treated people with honour. In 1949, when the government of the Republic of China moved to Taiwan, he abandoned his studies to join the military. To save the nation, he was positioned as a Captain of the Anti-Communist troops on the Yunnan-Burmese border and performed many successful assaults on the mainland. The effort took its toll on him, and he returned to Taiwan unwell. He finally retired at Erjia Mountain Villa and spent his later years gardening. He had a good life, and about him there is only praise. God, why have you chosen to summon this man to your side? His memory will remain in our hearts for all eternity."

"Mr Zhao Laoer hailed from Shunning, Yunnan Province. He leaves behind his father Zhao Lin, his mother Wang, his wife Yang, as well as a son and daughter, all of whom remain imprisoned in the iron wrought gates of the mainland, their fates unknown. Mr Zhao lived simply. He devoted his life to serving the nation by joining the Anti-Communist troops and

participated in guerrilla warfare on the Yunnan-Burmese border. In 1954, he followed the anti-communist troops into Taiwan. In 1959, he retired from military duty. With no kin to turn to, his life was difficult, and he spent the remainder of his life alone. Fortunately, he was diligent and resourceful. He saved up money and created a scholarship fund for students. He gave his love to the people around him. He is an example for future generations to admire and emulate."

These epitaphs had all been written by my father. Lighting an incense stick, he bowed and spoke at the graves, as if conveying everyday matters. I hunched my back, mimicking his every move.

I must get someone to trim the grass, my father would say. Or he'd notice someone's tombstone had sunken in, and say we must hold a meeting and collect some money to fix it. Every now and then he would place his hands on his back, and survey the burial ground, the final resting place for his guerrilla brothers. Deep in thought, he'd say, as if to himself, that when they were alive they did it all with their own hands—digging the graves, engraving the epitaphs, trimming the grass. Now so many of them were dead, that wasn't possible.

Several times I witnessed my father acting as pallbearer for his old comrades. The retired male guerrilla fighters wore white, with strips of white cloth tied around their heads, and marched with dignity along Taiwan's east coast. Residents and shop owners stood along the sides of the road, bearing silent witness to this strange and solemn procession of men.

I did not understand why my father had to be the pallbearer. My father's world was incomprehensible to me until one day I saw news reports about ex-guerrilla fighters from the Irish Republican Army—the IRA. Gerry Adams, the Sinn Féin Party leader was all in black as he stood sorrowfully before the procession of pallbearers, guarding over comrades of his who had died amidst the gunfire. It was a silent protest of grief-stricken frustration. Perhaps it took one who had gone through a similar situation to understand this grief. Just like those stone inscriptions—what did they think they were leaving behind? In a few hundred years would anyone come across these inscriptions hidden among the weeds, written in their blood and tears? The stone inscriptions were written by a small group of guerrilla fighters who'd never expected to end up in the southern island of Taiwan. After their retirement, they retreated to the mountains, which looked like Yunnan, their homeland. Not only did they engrave words on one another's tombstones, they also transcribed Sun Yat-sen's will and distributed it around. They even got the words tattooed on their bodies. Approaching death, they still believed fervently that their lifelong dream, of taking back China from the Communists, would be fulfilled.

The war had never ended. Every minute of it was relived fresh in my father's memory.

Whenever we came home after sweeping the tombs, my father would have the same dream.

Machine guns firing in all directions. Bullets whizzing past, a hair's breadth from his skin. Hollering at his comrades to wake up, wake up quickly, and get into position, to attack with all they had.

Enemy soldiers ambushed them several times on the mountaintop. Warm blood spurted everywhere as bullets made holes through the bodies of my father's fighting friends. Doctor! Doctor! Where's the doctor? My father would scream. But there was no doctor, only the blue smoke of gunfire and the blasting of bullets. My father held a young soldier in his arms, only eighteen years old. "Don't die on me," he yelled. "What will I say to your mother? She's back home, waiting for you to come home and get married!" His words fell on deaf ears as the soldier fell limp in his arms.

Father flew, holding his machine gun and continuing to fire. Bang—bang, Bang—bang—bang.

"I was back on that mountaintop, flying around," my father would say when he woke up.

His sleep was invaded by that recurring dream. Sometimes he was the only one left in the mountains. He was lost, racing forward, enemy soldiers in close pursuit. All around him were the bodies of his fallen brothers. Just as when he thought all hope was lost, his father—my grandfather, who had died on the way to trade with the English businessmen—would appear. My grandfather would stand some way off, smiling kindly at my father, and then turn and point out the way to escape.

Sitting up in bed, my father's face would be drenched in tears.

After waiting nearly forty years, he could finally go and see his family again. Cross-Straits relations had improved by then, and Taiwanese residents were allowed to visit the mainland. He could finally return home.

He and my uncle had made a promise to each other. My uncle gave my father the high US-dollar salary he was earning as a spy so that he could buy the Leica camera. My father wanted to use the camera to photograph the beautiful sights of Taiwan. One day he wanted to show the pictures to his family back home. But his wish was never fulfilled. He'd been involved in intensive military training at the time, with missions that sent him to Jade Mountain, 3952 metres above sea level, and Gui Lake in the Dawu Mountain, a name that struck fear even into the hearts of the local aboriginals even. He spent several weeks in the wilderness of that treacherous mountain, learning how to survive. To complete the task, he'd had to get to the meeting point to rendezvous with the others. He'd brought along his beloved Leica camera, as well as a harmonica purchased from the English businessmen in Burma. During the icy cold nights, under the twinkling stars, accompanied by the distant sounds of the wilderness, he'd blow a tune into his harmonica, to chase away the loneliness and the terror in his heart. He did not have a single soul to speak to during that time, and so he had used this much admired Leica camera— and shot surreptitious pictures of clouded leopards, leopard cats and the Taiwanese black bear. But on a diving training mission, as the rubber boat rocked about on the waters, the camera slipped out his pocket and disappeared into the deep dark ocean.

He thought about photography all the time. Not long after, he was sent on a secret military assault against an enemy base. He gave up his dream. That was a few years before he met my mother.

There was a breeze blowing that evening. He'd been strolling in a field, chatting with a couple of his of his military school friends after dinner, when someone informed him that the director had something urgent he wanted to see him about. My father raced to meet him. The director had always looked so severe and authoritative, but seeing my father now, he fixed him with a kindly look.

"When your country needs you to give up your precious life to infiltrate the enemy base, will you do it?" he said gently, almost humbly, patting my father's arm.

"Of course," my father answered loudly and with conviction, not even having to think.

"Do you still have family in Taiwan?" he asked.

"My brother."

"Let's draft a will to your brother in that case," the director continued. "We will notify your brother when he can come and pick up the settling-in allowance."

My father knew that the time had come.

That night he boarded a helicopter, along with a group of assault troops he didn't know, everyone in full military gear, armed to the teeth. They had no money with them, the only thing of value a gold chain they had each just been given.

None of them knew where they were being dispatched. They clutched their rifles tightly, knowing that as soon they left the helicopter, the battle would begin. No one knew they had been sent away, apart from their families who had received the wills they'd written, but there had been no time for tears.

My father gazed down on Taiwan from the high vantage point of the helicopter. He didn't know if he would ever return to the island that had become a second home. As the night drew in, the lights on the island gradually flickered out, and it sunk into a serene dreamland. They could hear gunfire in the distance where they were heading, and my father knew he would use his body as a human shield against the volley of bullets, if it kept that distant gunfire at bay and allowed Taiwan to continue developing peacefully. Taiwan's economy was just beginning to emerge from the trenches of poverty. Factories were springing up. Democracy and elections, things that people on the island had never before enjoyed, would soon be taking root. The next generation and the generation after that would enjoy improved education and better lives. With these thoughts in mind, my father flashed a naïve smile in the direction of the island he was departing, the smile of a soaring angel.

A few hours after he got off the plane, my father realised he was back at the disputed Sino-Burmese border. At the other end the Southeast Asian mainland, the Vietnam War was just beginning.

The French colonists had recently been driven out, and civil war had broken out. North Vietnam was gaining strength, while the situation in South Vietnam was precarious. Monks self-immolated on the streets, as political power kept changing hands. The US, which had secretly been providing South Vietnam with weaponry, ended up becoming its protector.

My father could sense the atmosphere in the region. The terror spread, that familiar undercurrent of people running for their lives. War was just around the corner, my father knew from experience. Of course he didn't know it was the Vietnam War that was about to start, or that it would shame America and nearly cripple them.

Guerrilla troops were waiting for them when they landed, made up of Chinese soldiers who, like him, had been living overseas. They didn't even have time to rest before the orders were sent down that they were to infiltrate the enemy base.

Attack the People's Communes. Raid the enemy's arms depot. Destroy their rations. Distribute flyers laying out Sun Yan-sen's *Three Principles of the People*.

Kidnap the regional head. Destroy their vital transport routes.

My father thought that each mission would be his last, but clearly fate had other ideas.

No one could have anticipated that each assault would be more successful than the last; that they would go from strength to strength. Chinese men from the Southeast Asian mainland join them, including Chinese businessmen and their mule caravans from the Tea Horse Road. They provided money and strength, and together they advanced inland towards Yunnan.

"We will recapture the land we have lost! We will recapture the land we have lost!" After every successful assault on a city, the troops would break into victorious cries, their spirits soaring.

My father discovered that after its series of defeats, their enemy had changed its battle tactics.

In the dark night, as the wind howled, the sound of his mother, my grandmother, came from afar. She was weeping and pleading, her voice echoing through the mountains and trees. The feeble voice of an old lady repeated sorrowfully into the loudspeaker: "Return to me, my child! Please stop fighting among yourselves. We are all very well. But we miss you so much. You have been gone for a long time. Don't you miss us too? I am getting old, and I worry I do not have long to live. It is time for my son to look after his mother! Our lives are better than before. We are happy with our lot. Summon your fighting brothers, tell them to set down their weapons and surrender! The Party has promised to reward you with high positions. The Party will take care of you and your brothers. Your mother is waiting for you, come back to me! Don't give up your life in vain."

My father's guerrilla brothers crowded around him, tears streaming down their faces.

"I miss my home. Commander, I miss my mother!" A young man, barely twenty-years old, wailed like a child. "I want to go home," he howled.

"No," my father barked. "Going home means certain death. The enemy is tricking us."

My father didn't manage to curb the show of grief from these soldiers, who had lived through so many fearsome battles, and one by one they burst into tears. Big strong men, who had not showered in days and were infested with fleas and lice, all crying, tears and snot running down their faces.

My father hid his face with the blanket, and covered his ears with his hands.

Beneath that blanket, he too was crying.

"Commander, are you crying?" a young soldier asked unthinkingly, in among the sound of all the wailing.

The soldier had meant no harm with his question, but my father exploded.

"Go back to sleep!" he bellowed.

Back in Taiwan, my father sometimes sang Yue Fei's song *When the River Runs Red.*

My hair pricks up in fury,
Standing beside the railings, I
see the rain has stopped,
I lift my eyes to the sky and call out,
Intense emotion filling my chest, Thirty
years of efforts turned to dust,
Eight thousand li battling night and day,
Youth must not be squandered,
Or old age will be spent in sorrow,
The humiliation of the Jingkang reign yet unforgotten,
The hostility of his courtiers lingers on …

With his hands behind his back, a low and sorrowful tune would rise from his throat. His thoughts would return to the flames of the battlefield. The only one who knows my heart is Yue Fei, he'd murmur to himself. Has there ever been such a situation, troops ordered to retreat despite successive victories? Yet that was what my father had to face. At first he couldn't believe it. He thought that the dream he shared with the comrades he'd been to hell and back with, was the same dream shared by everyone in Taiwan. Later he discovered this was not so. First it was rations cut, but then it was all supplies. They were facing one problem after another. He finally followed the orders from Taiwan to retreat and abandon the mission—including the return of all the cities and land they had recaptured. He reluctantly returned to Taiwan, where he discovered that he been demoted, and all his battle comrades discredited.

Not one person thanked them for what they had done. No one was moved by their military achievements, achievements that had sent them to hell and back, and would in ordinary circumstances have been lauded for. Some people even called them foolish.

Later he discovered the truth. As he'd been on the frontline, the high up officials sitting in their air-conditioned offices in Taiwan had started a rumour. That the real motive of these young, unruly soldiers fighting on the frontline was to seize power. When the area of land they had taken back had exceeded the area of Taiwan, the rumour was that they planned to start an independent plateau government and make an appeal to all overseas Chinese to join their fight against the Communists.

After returning to Taiwan, my father lived like Yue Fei from the Song Dynasty, full of grief and indignation. He'd sing *When the River Runs Red* in a low voice as he clutched my tiny hand and taught me calligraphy. The sentences I wrote with my brush were either from Yue Fei's *When the River Runs Red* or Wen Tianxiang's *Song of Righteousness.*

Finally, after many years, he was able to return to his old home for a visit. He took a Nikon camera with him. Along with relatives from his old home, he paid a visit to the battle zones that he had once fought in. For a long time he stood before the memorial tablets to fallen soldiers. Reading through name after name in the list of the enemy troops who had died, their ages and places of ancestry, he was shocked to discover that many among the dead had been childhood playmates or school-mates.

At night in that battlefield bullets flew around in every

direction. They pierced through chests and sent bodies crashing to the ground. On the other side of all that blood, the gunfire, and the wails of pain had been my father's old friends.

He only discovered this more than three decades after the battles, during that trip to the mainland. The knowledge of it induced a panic attack.

He stood before the memorial in for a long time, feeling out of control. His skull felt numb, and he broke out in cold shivers, he thought he might collapse. How could this have happened? It's been many years, he reminded himself..

When he returned to his hotel, he found that his Nikon camera, which he'd put in the wardrobe drawer, had gone. The undeveloped films of the photos he'd taken in his hometown in Yunnan, which he had wanted to take back to Taiwan and show to us, gone too.

Back in Taiwan he told my mother that having his camera stolen was probably an act of revenge by the descendants of the fallen soldiers.

It was then my father began to experience his recurring dream. He was always flying above the mountains, accompanied by the blasts of gunfire. I could not know exactly what he dreamt, but I thought it must have been like those martial arts scenes from films, when the actors fly.

But for the war, my father might have become a photographer, my mother a writer. But my father's beloved Leica was lost forever beneath the icy dark ocean and his dream was never fulfilled. His family back home never saw the fruits of that noble promise he'd made to my uncle back then, to use the camera as a pair of eyes, to record the beautiful scenery of their new island to show the folk back home. And we, his children, never got to see the wonderful photos of his childhood home in Yunnan that he'd finally been able to take.

But I saw the photographs he took every now and then, shot after shot of broken-limbed old guerrilla fighters, miserable in old age. They were his compatriots, his brothers. They were memories of the youth he lost, coupled with a sort of loneliness and solitude that we who came after could not comprehend.

He had once thought that my mother, who had once gazed up at him with the adoration of a little girl, would spend her whole life treating him with that god-like reverence. That he would be able to tell and retell his fearsome battle tales. But after we were born, our mother lost interested in our father's guerrilla warfare stories. "Enough of this!" she would snap decisively, each time he started to become animated over a story. My father's memories of his courageous guerrilla fighting days became a burden my mother had to bear. All the guerrilla brothers who had been to hell and back with my father, my mother saw as a burden.

My mother did not understand this solidarity these men kept harping on about. It did not compute. What was important to her was that her children had enough to eat. Every so often my father's guerrilla brothers would knock on our door, asking him if they could borrow some money, which my father would hand over without a second thought. Quite often that would be the last we'd see of the cash. And our mother would transform from a demure and pleasant housewife, into a fearsome tigress with sharpened claws.

"Those friends of yours have latched onto you." Thirty years later, my mother still gnashes her teeth in fury when she thinks about it—my father's sizable military retirement fund, frittered away on his friends. My father remained unmoved. What money compared to the aspirations and ideas they had all shared, and the friendship they had fostered through the smoke of war, going to hell and back.

My mother felt that my father immersed himself in all that was glorious in the world, and left her with all the crap.

She would always remember washing the shit from the underwear of one of my father's sworn brothers.

This man had been with my father during his guerrilla fighting days. My father referred to him as his big brother, and we knew him as Uncle Yang. He suffered from tuberculosis and coughed incessantly. A few years after he came down with the illness, his wife packed her bags, took their two sons and left. He wrote to my father describing his desolate situation and my father invited him to stay for a few months, to see if he could get better. That's when my mother's luck turned.

After she'd finished preparing the family meal, my mother would have to cook something else up, that could be easily eaten by Uncle Yang, who was losing his teeth. After the whole family had finished eating, she would squat in the courtyard under the dim orange lights, cursing as she washed the whole family's clothes. "Look at what your father's good deeds are doing for me," she'd say between clenched teeth.

She'd never had a desire to throw up when she was cleaning her own children's nappies. But washing Uncle Yang's large white underpants, which, because of his tuberculosis, would sometimes contain piss and shit, she would gag all the time.

Uncle Yang coughed all day long. I was often stirred awake by the sounds of his coughs from the other room. It was as loud as thunder, as if he were trying to cough up his internal organs. My mother would soak Uncle Yang's chopsticks and anything else he'd used in boiling water for a long time, and refused to let us to touch them. "Be careful or your whole family will get tuberculosis," she'd say fiercely, as if she herself wasn't part of our family. But our family's fate was intricately entwined with the fates of the guerrilla fighters; their life and death struggles became our undertaking, this duty passing down for generation after generation. It was our family's fate, but my mother didn't want to immerse her feet in these muddy waters; her life had already been far too difficult.

She cursed as she scrubbed, cursed my father and that past of his that she had once gazed on with such reverence.

His guerrilla brothers started getting old, getting diseased, dying one after another, and my father's life became lonelier.

The war never ended for him. When mainland China started shooting missiles into the Straits, he thought another war was imminent. He went out to the market and bought us a year's supply of rice. We gaped as we watched him struggling to unload the goods from the car, sweat pouring down his back. We asked why he had bought so much rice—wouldn't it go to waste? Go bad if we couldn't finish it?

He gave us a stern lecture. "There is a war coming. You don't know how terrifying war is. Soon we will not be able to buy grain from the market. And food shortage is always followed by inflation."

Even after the crisis was resolved, and it was proven that the missile had only been an empty shell, my father still believed war was imminent.

The memories of war stayed with him. In my father's world, the war never truly ended.

He continued to fly around in his recurring dreams, above the mountaintops, amidst the gunfire.

Conflict Twenty One

When I was older, I realised that my father's turbulent memories of deprivation and dispossession were rooted in Western colonisation and aggression.

I used to think that my father recalled his childhood with fondness, those beloved English leather Oxfords, and those exotic treasures my grandfather gathered from across the ocean, which had made my father the envy of all his peers.

Later, I discovered that this was not the case.

I brought Lawrence home for a meal once. At the dinner table, my father made a revealing comment in front of my blonde haired, blue-eyed boyfriend:

"Chinese people and dogs used to be forbidden from parks in China's British concessions."

Lawrence couldn't comprehend what my father was saying. He'd never even heard of the Opium Wars. In his world, that had been his country's proudest time: citizens of the British Empire passing on their highly advanced civilisation to other countries. Unlike nowadays, British citizens had been allowed to go anywhere they wanted without having to bother with visas. That was the glory of having an Empire. Every colony belonging to the Empire: India, Myanmar, Hong Kong, Singapore, weren't they all indebted to colonisation by an Empire that governed them better than their own people ever had? He hadn't heard of the unbearable injustices suffered in those colonies.

So my father's comment about Chinese and dogs forbidden from parks shocked Lawrence.

The night before I moved to England with Lawrence, my mother prepared a lavish meal for me. The whole family had gathered to send me off, everyone except my father. He, usually such a rational man, suddenly became awkward, thorny and childishly unreasonable.

He locked himself up in his bedroom and refused to come out. The bedroom was completely dark. He wouldn't even turn on the lights.

My mother stood outside the door shrieking at him. "You rotten old man, what's wrong with you? You're completely ruining your daughter's farewell dinner."

But no matter how my mother cursed and yelled, the door remained shut.

Grabbing a set of keys from the teacup, my mother told me to open the door and get my father out.

The room was completely dark. I fumbled around for the bedside lamp and turned it on. In the dim light I saw my father slumped in the rocking chair, hugging a pillow. He seemed to have regressed back to childhood, and was muttering to himself in a lonely, grief-stricken way.

"They want to rob me of everything. They're even trying to

take my daughter."

I knelt down, leaned towards my father and stroked his knee. Who was trying to take me away, I asked. "Bandits," he told me. "Bandits in suits and ties, fake gentlemen." He fell back into the swamp of his memories, a spirited youngster once more, living on the plateau.

"They stole our plateau's gold. Just because they had advanced mining technology, and greed of course. It was our land, our resources. They hid behind their company names to exploit us mercilessly. They bought our people for next to nothing, used them as coolies, forced them to work brutally long hours. A labourer named Daniu, sneaked off despite our warnings. He died in a cave from breathing in poisonous gases. There offered no compensation to any of us. They were ruthless, selfish, greedy bloodsuckers," my father said.

A past event, which had filtered out of his mind like smoke into the air, suddenly reappeared. One afternoon he and some friends from town had gathered a crowd together. They had set off into the remote mountains, where the mining took place. They beat up every Westerner they saw and chased them away shouting, "This is our land and our resources. Go back to your little island."

When they saw what was happening, the British gathered their own group together, and an argument started. In the end a fight broke out, with people seriously injured on both sides.

But the British did not stop mining. They continued to recruit large numbers of coolies to do their work, and even hired strong, able-bodied, rifle-wielding men from Burma and Nepal to safeguard their operations. "We discovered these minerals. If it weren't for us you'd still be thinking these mountains were nothing but wasteland," the British said self-righteously, using guns and bullets to protect their hard-earned discovery.

"They want everything, even my daughter. They are exploiters —it's in their blood. Wolves in sheep's clothing. They think that what they're doing is completely justified, because they don't see other races as human beings. As well as looting our palace treasures, they chased the Burmese royal family from their palace as if chasing some despicable dogs onto the streets. They've never shown us any goodwill. They are greedy and self-serving, only watching out for their own interests, and judging other people from their own narrow viewpoint," my father said, lost in his memories, angry and indignant. After he'd finished castigating the British, he turned to the Americans. "The Americans can't be trusted either. During the guerilla fighting American missionaries came to visit aboriginal tribes in the mountains and forests of the disputed Sino-Burmese border. They appeared to be kind, wanting to share their religion and teach English. They befriended everyone. We later discovered that they were undercover CIA agents who'd been sent to collect information from us. None of them can be trusted. They are all pieces of work. You just don't understand," my father said in anguish.

There was a photo album on the chest of drawers next to the rocking chair. It contained shot after shot of black and white photographs that my father had taken of me as a child. Looking like a little Miss World before the Queen's Head rock at Yehliu Park on one of our day trips, my eyes narrowed as I withstood the icy wind. Clutching my cat Pepper and grinning, revealing a tiny fleck of tongue. Riding my father's first Vespa Piaggio, looking like a courageous horsewoman. My first school dance performance, *Thumbelina*, with a basket of wooden fruit balanced on my head. Sitting comically before the piano with my bowl haircut, playing Schumann's *The Happy Farmer* ...

My father had kept every last childhood photo of me. But I was grown up now.

"I'm still here, father," I said. Standing beneath the dim lights, I saw the insolent young man from the plateau who believed he could shoulder the weight of the world. The passionate young man, who had appealed to his compatriots and rallied them together to protect their resources and drive the intruders from their land.

I still went to England. I lived there for two years, before deciding to return to Taiwan. In the beginning, my relationship with Lawrence was calm and stable. I was very happy with life in England. But as time passed, I started feeling homesick. I craved Chinese food, began to wish for people to speak to in Chinese. When I did get to speak Chinese, I found my vocabulary had diminished and I had trouble constructing a perfect sentence. I had a growing fear that if I were to stay there, my future children would be a different nationality to me—they wouldn't understand my background. I felt a chill running through my body whenever I thought about this. I felt as if the country that I came from was disappearing, from inside me and on the outside, the good parts and the bad. I started to hate the sound of my increasingly authentic English accent. I even started to doubt I'd ever be able to write in Chinese again.

Lawrence understood my anxiety, but he was unable to help me.

One day Lawrence took me on a seaside getaway to the Seven Sisters in Sussex. As we walked along the white-stained undulating cliffs, Lawrence began to complain about how British taxes were rising again. It was extremely frustrating, he said, his country was becoming more and more like a third world nation. Look at London. Foreigners have taken over. Going there feels like going to a foreign country. The taxes are so high, and most of it goes into the pockets of Indians and other immigrant groups. They have so many kids, and think up schemes to get their friends and family over as well. They take our resources, abuse our welfare and benefit systems, and drag our country down. Meanwhile us Brits have to pay these high taxes. Those damn immigrants, he said without thinking. I exploded.

"Damn immigrants?" I said. "That's me you're talking about." "No, I meant the damn Indians. The immigrants who sign up for benefits. You're different. You're living with a British family. You're British," he explained hurriedly.

"I'm not British, I'm from Taiwan. I will never, ever be British," I said furiously.

Less than two months later, I moved back home to Taiwan. Lawrence grudgingly followed me back, but our relationship was on its last legs, and eventually collapsed.

After our break-up, Lawrence began dating someone else and I decided to leave again. I quit my job, gave notice to my landlord, sold my car, and decided to travel. I used to believe I could be in a close and stable relationship with a man, creating a solid family on the basis of this shared love. But I discovered it was a pipe dream, creating a solid family was impossibly difficult, while tearing one down was easy. And at the end of the day, you couldn't even trust the close relationship not to become the razor blade you'd both use to slice at each other with in that age old battle between the sexes, continuing that way until you were both too tired to go on. This is partly why you find me here, walking the streets of a foreign country alone. I thought that by going there I might be able to clear my head, to find an answer to my many lingering doubts.

I don't know. It was the only thing I could think to do, foolish though it might be.

My plan was to leave South Korea for London to catch up with a couple of old friends, and then fly to Greek alone. Greece was somewhere I'd always wanted to go to, but had never had the chance. I planned to rent a little holiday cottage on an Aegean island and stay there for a while. I would do nothing apart from read, swim, sunbathe and relax. And maybe, maybe, when I returned to Taiwan, a new life would await me. At least, that's what I told myself.

I went to the travel agent and booked my ticket, and was about to find Judy to say goodbye. The future. What would the future hold? Would two strangers brought together by chance ever see each other again? Who knew. And where was that Korean man Park Chang-chuk, who loved Teresa Teng? I would say goodbye to him too if I could, but he was probably still being detained, paying the price for the Itaewon anti-American protests that got out of hand.

On my last night in Seoul, Judy and I went to a trendy Itaewon bar. She told me with excitement that she was bringing her mystery man to meet me. I guessed she was referring to the guy she'd told me about before, the Taekwondo national team member. She was so spellbound and smitten she seemed to have completely forgotten the heartbreak she'd felt for her old boyfriend.

The bar was called *Manhattan*. It was like a mini United Nations, with people from all over the world. It was similar to the bars you find in Taipei near the National Normal University or on Shuangcheng Street, with ear-splitting music, dingy lighting, and suffocating smoke. There was one bunch of people squeezed together in front of the bar, and another on the dance floor shaking their bodies and bobbing their heads to the beat of the music. People who wanted to have a conversation in there had to shout directly into each other's ears to have a hope in hell of being heard.

I wondered if Judy's infatuation with eastern men was a kind of jungle fever too. Or perhaps it was just her situation, living in the east, no real option other than to seek out these foreign lovers to meet her emotional needs. But she didn't really understand them. But maybe this ambiguity only intensified her love for them. Judy enjoyed this enigmatic pursuit. In the youth hostel dormitory, I came across a book on the floor next to her bed once. A photo had fallen out from its pages, of a guy. I had tentatively picked up the book and photograph and placed them both next to her bed, carefully so as not to wake her, while stealing a curious glance at the guy in the photo. He was Chinese. Zhou, I imagined. He was standing in front of an antique bookshelf inside a vintage bookshop, in Tokyo by the looks of it. He was a pleasant looking man with narrow eyes and long hair tied in a ponytail. He was holding an old book open and reading it. On the cover in big letters were the words: *The History of Sino-Japanese Relations*. It looked as if Judy had taken this photo of Zhou on the sly. One corner of the photograph was water-damaged and creased. Perhaps from Judy's tears.

Judy didn't understand Zhou. Even when they broke up she didn't understand him.

During my last week in South Korea, Judy and I took a train trip around the country. We visited Suwon, Gunsan, Jeonju, South Jeolla, Busan and Gyeongju.

One day, we found ourselves in a mountain somewhere in the centre of the country, surrounded by sturdy pine trees. We made our way up the mountain via a series of wooden steps. As we were nearing the top, we saw murals on the rock cliffs, weather-beaten Buddhas engraved into the stone. The engravings looked very similar to the Dunhuang stone Buddhas in western China, I told her with surprise.

"They've travelled a long way. It must have taken at least a thousand years," Judy said. We were both awestruck by the engravings on these stone cliffs, hidden in the mountains amongst the leaves in the quiet forest.

"Why can't humans move around carefree like these engravings, without any borders?" Judy said.

"Because humans aren't like Buddha. Humans have emotions—hatred, oppression, jealousy, madness. Maybe it's in our genes to gravitate towards conflict and destruction," I said.

"Well, I believe in a borderless world. Nations have absolutely no meaning to me. Just like the idea of home. I don't need that kind of sense of belonging. I've never really had a home anyway." Judy told me about her experiences growing up.

Her mother was from Britain and her father from France. She was born in Australia. Her parents were part of the hippy generation. The passionate pair met in the height of the 1968 student movement in Paris. Seeking a new life and spurred by their dream of setting up a farm, they left the ancient continent of Europe and travelled to Australia, where eventually they did establish a huge farm and had several kids. But later they separated, and each met a new partner. Her mother moved back to Europe with her new boyfriend, while her father remained in Australia with his new girlfriend, running the farm. They each had kids with their new partners and whenever Judy saw either of them it was with these new partners and children in tow. The concept of family was no longer important. The concept of nation didn't seem important either. The essential thing was the quality of the relationship. The world had changed and was still changing, she explained. Her father was French, her mother Scottish. Their families had different nationalities to her, too. The existence of nations didn't mean much to her. Yet wars were still being waged in the name of nationhood.

It was a wonderful trip. I'm eighty to ninety percent certain I'm going to stay in Seoul, Judy said.

* * *

Ahn Yeon-uk was shy, not a big talker. He nodded politely when Judy introduced us, then slipped his arm around her shoulder, and teased her hair with the tips of his fingers. Judy looked incongruous next to this towering figure, like a child. "That tickles!" she told him with a giggle.

They spoke to each other in a mix of broken English, Korean and Japanese, resorting to hand gestures when none of these worked.

When they started speaking in Japanese, Judy must have sensed my astonishment, as she turned to tell me that Ahn's parents did business in Japan. They had sent him to school in South Korea, where he'd lived with his grandparents, but he went back to Japan regularly and had no trouble speaking the language.

"Guess what business his parents do in Japan?" Judy said, keeping me hanging.

"Japanese arcade gaming. You'd never have guessed, would you? They're filthy rich," Judy said. "I was dumbstruck the first time I saw him in his red Ferrari. I thought to myself, how does a bartender have this much money?" Judy was talking very animatedly. Next to her, Ahn was expressionless. It felt like Judy was talking about someone else. He was still curling Judy's hair around his fingers as if he wasn't even aware he was doing it.

"I asked him, why did you decide to become a bartender if you're so rich? Guess what he said?" Judy's eyes shone with excitement as she gazed up at Ahn. "He said, not many things in this world interest me. Driving fast cars and bartending are about the only two things I find remotely interesting. Isn't he cool?"

This time she actually got a response from Ahn, who clearly did like to play it cool. He blushed and lowered his head.

To make things less awkward, I decided to strike up a conversation with him.

"So I heard you used to be a taekwondo expert?" I said.

"Yeah," he said. After a pause, he continued, "I was injured in a competition, and had to stop after that."

"That's a shame," I said.

"That's why his father sent him to Korea to study. He hoped he'd join the national taekwondo team and get an international gold medal!" Judy said.

"That's in the past now," Ahn said. He took Judy's hand and led her to the dance floor.

The bar was filled with smoke. I stood alone at the bar, watching Judy and Ahn moving to the beat of the music.

They were playing Korean pop songs that were heavily influenced by hip-hop. Lots of people on the dance floor were trying out hip-hop moves too. People on the dance floor raised their arms as they moved, rapping along to the Korean lyrics, completely lost in their own worlds.

Ahn was an extremely skilled dancer. He did splits and somersaults. He didn't look at all like he was dancing, more as if he were boxing or doing some kind of physical stunt. He looked completely different to the shy guy I'd been speaking to just moments before. His T-shirt clung to his upper body, accentuating how toned he was, and his tight jeans revealed his firm butt. As he moved to the music, he gave off a manly sensuality. I began to understand what Judy meant when she'd said how devastating he was on the dance floor. All this time Judy was moving her body too, while gazing with adoring eyes at this new beau who'd been so integral to her decision to stay in Seoul.

The fast song finished and a romantic one began. The dance floor lights were dimmed.

Ahn held Judy in a tight embrace. Their faces touched as they slow danced together.

In the dim lighting, Ahn's fingertips slid snake-like over Judy's body, stopping at her buttocks. With slightly more force, he pulled Judy's hips in against his groin, his legs squeezed around her thighs. His fingers continued to move over her body, touching her skin sensually and hungrily. He lowered his head and buried his face in Judy's neck, nuzzling her. Judy kept her arms around him as they continued to dance, not responding with much eagerness.

After the song ended, they walked back over to the bar holding hands, grabbed their beer mugs, and glugged down their drinks. Judy suddenly edged towards me and in my ear, so that only I could hear, she whispered,

"I'm not going to make the same mistake. You have to wait longer before sleeping with an Asian man, I don't want to be taken for a slut again."

Because my flight to Europe was early the next morning, I had to move my bags to the airport transit hotel where I was spending the night. So I said goodnight to Judy and Ahn Yeon-uk at the bar. I exchanged email addresses with Judy and we promised we would meet again one day.

Conflict Twenty Two

Some people disappear before your very eyes, but you don't even notice them disappearing at first.

While travelling, I used to find an internet café every week or so to check my emails, and update friends or family about my trip. Sometimes I'd receive replies from friends, but Judy was among those who never responded. At first I thought nothing of it, imagining it to be down to her laziness. It was only when I was in the airport on the Greek island of Rhodes, about to get a flight back to London, and then on to Taipei, that I saw the news. An Australian woman had gone missing in Seoul. Her divorced parents were both flying to Seoul, one from Australia, the other the UK, to search for their missing daughter. A photograph of a woman with a brilliant smile flashed onto the screen.

It was Judy. Judy who I'd hugged goodbye only months before at that Itaewon bar.

Where had she gone to? I felt a stirring unease.

I flew from Rhodes to London, where I stayed for a couple of days before flying back to Taiwan.

I thought my new life was about to begin. But after finding a new apartment, getting a new phone number and re-establishing contact with old friends, my luck started to turn bad.

"Didn't you know, Fat Luo wrote you into his new novel. It's vicious! How did you manage to piss him off so badly? Everyone's talking about it!" A long-time friend told me anxiously over the phone.

I thought Fat Luo had disappeared from my life a long time ago. But it seemed he had never truly left. He was only hiding there, waiting like a time bomb ready to detonate.

"What did he say?" I asked.

"He said you were a 'banana'—yellow on the outside, but white inside. That you went to bars just to hook up with Western guys. He said you deeply despised your heritage and your home. He said you'd happily kneel down to lick a Western man's toes. But you were completely indifferent towards men of your own race and culture and didn't see them as equal to Western men. He was pretty disparaging about your English boyfriend. He called him a sissy, a kept man, a dosser and a reprobate. And he called you the perfect example of an Asian prostitute—keeping her legs clamped tight until she came across a big Western cock.

"Oh, and didn't you used to have a close friend called Taomei or something? He called you both a pair of "masked dolls". He said all Taomei was chasing after was the fruits of knowledge, that she'd only sleep with guys who had power. He called her a slutty bitch and a public toilet."

"Oh. Really? So some nightmares you just don't wake up from," I said. "I'm just going to ignore him. All he wants is pity and attention."

I thought if I ignored what was happening, that would be that. But the phone rang non-stop, friends calling to find out what was going on. Even my family were dragged into it.

"Is that the ugly boy who chased after you at university?" asked my mother, who seemed a lot older now.

"Yes," I said.

"To think we treated him with such warmth and hospitality when he came to our house. I thought he was your friend." My mother shook her head, lost in her thoughts. "People! You think you know someone … He seemed like such a decent, honest boy."

"Perhaps he once was. Let's just ignore him. It will die down eventually." I felt like a wise adult consoling my mother, who had over the course of time transformed into the upset child.

"But you're my daughter," she howled and burst into childish tears.

It didn't end there. Fat Luo and his publishing house launched a new marketing campaign to promote the new book, in which readers were offered a Masked Doll when they bought a copy. These Masked Dolls eclipsed Hello Kitty even, and became an overnight sensation in Taiwan.

Fat Luo's fictional fantasy sold like crazy. He went from being an impoverished writer to a national sensation. The newspapers called him the hottest writer in the past decade, and praised him for revitalising the stagnant waters of the literary world. Fat Luo was invited for book-signing sessions at every writing seminar, and chain bookshops and publishing houses promoted his book by holding a midnight book launch. On the day of the launch, there were hordes of people clamouring to get a glimpse of him, so many people that the bookshop window was shattered by accident.

"*The writer reveals, in its full naked glory, the jealousy, fury,* revenge and madness of human nature. He has transformed wretchedness into literary marvel, and used it to create his own aesthetic style. On the merit of this alone, it is safe to say that his literary achievements have surpassed those of his experimental mentor, Gary."—This was what a well-respected literary critic wrote about Fat Luo's work in a major national newspaper.

"A collective memory of humiliation and sorrow condensed into a hopeless, heartrending love story. Conveyed with poetic lyrical narrative, this tragic memory is relived over and over again. We experience defeat and a distorted portrait of ourselves. After Italo Calvino, the outside world gave us another literary star, Edward Said, who has helped to shape our national intellectual scene. We should be thankful that we now have the wise voice of Mr Luo, a man who scrutinises our collective sense of inferiority in all its absurdity. He has emerged from the dingy decadence of the ancient palace, making his way through the corridors of Western Baroque and leading us into turn-of-the-century Taipei, the amusement park where loud, noisy teenagers abound."—This was written by a poet, cultural critic and political activist whose writing career ended early.

We've had Portuguese custard tarts, Tamagotchi and Hello Kitty; the mass fever in Taiwan is now Masked Dolls …

Fat Luo's publisher, having discovered that the sales of Masked Dolls was overtaking even those of the books, jumped at the opportunity to mass produce them. Posters advertising the dolls read: "If you were ever looked down upon by scornful girls while you were growing up, if they rejected or humiliated you in any way, your time for revenge has come. Masked Dolls will heal past scars, and provide you with power for the future."

As I was walking through a neighbourhood alleyway, I noticed that a couple of grabber machines in front of the grocery store had replaced all their stuffed toys with Masked Dolls. Some dolls had "Tao" written on their dresses, other dolls had "Jia", referring to Taomei and me, I supposed. I went over and saw some teenager boys hooting and cheering. They were competing with each another for a chance to grab one of the dolls.

"Almost got her, almost got her! Jia, don't run baby, I promise you I'll give your hole a good time," one teenager said excitedly.

The rest of them burst out laughing.

"What's the big deal about foreign cocks anyway? Mine's better, it's just like a giant cannon. Boom boom," said the boy with the pierced ear.

I stood by the convenience store, watching them try to grab the dolls, confused. Hole? What did they mean? What was going on? When they finally managed to grab the doll, it all became clear.

The guys picked up the Masked Doll and pulled up her skirt to reveal that she had a hole down there. The boys were beside themselves when they saw this hole. They started jeering loudly, out of control, like a pack of wild animals that had finally brought down their prey.

"Let's get a plastic slingshot from the shop. When we get home we can have a competition, see who can shoot her in the hole," one of them said.

"Let's nail her to a wall first," another said.

"No problem, I can sort that out. Come to my place tomorrow when my mum's out. The doll can scream all she likes," the boy said, laughing nastily. He bought a plastic slingshot from the shop and the lot of them dispersed.

I stood frozen to the spot. Those teenage boys had suddenly taken on the face of the young Fat Luo. The shop owner asked me several times if I wanted anything, but I was too lost in my own thoughts to answer.

I walked out of the shop to discover that in my panic-stricken scramble to purchase something, I had somehow managed to buy a packet of sanitary towels. Perhaps it was an unconscious reaction, as if I were the one that had been pierced by that tirade of arrows and was bleeding from down there. I felt as if the Masked Doll might be made of flesh and blood, and like me, could feel pain.

Masked Doll fever continued to spread throughout Taiwan. They weren't just found in grabber machines; another game had evolved too. It was like darts, but the doll was the dartboard and the bull's eye was between her legs.

This Masked Dolls game spread over Taiwan like a summer typhoon and had soon developed into a computer game too. The Asian men in the game were handsome and strong. Their task was to overcome hurdles and defeat the evil foreign men one by one. The Masked Dolls were there for them to abuse at will, and would open their legs at their command. They could use sexual means to overpower her and punish her for dating foreign men and overlooking them.

It was the game Fat Luo had used to enjoy playing.

"Being wretched isn't a sin, it's an integral part of humanity. The story allows us to pull back the mask of wretchedness and to co-exist with it peacefully, recognising its need, like that of sunlight, air and water." One day I walked into the twenty-four hour bookshop, which reeked of the petit bourgeois. I saw a large poster of Fat Luo's book hanging from the ceiling with a couple of sentences about it. There were huge piles of Fat Luo's new novel on display, with a side profile headshot of him that filled the cover page.

Fat Luo had aged. He looked like a fully-fledged middle-aged man.

I picked up a copy of the book from the display, flicked to a random page and started reading. I found myself in the middle of an incident where Fat Luo, in a fit of rage, was attempting to hit a drunk Western blond-haired man at a bar on Shida Road, while I, Jia in the book, was trying to stop him. He's just a drunk who's wandered over here lost, I said. What's the point of beating up a drunk? You won't feel proud of yourself even if you win. With his clenched fists raised a hair's width from the drunkard's face, Fat Luo huffed.

On the next page, he started with the insults about Jia's Western boyfriend.

A downtrodden Marxist whose only talent is spending a woman's money. A tramp who leeches off state benefits. He's crap in bed, but he just happens to have been the top history student at some distinguished private school. Of course you can't tell by looking at him.

As for that slag Jia. She wears Givenchy underwear worth thousands of dollars while her father, an ex guerrilla troop commander, moved to Taitung in Taiwan alongside his fellow guerrilla fighters after suffering defeat in the war. He even tried chasing that blonde-haired, blue-eyed Western man from his house once! What a hero!

I shut the book and gave a long sigh. Ten years. Ten years wasn't long enough to defuse a person's rage. Some people would remain submerged in the swamp of revenge and humiliation forever. They would harp on about it for eternity, refusing to move on. Revenge and humiliation provided a driving force for living things, an instinct for survival, to go on no matter what. It was a strange force, a marvellous, constant energy that brought about both destruction and regeneration, and without which the universe would not be able to keep its balance and carry on spinning.

I walked away with a tinge of grief and sorrow. Fat Luo, the boy who used to stammer and get stomach-ache when he saw Gary, had aged. He looked even older than I remember Gary looking. This decade had passed in the blink of an eye. I hadn't seen Fat Luo in ten whole years, not even once. Since leaving our shared student house, I went back only once to have a look. That house we had thought of as a fairytale castle. While that notion had turned into rubble, the house still inhabited that quiet nook between the mountains. Ten years had passed by like a day, but we were the ones that had changed.

I could smell that same odour seeping from the house. It was thick, entrenched in the swamp and dust of memory: our missing underwear, Fat Luo crouched clumsily in the bushes, Ying's attempted suicide, me lecturing Fat Luo on his lack of morals, the voice of Gary haunting us with his midnight phone calls, and Taomei starting to mumble to herself in the house, like a lost soul …

In the end I went back to the shop in the noisy district where I'd first come across the dolls with those teenage boys. I bought two Masked Dolls. One of Taomei, the other of me. Perhaps I did it as a tribute to our lost youth.

I bought the Masked Dolls home, and with needle and thread I sewed thick nappy-like pants for them to wear. I placed them on the bed, cooing to them like a mother, murmuring, Don't be afraid, you're safe now. No one can hurt you anymore.

All their features were visible under the light. Their hair was made of thick dark thread. They had round faces with black lashes and black eyes, and were wearing red silk slips, and nappies wrapped round them now. The Masked Dolls were finely crafted with adorable faces. I stroked their cheeks, thinking about heading south to pay Taomei a visit. Perhaps I could bring her a Masked Doll too, help her while away the dull hours in the ward.

* * *

Taomei's condition was deteriorating. She didn't recognise my face anymore. Her mother told me that she had started to become aggressive. If she ever heard insults like prostitute, slut, or public toilet, she'd sling shit at the person who'd said it.

"We had no choice but to send her to a care home. We're too old, we can't spend the rest of our lives looking after her." Taomei's mother's voice, on the other end of the line, was beseeching. "You're her good friend, aren't you? You must know what happened to Taomei while she was in Taipei? What happened to make her like this?"

I couldn't say a word into the receiver.

It was around this time that my father began writing letters to the Queen of England. His handwritten calligraphic letters told the Queen to please return the treasures that had been stolen from China. My uncle and all the surviving guerrilla fighters co-signed the letter. Our noble dream hasn't yet been fulfilled, he'd tell my mother. By this time my mother was used to turning a deaf ear to him.

My mother told me that my father had been planning this since coming to see me in England and visiting the museums. He said that those stolen treasures on display in English museums had been calling for him to take them back home.

There were tears running down my father's old face whenever he talked about this, my mother told me with a baffled shake of the head.

233

Conflict Twenty Three

I learnt of Judy's death from the news on television. A dismembered female corpse, badly decomposed, had been discovered by the police, in a cave by a seaside resort mansion owned by Ahn Yeon-uk. DNA tests on the bones confirmed that it was Judy, who had been missing for many months.

According to the news reports, Ahn frequented bars to get close to Western women. He'd been linked to the death of another British woman while living in Tokyo. She'd started vomiting in Ahn's mansion, after an accidental overdose of ecstasy and alcohol. Ahn took her to the hospital on the verge of death. After she'd died, Ahn told the police that it had been her first visit to his place. He told them he hadn't been aware she'd taken ecstasy, but that he'd taken her to the hospital as soon as she started vomiting. It was too late. When this woman's parents arrived from Europe, he had entertained them and even tried to console them. The police suspected Ahn of killing the woman by spiking her drink with ecstasy. They uncovered a large collection of videotapes at his place that showed him raping Western women. When they woke up many hours later, the victims weren't even aware that they'd been sexually assaulted. They thought they had just drunk too much. Judy's death must have been similar to the British woman's. She must have died from an ecstasy overdose, and then been cut up and disposed of by Ahn afterwards.

According to news reports, Ahn had been a taekwondo expert on Korea's national team, with a bright future ahead of him. However, during an international competition against a European team, he'd been injured by his opponent, and forced to withdraw, both from that competition and participating in competitive taekwondo again. The injury had also made him sexually dysfunctional. This massive blow had caused Ahn to slip into darkness. He spent his nights going to bars. He received a huge pile of speeding tickets from driving his fast cars. He had nothing else to do with his time. His life had been destroyed.

I saw Ahn on television in handcuffs, surrounded by reporters and journalists. "Conclusive evidence has been found against you. What do you have to say to this?" one reporter asked. His answer left me stunned.

"An eye for an eye, a tooth for a tooth. The war never ended. The day will come when the oppressed will rise up."

He said this with coldness and arrogance, not a trace of remorse. I foresaw Judy's death, but I had no way to prevent the tragedy. First, Taomei. Now, Judy.

In every stage of my life I had been carried along by this unnamed powerlessness.

I became afflicted with a bizarre illness in which my limbs lost all their strength. For two whole weeks I lay in bed, unable to move. My mother came to my apartment every day to take care of me, but whenever she saw me lying in bed, tears would roll down her face.

"My darling daughter, what's happened to you?" she cried. One day she could no longer cope with seeing me declining food and water, or refusing to see a doctor. She hurled a bowl to the floor and began to wail. For a minute, she was like her old self, feeling as if the whole family had taken advantage of her, ungrateful despite all she'd done for them.

"Lord Almighty, did I sin in my past life for my daughter to be struck down with this strange illness? What kind of world has it been for me? What kind of family have I become entangled with? My children have all taken after their good-for-nothing father—what's the matter with them all? I come to her with food and water, but she refuses to budge an inch. All this while her good-for-nothing father spends his days writing calligraphy in his letters to the Queen of England, and for what? To get back our national treasures, he says. Do you think those Westerners give a damn about your calligraphy or your letters? Do you think they understand a word of what you're writing? You're mad—the whole lot of you. You've all got screws loose. The cherry on the cake is that amazing father of yours. National salvation, national salvation. What's the use of national salvation if you can't even save your family? Your uncle was right all those years ago. How do you help your country if you can't even help yourself? Your father made sacrificial lambs out of his whole family in order to save the country. Now he wants to get back some national treasures. Take a good look at yourself in the mirror, old man, look at how old you are. The Opium War was a hundred years ago. It's in the past. You're crazy, the whole lot of you. It's because of him that his daughter is like she is, spending her good years wandering around the globe like a ghost, rather than finding a good husband. It's my rotten luck to have chosen this man, to be still working like a slave in my twilight years. Dear God, I must have done something wrong in my past life. If my daughter continues to roam from place to place like this, she will end up like that girl on TV from whatever country who got murdered in Seoul ..."

My mother wept.

I listened to everything she said. I didn't argue with her. I didn't say a word.

I could not find the words to tell her that the Australian girl on TV, the girl who'd just been murdered, was in fact someone I knew. That we'd shared the same dormitory in a youth hostel in Seoul. I foresaw her tragedy, just like I'd foreseen Taomei's, but had been helpless to do anything. I couldn't find the words to express why I'd been compounded with such immense guilt from learning of Judy's death. I wasn't sure where the guilt came from, or why I felt I should that it should have been me instead. All I told her was that I was searching for a ray of light. When I found that ray of light, when I felt its warmth, I would get better.

My mother didn't look at me like I was crazy. Instead she stopped crying, as if she too was searching for that ray of light.

I began to have a recurring dream. I was in a long, deep seemingly never-ending tunnel. I walked on and on, searching for a way out, an end I couldn't find. The tunnel was pitch-black and humid. I heard the echoes of my footsteps as I stumbled along. From time to time water would trickle down onto me. The tunnel was deep, so deep it felt as if it ran down to the centre of the earth. As I walked along it, people I knew, acquaintances and loved ones, would materialise before me, one after another. My father, a spirited plateau youngster, sitting astride a white horse, galloping along with a troop of people following him. Imperialism, and all foreign-imported ideals will be destroyed, he shouted to his brothers. We will never allow them to plunder our resources again, or take our food. My father and his troop vanished. Now it was my grandfather's old and sunken face. He was slouched in his rattan chair, his expression grief-stricken as he faced my step-grandmother: *It's not my fault, it's not my fault. Everything was caused by the war!*

I walked on. The cold dank tunnel air made me shiver. Park Chang-chuk's face floated before me above the riotous crowd. His expression was twisted into a mask of pain. *Rise, people of Asia, rise!* he was yelling. *Economically and culturally, we must stand up and take control! We will be a colony no more! We will be a colony no more!* Next it was Fat Luo's turn. He had a crestfallen expression on his face as he whispered, *Jiaying, this is our little secret. Guard it well. That is, I. Love. You. One day I will be strong and powerful, just wait and see.*

The last to appear was my uncle. He was sitting by the window, combing his hair, just he had in my youth. Light appeared at the end of the tunnel, and it illuminated the dandruff falling from his hair, white as the snow of Korea. He carried on wordlessly as I stood beside him and gazed. I heard the voice of his heart speaking to me: *Now you finally understand my agony of losing Seol-hee and your little cousin. I cordoned myself off in loneliness, because there are indescribable moments in life that you just can't face. The sorrow of life doesn't stop; it continues to fall on us all. It is an eternal symphony.*

As I continued to walk, I felt people taking my hands in theirs. Taomei and Judy. *Of course we must walk with you on a journey like this,* Taomei and Judy said as one.

Hand in hand, the three of us made our way towards the end of the tunnel.

"Do you see the light?" I asked.

"Yes," they answered.

"That's our destination!" I said.

But then they vanished. They transformed into Masked Dolls and disappeared completely.

I made my way towards the light.

That ray of light was extraordinarily beautiful, like golden dust. It appeared at the end of the tunnel. I walked towards it, but as I drew close it seemed to be moving away.

Sometimes it would disappear at the end of the tunnel.

I moved towards it, step by step. I had to find it. It would give me light, hope and warmth. I felt extraordinarily weary. My eyes began to close.

If, if you see that ray of light, please wake me up, and tell me.

Notes

Conflict 1

p.8, *Kim Dae-jung* (1924–2009): South Korean politician. Worked as a reporter in his early days before beginning his political career as an advocate for human rights and democracy. Between 1971 and 1987 he suffered periods of exile, imprisonment, kidnapping and house arrest. In 1997, he became the first South Korean president to emerge from an opposition party, and in 2000 he embarked on a process of reconciliation with Kim Jong-il to improve North-South Korean relations. He was subsequently awarded the Nobel Peace Prize for his efforts.

p.8, *Kim Jong-il* (1942–2011): North Korean politician. The second political leader of North Korea, who succeeded from his father, Kim Il-Sung. He ruled North Korea for 17 years.

p.9, *Teresa Teng* (1953–1995): Taiwanese singer. Achieved massive popularity in mainland China in the 1980s. A popular Chinese saying at the time went: "Pay attention to Old Deng in the daytime; listen to Little Deng at night; the latter is far better than the former," "Old Deng" referring to then-political leader of China, Deng Xiaoping.

p.10, *Leon Lai (Li Ming)* (1966—): Actor. Born in Beijing, later migrated to Hong Kong. He became active in the Chinese entertainment scene in the 1980s. In 1996 he starred in a movie alongside Maggie Cheung. Its title was adapted from one of Teresa Teng's songs "Tian-Mi-Mi" (You Smile So Sweetly) (Official English title: "Comrades: Almost a Love Story").

p.10, *Maggie Cheung* (1964—): Actress. Born in Hong Kong, raised and educated in the United Kingdom. Her career kicked off in the 1980s in the Hong Kong entertainment scene and she subsequently received the Best Actress Award at the 42nd Berlin International Film Awards and the 57th Cannes Film Festival.

p.10, *Chiang Kai-shek* (1887–1975): Chinese/Taiwanese politician. Born in Zhejiang, China, and attended military school in Japan. Between 1928 and 1949, he was the political and military leader of China. In

1937, with the Japanese invasion of China, Chiang led the country in a series of anti-Japanese strikes which led to Japan's defeat in 1945. Between 1946 and 1949 Chiang's political party Kuomintang fought against the Chinese Communist Party fronted by Mao Tse-tung, but was defeated by them in 1949. In the same year, Chiang fled to Taiwan with troops of over six hundred thousands. Under Kuomintang rule, Taiwan was subjected to a period of martial law that lasted thirty-eight years.

p.11, *Chyi Chin* (1960—): Taiwanese singer, active in the Taiwanese pop scene in the 1980s. Now lives in Beijing.

p.11, *Joey Wong* (1967—): Taiwanese actress, active in the Taiwanese entertainment scene in the 1980s. After leaving the entertainment industry, she migrated to Canada. Her 16-year relationship with Chyi Chin has been the subject of intense media scrutiny in the Chinese media.

Conflict 3

p.21, *Clay Figures*: A classic love song composed in 1953 by Li Pao-chen while on a road trip in the United States. The song was adapted from a poem by the Yuan Dynasty poet, Guan Daosheng. In the late 1980s, the song was performed by Teresa Teng and become popular in the Chinese-speaking world.

Conflict 4

p.28, *Ryan's Daughter*: British film from 1970 about the 1916 Easter Rising in Ireland. It tells of an Irish married woman who fell in love with British military officer.

p.28, *"Between the earth and sky, there is justice to abide by"*: This verse is taken from the classical poem Song of Righteousness by Song Dynasty poet, Wen Tianxiang (1236–1283). When Kublai Khan led the Mongols in the invasion of China during the Song Dynasty, Wen Tianxiang was defeated and captured. He wrote this poem during his time in prison.

p.29, *Tamsui River*: A river in northern Taiwan. It is Taiwan's third largest river, and flows through the greater Taipei city district and northwest into the Taiwan Strait.

p.30, *Mao Tse-tung* (*Chairman Mao*) (1893–1976): One of the founders of the Chinese Communist Party (CCP). In 1949, after being defeated by the CCP, the Kuomintang fled to Taiwan. The People's Republic of China was established, and Mao Tse-tung became the first political leader of the CCP, ruling until his death in 1976.

Conflict 5

p.33, *Eileen Chang* (1920–1995): One of the most influential Chinese writers. Born in Shanghai, she studied at the University of Hong Kong before moving to the United States in 1955. Her works includes fiction, essays and plays. Her novel *Lust, Caution* was adapted into a film by Ang Lee.

p.34, *San Mao* (1943–1991): Taiwanese writer. Her collection *Stories of the Sahara*—travel stories set in the Sahara desert—was popular during the 70s and 80s in Taiwan and mainland China.

p.34, *Yukio Mishima* (1925–1970): Japanese novelist, playwright, reporter and filmmaker.

p.34, *Yasunari Kawabata* (1899–1972): Japanese writer, awarded the 1968 Nobel Prize in Literature.

p.34, *Lao She* (1899–1966): Chinese writer. His father was killed when the Eight-Nation Alliance invaded Beijing in 1900. He taught Chinese at the School of Oriental and African Studies (SOAS), University of London between 1924 and 1929. During the Cultural Revolution, he was publicly denounced by the Red Guards and savagely beaten. Humiliated both mentally and physically, he committed suicide by drowning himself in 1966.

Conflict 7

p.45, *Lee Teng-hui* (1923—): President of Taiwan between 1988 and 2000. Born in 1923 in Tamsui District, Taiwan, which was then under Japanese colonial rule. From 1943–1946 he studied at Kyoto University. During this period, Lee was called up by Japan to serve the Japanese army. His brother Lee Teng-chin (1921–1944) served the Japanese army in the Philippines. He died in Manila and was enshrined at Yasukuni Shrine in Tokyo.

p.45, *Jadeite Cabbage*: Nineteenth-century Chinese treasure, part of the collection at the National Palace Museum in Taipei.

p.45, *Travellers Among Mountains and Streams*: 11th century painting, by Fan Kuan, North Song Dynasty, part of the collection at the National Palace Museum in Taipei.

p.45, *Song Huizong* (1082–1135): The eighth emperor of the Song Dynasty.

Conflict 11

p.71, *Lu Xun* (1881–1936): Born in Zhejiang, Lu Xun studied medicine in Japan between 1902 and 1909. Also known as one of the leading figures of Modern Chinese Literature, Lu Xun's works include novels, prose, essays and poetry. His short story *A Madman's Diary*, published in 1918, is the pioneer of vernacular Chinese literature.

p.71, *Ding Ling* (1904–1986): Born in Hunan, her works include novels, essays, and poetry. Her novel *Miss Sophie's Diary* is renowned as China's first feminist literary work.

p.71, *Pai Hsien-yung* (1937—): Taiwanese writer, moved to the United States in the 1970s and taught at the University of California, Santa Barbara. *Taipei People* is his most famous work of fiction.

p.71, *Huang Chun-ming* (1939—): Taiwanese writer. His writings are representative of the nativist literature movement. His works include novels, poetry, children's literature and drama. Author of numerous short stories, the most famous of which includes, *His Son's Big Doll, Sayonara/Zaijian* and *A Flower in the Rainy Night*.

Conflict 14

p.104, *Ah Q*: A character in Lu Xun's novella *The True Story of Ah Q*, published in 1922. The novel uses the character of Ah Q as a conduit to criticise the collective character of Chinese people, and their semi-feudal, semi-colonial society.

p.104, *Marco Polo Bridge Incident*: A bridge located fifteen kilometers southwest of Beijing. In 1937, the Japanese army stationed in China were carrying out military exercises in the area. Claiming to be missing a soldier, they requested entry into Wanping town to conduct a search. When the Chinese refused, the two sides clashed. This was the inception of World War II in Asia.

p.106, *Nanjing*: Located in central China, China's capital during KMT rule.

p.114, *Quanzhou*: Located in Fujian Province, southeast China, Quanzhou marks the beginning of the maritime Silk Road. It acted as one of the world's major trading ports between the 10th and 14th centuries. It was also the port Marco Polo left from to go back to Europe in *The Travels of Marco Polo*.

p.116, *Dali Kingdom*: Located in Yunnan Province, southwest China. Historically several independent countries have been formed in this area, including the Dali Kingdom, established by the Bai ethnicity between the 10th and 14th centuries.

Conflict 16

p.133, *Clon*: South Korean dancing duo, popular from 1996 in Korea, Taiwan, Hong Kong, and mainland China.

p.134, *"The World of Suzie Wong"*: British writer Richard Mason's 1957 novel. It tells the story of an American man who fell in love with a prostitute, Suzie Wong, in Hong Kong.

Conflict 17

p.145, *Dai*: An ethnic minority group in southwest China, with a population of about 1.26 million.

p.146, *"The song girl understands not the destruction of the nation, From the other side of the river she still sings her palace song"*: A line from a poem by Tang Dynasty poet Du Mu, titled Boarding at Qinhuai River.

p.147, *Hui*: A Muslim ethnic group in China.

p.148, *Lolo*: An ethnic minority group in the southwest China, with population of about 2 million.

p.148, *Annam*: The name of Vietnam, used prior to 1945.

p.149, *The five black categories*: During the 1965–1975 Cultural Revolution, the Communist Party identified groups that were considered as enemies, including: landlords, wealthy farmers, anti-revolutionists, bad influencers and rightists. They were all subjected to brutal struggle sessions.

p.150, *Gayageum*: Traditional Korean instrument which had been in use for more than two thousand years old.

p.151, *Fu Manchu*: A fictional character invented by British writer Sax Rohmer in the second half of the 20th century. He later became a Hollywood film character.

p.151, *Bruce Lee* (1940–1973): The most famous Chinese martial arts star. He was active in the Hong Kong and Hollywood film industries.

p.151, *Boxer Rebellion*: After the national weakening of China in the nineteenth century, the Western and Japanese imperialist powers invaded. The Qing government's lack of resistance lead to widespread resentment among the people. The Boxer Rebellion broke out between 1899 and 1901, with people attacking and killing Westerners and Japanese with their bare hands.

p.153, *Yuan Shi-kai* (1859–1916): Political figure in the late nineteenth century. He was deployed by the Qing government to Korea to assist in training a new Korean army and help Korea repel the Japanese.

p.156, *Taichung*: the largest city in central Taiwan.

p.156, *Lee Young-ae* (1971—): Famous Korean actress, with a large fanbase in South Korea, Taiwan, Hong Kong, and China.

p.157, *Lin Yutang* (1895–1976) Writer and linguist. He taught at Peking University and the Chinese University of Hong Kong.

p.157, *Su Tungpo* (1037–1101): Famous politician and writer in Song Dynasty, who was demoted and exiled to Hainan Island.

p.157, *Amis*: A Taiwanese aboriginal tribe found mostly in eastern Taiwan, with a population of about 200,000.

Conflict 18

p.170, *The Unbearable Lightness of Being*: A novel by Czech writer Milan Kundera, published in 1984.

p.175, *Nietzsche*: Friedrich Wilhelm Nietzsche (1844–1900), German philosopher and poet.

Conflict 19

p.185, *Ernst Wilhelm (Wim) Wenders* (1945—). Famous German director, with many Taiwanese fans in the 1980s and 1990s.

p.191, *André Paul Guillaume Gide* (1869–1951). French writer, winner of the 1947 Nobel Prize in Literature.

Conflict 20

p.201, *Sun Yat-sen* (1866–1925): Born in Guangdong, and educated in Hawaii and Hong Kong. He founded the Revive China Society (precursor to the Kuomintang) to overthrow the Qing Dynasty. During this time, he was exiled to Japan, the US and Britain. He was arrested in London in 1896 by the Qing Embassy in Britain, and was rescued by his British teacher, Sir James Cantlie. After eleven failed revolutions, he finally overthrew the Qing Dynasty in 1912, and established the Republic of China, of which he became the first president.

p.202, *Jade Mountain*: Highest mountain in Taiwan, with an elevation of 3952 metres. Situated in central Taiwan.

p.202, *Dawu Mountain*: Located in southern Taiwan, with an elevation of 3092 metres.

p.207, *Yue Fei* (1103–1142): The most famous general of the Song Dynasty. He led many successful assaults against the Jin Dynasty, and regained much of the land that had been taken by the Jin. He was later accused on false charges of trying to overthrow the Emperor. He was summoned back from the frontlines, sentenced to death and executed.

p.213, *The Opium Wars* (1839–1842): The Opium Wars took place in the 19th century, between 1839 and 1842. The British East India Company profited greatly by selling opium to China, in exchange for silver. Drug addiction in China led to severe social problems. Because of this opium trade, the British managed to turn their trade deficit into surplus, causing China and its people to sink into poverty. In 1838, the Qing Dynasty sent Lin Zexu to Guangdong to investigate, ban the sale and destroy the supplies of opium. All remaining supplies of opium were incinerated at Humen and the fires raged for 22 days. This incited a series of conflicts between China and the United Kingdom, and in 1840 the British declared war on China. In 1842, China was defeated and Hong Kong was ceded to the British. This event has always been seen as a source of national humiliation for China.

Lightning Source UK Ltd.
Milton Keynes UK
UKOW04f1859210316

270615UK00001B/47/P